# THREATENED

# THREA

## ELIOT

# TENED

## SCHREFER

SCHOLASTIC PRESS · NEW YORK

# FOR ERIC,
# HOME

Library of Congress Cataloging-in-Publication Data

Schrefer, Eliot, 1978– author.
Threatened / Eliot Schrefer. — First edition.
pages cm
Summary: Luc is an orphan, living in debt slavery in Gabon, until he meets a Professor who claims to be studying chimpanzees, and they head off into the jungle — but when the Professor disappears, Luc has to fend for himself and join forces with the chimps to save their forest.
ISBN 978-0-545-55143-4 (jacketed hardcover) I. Orphans — Gabon — Juvenile fiction. 2. Chimpanzees — Juvenile fiction. 3. Animal rescue — Juvenile fiction. 4. Wildlife rescue — Juvenile fiction. 5. Adventure stories. 6. Gabon — Juvenile fiction. [I. Orphans — Gabon — Fiction. 2. Chimpanzees — Fiction. 3. Animal rescue — Fiction. 4. Adventure and adventurers — Fiction. 5. Gabon — Fiction.] I. Title.
PZ7.S37845Thr 2014
813.6 — dc23
2013018599

10 9 8 7 6 5 4 3 2 1    14 15 16 17 18

Printed in the U.S.A.    23
First edition, March 2014

The text type was set in Centaur.
Book design by Whitney Lyle

"THE CLOCK IS STANDING AT ONE MINUTE
TO MIDNIGHT FOR THE GREAT APES."

— KLAUS TOEPFER, EXECUTIVE DIRECTOR
OF THE UNITED NATIONS ENVIRONMENT
PROGRAMME

# GABON

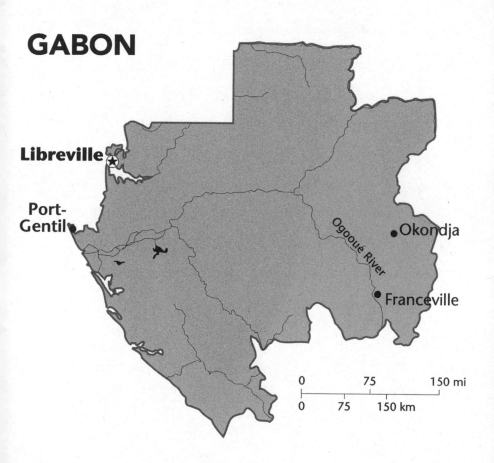

# PART ONE:

## OUTSIDE

# ONE

I'd never seen a mock man until the Professor showed me one. I'd heard them, of course — many evenings the chimpanzees would scream within the dark trees surrounding my village, their cries too strange for a person and too intimate for an animal. I still hear those shrieks, these years later. Whenever they got too loud, my mother and I would huddle on the floor of our hut, her arms wrapped tight around me. "This is why you must promise always to be home before dark, Luc," she would whisper. "If you're not, you'll become one of the *kivili-chimpenze*." The mock men.

I'd lean into the scratchy fabric of her *boubou* and wait for a hairy hand to come through the window. I'd imagine a lumpy head sniffing the air, black eyes staring into mine, lips pulling back from sharp teeth as the mock man lunged. I'd see us carried off into the jungle, one under each of the beast's arms.

My mother's warning worked; I was always home and at her side before dark.

Even when I was a little older and my village and my mother felt long in my past, I turned quiet and watchful at dusk. I would have loved to be safe in a home before the sky turned black. I just didn't have one to go to.

I worked long into the nights at the *paillotte* across from Franceville's best hotel, where the foreigners with their American

1

dollars piled in after the day's train arrived. No one knew quite when that would be — the trains were always hours or days late. If one appeared to be arriving on time, it was probably from last week.

When I heard the whistle of a locomotive, I'd dash through Franceville's dusty streets to the Café de la Gare. There, beneath a string of naked lightbulbs, I would clean glasses, rubbing each with an old wet rag until the spit on the rim and the line of dried beer foam had merged and it could be filled again. I didn't get paid, but sometimes foreigners would leave me coins on the table and the lime twists at the bottoms of their drinks. Between coins and peels and the occasional snack swiped from the center market, I survived. At least I didn't have to rummage my food from the dump.

The city was loud at my back, but when I faced the trees all I could see were plastic tables tilting into the mud against the silhouette of the jungle. The streets were gone, the hospital was gone. Sometimes, when there were no more glasses for me to wipe, I'd stand at the forest line and listen under the music for the calls of the *kivili-chimpenze*, straining to hear the angry screams that said they'd once been men and now were not. I hadn't heard them since my mother had died, and I'd begun to wonder if the mock men had ever been out there, or if they'd been an illusion she'd conjured and the spell had died with her.

The night I met the Professor, a fleet of logging trucks had arrived at the same hour as the train, so I was very busy. It was all I could do to get the glasses wiped before they had to be filled and back out onto the tables. I worked hard and kept grinning, wiping sweat from my forehead with the ragged hem of my shirt. I'd smiled through all the bad moments of the past year: surfacing memories of my mother or sister; the times hunger's blade went from flat against my belly to jabbing its tip; the diarrhea I kept clenched inside my body until the bar closed and I could flee into the trees. I kept smiling because the bar owner could replace me at any time with one of Franceville's other street boys. I kept smiling because if I didn't have an occasional coin to bring home to Monsieur Tatagani to put toward my mother's debt, he would throw me out in the street. Or worse.

I didn't notice the Professor at first, not until he said the word *chimpanzee*. I thought right away of my mother's warnings about the mock men, and gaped at the man. He looked to be an Arab, at least forty years old, and was seated all by himself. I decided to clear the table next to him as an excuse to draw near. I expanded time by scrubbing hard, as if hoping to find a new and better plastic table beneath the surface.

The man was a foreigner, but not too much so. He spoke good French like a normal person, and was darker than the Chinese bosses who ignored us and the American missionaries who didn't ignore us enough. He definitely wasn't Christian: He wore a tight woven cap, a taqiyah.

Unlike the other bar customers, this foreigner wasn't taking the fastest path to drunkenness — he'd ordered a mint tea. He was here for the company, I guessed, since he let his drink cool while he leaned far over the back of his chair to talk to a man at a nearby table.

"There have been other researchers who have come to these forests," the Arab was saying, "but none so famous as me. This conversation we are having might not seem like much now, my friend, but one day you will brag about it."

Maybe if the Arab had said he was a rich businessman, the man would have been impressed. But a researcher? What did that even mean?

"You have heard of janegoodall?" the Arab continued. "No? Well. Many important people came together to make a vote. And do you know what they concluded? They have decided that Africa should have its own native janegoodall. And that person is to be me!"

It was clear that the man did not know what the Arab was talking about any more than I did. I figured, though, that if a janegoodall was something all of Africa could have only one of, it had to be important. I edged closer, deciding this was the time to give the nearby chairs a good rubdown, shining them like lamps. It brought me even nearer to this strange man who had said my mother's word. I smiled for real as I worked, without knowing why I did.

The neighbor asked the Arab his name. "I'm Professor Abdul Mohammad of the University of Leipzig," he replied. "But most people call me Prof. It's less formal that way, you understand. I don't need to be flattered by formalities."

There was a flurry of motion below the table. A monkey emerged from the Arab's belongings, nearly knocking them over as it scampered up his back and onto the tabletop. "And this is Omar the vervet. Also of Egypt," Prof said.

Startled, the other man sprang to his feet.

A monkey was nothing unusual — they were frequently chained up at the side of the road to offer as pets, or gutted and hung for sale in the bushmeat markets, their dead mouths sucking on sky. But this one was fearless and tiny and silver with a soft black face. We didn't have monkeys like that in Gabon. Omar flicked his gaze to his master and then paced the table, lurching from one leg to the other as he stagger-walked. After testing the tea with his finger and hissing, he sat down, scratched at a sore on his backside, and scrutinized me, as if figuring out how I might be of use. I returned my focus to the chair I was cleaning.

Prof didn't have the monkey on a leash, but Omar sat close, worrying his hands together and peering into his master's eyes. Prof plucked a salty nut from a bowl and offered it up. Omar looked at the single nut, then picked up the dish and wolfed down handfuls. "Omar, no!" Prof scolded. But his eyes were smiling.

Omar met all of our eyes in turn as he gobbled, suspicious of this good turn in his luck. The other man took advantage of the commotion to shift his seat so it faced away from the Professor and his monkey. Left without an audience, Prof caught my eye. "That chair looks very, very clean," he said. "You've done good work. Perhaps you can stop wiping it for a minute and talk to me instead. What's your name, boy?"

I was flattered — he had barely asked the other man a single question, but he was curious about who *I* was. I pretended not to understand him and headed away. I'd learned that all the worst things that could happen to you in the city came after being noticed.

Besides, I didn't want this man to remember my face. Not with what I was already planning to do to him.

Alongside his chair, where the monkey had been hiding, I'd spotted luggage. There was a huge leather valise, probably as old as Prof himself. But what had caught my attention was beside it: a metal briefcase with a sturdy combination lock.

I'd never seen anything like it in the real world. But I'd seen metal cases in the spy movies the vendor in front of the station sold from his wicker mat. He always had one of them playing on his tiny screen, and each day while I listened for the train whistle I would stand as near as he allowed and watch. In those movies, it seemed like every time a man carried a metal briefcase, it would wind up broken open. Money would flurry about, everyone desperate to catch it.

Of course, in those movies the cases were carried by handsome men in expensive suits, not scrawny professors. But that case still told me that Prof was something special. There was probably a lot of money inside. Or maybe fancy equipment. Whatever it was, it was valuable enough to lock away.

I maneuvered so I could watch him while I wiped glasses. He looked my way once in a while, offering an unknowable smile.

Eventually he pulled out a book, leaned it against the edge of the table, and began to read. I'd never seen anyone read at a bar.

I didn't *want* to steal. But I couldn't stay in Franceville forever. By the time my mother had died in the hospital, leaving me standing out front with a plastic basin full of her possessions and a baby sister on my back, she'd owed thousands of francs we didn't have. The hospital released me to Monsieur Tatagani, the bill collector, who let us live in a room crowded with other street boys working to pay off their debts. Of the six boys who'd been there when I'd moved in, three had gotten sick and died. Two had disappeared. The last had stolen a hundred francs from Monsieur Tatagani and fled. Monsieur Tatagani had gone all the way to Lastoursville to retrieve him, and after he'd brought him back he'd chopped off the boy's hands, right in the middle of Independence Square. The police had watched in case the boy tried to run. He'd died of infection not a month later.

If there was money or valuables in the metal case, I could pay my debt, get out of Franceville, and buy land somewhere. I could take the first steps to having a home, with breath still in my chest and hands still on my wrists.

Once Prof had finished his drink, he dropped some coins on the table and got to his feet, Omar scampering to his shoulder. I hadn't expected him to leave so soon, and hadn't yet come up with a scheme for getting the case. In an instant my heart went from quiet to thudding.

I decided I would put the glass I was wiping back in the slop bucket and get to the front of the bar as fast as I could manage. Skirting the wall, I eased around the corner. I didn't have to look far — the Professor was right there, facing me.

"*M'bolo,*" I said, shocked.

"*Ma wok ki Fang,*" he said slowly in my language, shaking his head.

"That's not a problem," I said in French. "I speak French, too."

"Oh, you must have gone to school," he replied, also in French.

I didn't know how to answer. I had gone to school until my mother had died. I had loved it. But you didn't have to go to school to learn French. It was the language of the radio.

Prof gave up on getting further explanation from me. "I'm looking for the Hôtel Beverly Hills," he said. "Do you know where it is?"

I pointed down the road. "It's the large building at the other side of town," I whispered. "Franceville's only painted hotel. You can't miss it. But someone important like you should be staying here at the Hôtel Léconi."

Prof had hunched close to hear me, hand cupped at his ear, and now shook his head. "The only thing African about this hotel are the flies. Does the Beverly Hills have beds?"

I nodded.

"Then it will do fine. I am going to live with apes in the jungle, after all. No need for luxury now! Would the bar's *papa* mind if you disappeared for a few minutes to help me with my bags? There could be a franc in it for you."

I filled with warmth. The Professor was singling me out, as I'd done him. I sized up the large leather valise and figured I could manage hauling it. I picked it up and fought back the wave of dizziness that tilted me. My worry was less about passing out and more that Prof would notice my strain and fire me before I'd begun. I lost sensation in my arms for a moment, but managed to fit them through the straps. Blood pounded in my head, pricking the hairs on my neck.

"Have you had anything to eat today?" Prof asked.

*Please*, I silently begged, *don't be nice to me.* I told him I had. I didn't tell him it was because someone had spilled pastis into a bowl of dried peas and I'd gone around back and downed the whole thing.

Omar, full of bar nuts, watched me passively from his shoulder perch.

"Do you need to tell your parents you'll be helping me?" Prof asked.

I shook my head.

He nodded sadly, as if I'd revealed myself, and I hated him for it. "Okay, let's get along, then," he said. "I know the bag is heavy. It might be worth five francs to carry. Or even ten. I am an important man, after all, on a very important mission, and important things are not cheap. Important things are either free or expensive." Pleased with himself, he scratched the silver-and-black scraggle on his chin.

I took a step forward and immediately stumbled. After a moment's pause, I made another step. Grinning to let the Arab know how enormously fine I was feeling, I freed a hand and reached for the metal briefcase.

"No, no," Prof said hurriedly, picking it up and clutching it to his chest. "I'll hold on to that."

Omar chattered at me and exposed his teeth. The stupid monkey had figured me out better than his master had. Muttering under my breath, I took one step and another toward the far side of the town.

Prof puffed with exertion, walking with a slight limp.

We weren't a hundred paces from the bar when we came across Monsieur Tatagani. He spent his days sitting in the center of Franceville so he could keep an eye on his boys. Squatting in the dirt, he wore a blazer that was so unclean, it was more the tan of dust than the black of fabric. Sometime in his life he'd been struck on the head hard enough to expose skull; he had a ring of white at the top, like an upside-down teacup saucer. When I had nightmares, I always knew Monsieur Tatagani had been the cause if the monsters had the same saucer of bone on their heads — and if, when I reached up my arms to defend myself, there were no hands at the ends of my wrists.

When he saw us coming up the walk, Monsieur Tatagani grinned hugely, exposing teeth unusually white and strong for a man of his age. He said nothing, though, I think because he sensed the chance for a payday. We were suddenly conspirators, he and I. The Franceville moneylender, the man generous enough to give me a place to sleep at night but cruel enough to cut off the hands of orphans who couldn't pay, saw into my wicked heart. Worse, he found himself there.

I avoided Monsieur Tatagani's eyes as I struggled under the valise. Soon he was out of view and Prof and I were stepping along Franceville's main paved avenue, kicking away garbage and excrement and the occasional stray dog.

"How old are you, boy?" Prof asked, gasping as we walked.

"I'm not sure," I said. It was the truth. The last person who'd acknowledged my birthday had been my mother. That had been my tenth. I thought that had been three years ago, but it might have been two.

"That," Prof said, pausing for a moment to catch his breath, "is my official answer, too."

We'd arrived at the Hôtel Beverly Hills, a dank cinder-block tower. It had painted walls, not because it was the fanciest building in Franceville, but because it had the most to hide. I let Prof lead us in.

Once I'd heaved the valise to the ground, Prof thanked me, placed a twenty-five-franc coin in my palm, and turned his attention to the desk clerk. Omar climbed down and sat on the floor, one hand protectively circling his master's ankle, his little monkey fingers working their way under the pant leg until they were against Prof's skin. I kneeled beside Omar, as if to pat his head. Prof noticed my attention to his monkey, smiled, and returned to haggling with the clerk.

Omar watched as I stroked his forearm. He watched as I stroked his shoulder. He watched as I inched my hand over to the handle of the metal briefcase.

Suddenly suspicious, the monkey bared his teeth and began squawking. Now that I was so close to him, I noticed that the skin on his arms was strange — it was almost like corduroy, and his palms were the slightest bit oily.

Though I was worried the monkey would bite me, I wasn't about to stop.

I tightened my grip on the handle.

I took a deep breath.

I ran.

There was shouting behind me, and motion. But I couldn't afford to look. I couldn't afford to do anything but sprint and dodge.

I knew these streets so well, and it felt like only moments before I had turned a half dozen times and thrown myself down countless alleys. I stopped against a tree on an empty street.

The briefcase was so solid in my arms. If it had money inside, I could escape with it come morning, hitch a ride on the next logging truck, and get away from Monsieur Tatagani and the police, into Angola or over to Libreville. If it was something other than cash, I could sell it at the market right as it opened and then either use the money to pay off Monsieur Tatagani or flee.

All I had to do was survive the night without getting caught. Because boys like me didn't go to jail for theft. Boys like me disappeared.

The night came, and grew long. I clutched the case to my chest. Avoiding the main road, I stuck instead to the edges of the city, creeping along farmland buffalo paths and the hunting trails I'd once prowled for bushmeat. The jungle loomed black off to one side.

It might have all been in my head, but for the first time in years I thought I could hear the mock men off in the trees, shrieking about how they had once been just like me.

# TWO

I was very late, which meant one of two things: Monsieur Tatagani would be awake and would beat me, or he'd have barred the door before going to sleep and I'd have to risk a night out on the street. I could see, as soon as I turned onto the dirt road that led to Monsieur Tatagani's house, that the lights were out. But he was waiting for me on the stoop. Moonlight edged the saucer of bone on the top of his head.

I had no saucer of bone to give me away under the moon, so I had time to figure out what to do. Simplest would be to press the case into Monsieur Tatagani's hands, tell him that whatever was inside could pay off my debt, and leave in the morning. The fact that the case was stolen would not matter; all he'd care about would be whether its contents were valuable enough.

Hiding behind a tree, I propped my head on clasped hands and stared at the glimmering metal briefcase. Its corners were reinforced, the combination lock sturdy as a stone, the dial engraved with numbers. Unable to resist, I tugged at the clasps, but they didn't give at all.

There was no way I was going to be able to get it open — not while I was outside in the dark without any tools. I'd been so focused on getting the case that I hadn't given a single thought to how to open it.

I crept around the back of the gnarled, lonely tree. An *iboga* bush grew alongside it, and when I nestled the case within its leaves it was out of view of anyone passing along the street. Heart pounding, I headed to Monsieur Tatagani's house.

The moment he saw me, he rose to his feet. "Why are you so late?" he asked. His voice was controlled, with no sign of irritation. "And why are you coming from that direction?"

"You saw me leaving the bar with the Arab, *papa*. I took him to the Hôtel Beverly Hills."

A smile, empty of happiness, spread on his lips. "Yes, I did see that."

"I thought he might have work for me to do," I said. An image of the case forced its way into my thoughts. I hoped Monsieur Tatagani couldn't see it flickering behind my eyes.

He laid a hand on my neck, like he was figuring out the force he'd need to break it. "And did he? Find work a boy like you could do? Are you finally going to pay back the thousands of francs it's taken me to keep you alive?" He laughed in his gray way. I could smell palm wine on his breath.

I shook my head, hoping to loosen his fingers. They only tightened.

"Is that so?" Monsieur Tatagani said, shoving me so I tumbled past the open front door and into the main room. I managed not to fall to the ground, which I knew would have invited more anger. Blocking the moon, Monsieur Tatagani was a figure cut out from the night, a beast come for a boy who'd stayed out too late. "You didn't ask for a coin for carrying that Arab's bag? You didn't slip a hand into his pocket and see what you could find?"

He flicked on a light, and the leer on his face was more ferocious than I'd expected.

Heart skipping in terror, I remembered that I *had* gotten something out of Prof that I could give Monsieur Tatagani. My trembling fingers searched through my pocket. There was a hole in the threadbare fabric, but the coin was too big to have fallen out, even during my flight.

"Here," I said, holding it out in my sweaty palm. "He gave me twenty-five francs."

Monsieur Tatagani looked skeptical. "Twenty-five? And all that weird old man asked you to do was carry his bag?"

I nodded, and the coin was gone. Having that much money taken from me would have been agony before, but all I felt now was relief.

"Maybe sacrificing so much to keep you alive wasn't a mistake," Monsieur Tatagani said. "You've finally paid for a tiny part of your keep. Go to bed. I'll wake you before dawn so you can get back to the Hôtel Beverly Hills before the Arab wakes up. You'll do whatever he desires, and you'll bring me thirty francs this time."

He nodded, and I ducked through to where I slept. Monsieur Tatagani had separated a drafty mud-walled room from the house with an old housedress that he'd hung as a divider. This was where he kept his boys. Monsieur Tatagani lived his life — cooking, sleeping, drinking with guests — on the other side of that tattered housedress, while we listened in nervous silence.

Two wooden benches lined either sidewall, and it was on those that I and the other boy who'd been with Monsieur Tatagani longest slept. The rest of the orphans were lined shoulder-to-shoulder on a rubber mat on the dirt floor.

The room was so silent that I knew they were all awake and listening, eyes scrunched shut, making no noise so as not to attract Monsieur Tatagani's anger. Pierre, the youngest, had taken advantage of my missed curfew and laid out on my bench. "It's okay," I whispered, lying alongside him. We fit, barely. "There's room for two tonight."

"Have you already had your pee outside?" he asked.

I nodded. We weren't allowed out of the room at night, but there was a can in the corner that we could use. Pierre claimed that the smell kept him awake.

On a shelf above my bench was a plastic basin that contained my few possessions. I reached up and took it down, taking advantage of the lamplight to examine the worn-rough ridge of the plastic, the frayed rope handles. I imagined my mom's and my sister's fingers on them.

Most of the boys paid their keep by hunting rodents and monkeys out of the bush that Monsieur Tatagani could sell to the market vendors. When they had a good day we'd eat the extra meat, but usually Monsieur Tatagani boiled up rice, shallow wooden bowlfuls for which he'd add a few francs to our debt. Whoever returned last got the sludge at the bottom, a cooked-down rice water that was gray and foamy. It looked like what you'd get if you milked a monster, but it was plentiful and filled the belly. I took a plastic bag from a hook on the wall and held the snipped-off tip to my lips. Some of the cooled dregs dribbled into my mouth, and I swallowed them and then some more.

Back when my mother had been alive, dinner had been fruit and a heavy slice of manioc bread, eaten at a sloping wooden table overlooking our field. My father was a road builder and almost always far away, laying pavement. There was never a lot to eat, but there was always enough, because when none of our crops were ready we'd find a neighbor who'd harvested. Other times we'd return the favor, so there was usually company at our table. When my mother got sick and my sister stopped growing, we had to move to Franceville for its hospital. I was too young to work, so I'd beg meals from the few family members we had here. But they were my father's family, and it had been years since he'd last been seen. Once they gave up on him, they gave up on me, and my meals became bar scraps and the milk of the monster.

I didn't usually allow myself to stew on the time when my parents had been around, but that night had been so strange — between Prof and the metal briefcase and the calls I thought I'd heard from the mock men — that I was cracked open. As I lay on the bench, I wished that my mother could place a blanket over me, like she'd once done. But she was gone. Even the blanket was gone. So instead I lay my arm across Pierre, blanketing him.

What I needed most was to get some sleep. But all I could think about was the metal briefcase and what it would look like placed alongside the rest of my possessions inside the plastic basin. Its four corners would just nest inside. Once that basin had held my sister, until she'd stopped growing and shrunk to nothing instead. Tomorrow it would hold this different treasure. Making soft *tuck-tuck* sounds, I turned the basin in a slow circle, the way I'd once done to coax Carine into sleep. I stopped only when Pierre fidgeted.

I allowed myself to dream. In my new life I could use whatever the case held to buy a hut and a plot of land. Once I had that, I could pay Pierre's debt and he could live with me. Or maybe my father, once he heard I was set up somewhere, would finally return. I could have a family.

# THREE

Usually I was woken by the clatter of Monsieur Tatagani rummaging through the kitchen pans, grumbling about his hangover. But today I woke to silence, which was worse.

I drew in my legs and sat up as quietly as I could. I was sore all along my back, my tight muscles pulling me into a curve. As I sat up my head hit the shelf, and without thinking I shushed, hoping my sister wouldn't make noise.

I must have forced Pierre off the bench during the night — he was now lying on his usual spot on the floor. I crept over to the housedress and peered around it.

A creature was in the doorway — a monkey with a silver body and a black face. Hand against the mud wall, he was peering in, the dingy dress-curtain piled on his head.

When he saw me, Omar perked up and squeaked.

The stupid monkey had tracked me. Behind him I saw Prof, kneeling on a small rug he'd placed in the house's main room, chest touching the ground. His lips were moving silently; he didn't stop his prayer as Omar chirped away.

I was trapped. The only way out was past five sleeping boys, a man who owned me, a crazy monkey, and a praying Arab.

It was hopeless, but I had to try. As silently as possible, I took the basin down from the shelf and slipped into the main room. Omar grabbed wildly for me as I crept by. He made contact, then wrapped his furry little arms around my leg and let himself be dragged, squeaking triumphantly.

The boys began to wake and stir behind me. Prof opened his eyes, got up from his mat, rolled it, and calmly placed it in his valise. It was strange to see no smile on his face, like his personality had turned sideways since last night.

"Good morning," he said coolly.

My first thought was to bolt. It must have shown, because Prof held up his hands warningly. "Be careful. Look around before you decide to run, my boy."

His eyes flitted to the kitchen.

Leaning against the woodstove was Monsieur Tatagani, staring at us with an expression of cold amusement.

He was going to let Prof turn me in. *My hands.*

Trembling, I stepped back into the sleeping room and drew the curtain, as if some mother's old housedress could protect me from what was about to happen.

"Stop, Luc," Prof said, his voice low. "I explained to the hotel desk clerk exactly what happened, and he told me that you lived on the streets but spent the night here with this Alphonse Tatagani. Then the monsieur here told me he would help get my case back if I paid him a finder's fee, and that as part of that fee he would take care of your punishment."

*Take care of your punishment.* My thoughts skittered around everything those words could mean.

I tried to fight it down, but what remained of the rice sludge I'd eaten the night before was crawling up my throat. I heard Monsieur Tatagani *tsk* as I spat it out on his rubber mat.

Once I'd finished retching, I wiped my mouth and glared up at Prof. Why was he telling me all of this if it didn't change what was going to happen? All he wanted was his stupid metal briefcase back, whatever the cost to me.

Monsieur Tatagani stepped forward, but Prof motioned for

him to stay. Surprisingly, the much larger man obeyed. Something about the professor had him spooked.

"You owe a lot of money to Monsieur Tatagani," Prof said to me. "How did that come to happen? Surely not from the small amount of rice you eat."

I shrugged and spat bile. I didn't want to drag my dead family into this. And the reasons for my debt didn't matter, anyway. The amount was real.

"I have a suspicion that it wasn't your fault," Prof said.

I looked up. I'd never thought it was my fault that my mom and sister had gotten sick, or that my father had never returned. But still I felt relieved to have it told to me.

"Why don't you tell Monsieur Tatagani what really happened with the case?" Prof said. "Then he can explain everything to the police and this will all be settled."

I didn't understand. Prof wanted me to confess? But I saw a crafty tilt to his mouth and realized he'd plotted something.

I took my time wiping my mouth, waiting for the right story to come to me. "I was waiting with the bags," I said, slowly and loudly enough for Monsieur Tatagani to hear clearly. "And a creature came up. I didn't recognize what it was at first. . . ."

I took a deep breath, then rushed forward with my tale. "It was a mock man, from the jungle! Hairy and mean. He grabbed the metal briefcase, and I ran after him. I didn't want him to steal it, you see!" Now I was getting into it. I kept my eyes wide and honest and nodded gravely. One of the boys listening behind the curtain gasped.

Monsieur Tatagani made a loud cluck. "The case was stolen by one of the *kivili-chimpenze*? In Franceville? And let me guess: This beast got away before you could stop him."

"No," I said. "I caught him. I fought him to the ground. I wrestled the professor's case away. The mock man escaped, though, and by then it was so late. I decided I would wait for the morning, when I'd walk the case back to the hotel and return it."

Prof clapped his hands. "See? I knew there had to be an explanation."

"Why are you even listening to this street rat's lie?" Monsieur Tatagani asked. I was wondering much the same thing.

Prof tapped his chin. "I am a world-renowned expert on chimpanzees, and this behavior is very likely for one of them. Last night this boy promised to come with me for a very important scientific study. I need someone to carry my things, and he has proven himself to be resourceful and courageous. He wrestled down an ape, after all!"

I stared at Prof, openmouthed. I was being saved with a fable. Why anyone would want me to be part of his life, even at this strange price, was beyond me.

"Isn't that right, Luc?" Prof asked me. "Isn't that what you promised?"

I nodded, slowly at first, and then energetically. "That's right. I promised that I would go with you."

Monsieur Tatagani grunted. "This boy is not going anywhere until he's paid his debts. His mother ran up a large hospital bill before she went. She had the worm."

"Luc," Prof said to me, his eyes smiling in deep crinkles, "if you tell me where my case is, I can get money out of it to pay Monsieur Tatagani."

I nodded numbly and pointed to the front door, for the moment beyond words.

As I stepped out, Omar remained clutched to my ankle, like a fur boot. Finally he let go and toddled next to me, my pant leg in hand. Prof and Monsieur Tatagani were close on either side, no doubt ready to grab me if I tried to run.

When I got to the *iboga* bush and pulled out the case, Monsieur

Tatagani coughed. "Why didn't you bring this case inside the house to keep it safe, boy?" he asked.

"Perhaps because he thought it was safer here," Prof snapped.

I frowned. All I needed was to get these two going after each other before the transaction was finished.

"Just open the case," Monsieur Tatagani ordered.

Prof shook his head. "Not here. Come with me." With Omar on his shoulder, he started down the road. At the corner I saw two men in police uniforms seated at a café table. I was relieved that Prof had already figured out not to transact with Monsieur Tatagani unless there were witnesses.

The policemen frowned when Prof explained that the case had been recovered by me and that he was paying my debt as a reward. "As you wish, monsieur," one of them said.

Prof laid the case on an empty table and rolled the combination lock. When it opened, we all fell into a stunned silence.

Francs. It was full of francs in paper-wrapped bundles. The kind of cash a movie spy would have had, only this money was African!

"How much does this boy owe you?" Prof asked.

Monsieur Tatagani surprised me by not exaggerating. "Nineteen thousand francs."

Prof danced his fingertips over the precious notes. I looked at them in awe, a purple drawing of a beautiful woman repeated from one side of the case to the other. "Now," Prof said, "we can do each other a favor. You would prefer to have United States currency, yes? So would I, but I will need these francs in the smaller villages. Will you accept traveler's checks instead, drawn from an American bank? For your trouble, I can raise your price to twenty thousand."

Monsieur Tatagani nodded solemnly, his excitement so intense, it had made his body go rigid. Only really important people spent

American money. This might be Monsieur Tatagani's first time to have any.

Prof reached into his valise and pulled out a floppy leather wallet. As he rummaged through it, receipts and slips of paper fluttered to the ground. I ran around and picked them all up, except for one, because Omar got to it first and ate it. I hoped it wasn't important. "The National Geographic Society will be happy to pay off this boy's debts in return for his service," Prof said with odd formality, like he was in a radio advertisement. "I am pleased to offer you twenty thousand francs' worth of United States currency."

I stared, openmouthed, as Monsieur Tatagani took a note into his hand, this one even more fine and intricate than the francs. "I don't know what you're on to, old man," he said, "but the check is good. The boy's yours." He leered at me. "What will I do now? My home will feel so empty!"

Unconsciously, my eyes went to Monsieur Tatagani's house. The other boys were lined up at the front door, staring at us. I wished I could take Pierre and the rest with me, both to get them away from Monsieur Tatagani and to have allies against this odd Arab.

Monsieur Tatagani slipped the check into his wallet.

"I hope," Prof said to Monsieur Tatagani, "that you will see this windfall as an opportunity to help those in need."

Monsieur Tatagani laughed. "*I* am in need! Even a money-lender can need money. This will pay the tax collector."

*With plenty left over for banana beer,* I thought sourly.

Monsieur Tatagani scowled at me, his expression angry but also somehow wounded. Then he headed back to his home, scrutinizing his check. My new owner and I stared after him as he swaggered away.

"Hurry up!" Prof said, snapping his fingers. "Get your belongings! The chimpanzees will be disappointed if we're late." Then his expression softened and he winked. "Unless that mock man you met last night told you otherwise."

Numbly, I tripped after Monsieur Tatagani. My knees were limp. I'd thought I'd spend the rest of my short and pointless life laboring under that debt. And this crazy foreigner had paid it on a whim. I'd seen the number printed on the traveler's check — fifty American dollars! I couldn't understand it.

As he approached the house, Monsieur Tatagani yelled at the boys lined up in front. "You know you're not allowed around here during the day! Go! Get hunting!"

They lingered, but when Monsieur Tatagani picked up his stick they hurried along the road. *What happened?* Pierre mouthed as he retreated, awestruck.

"Good-bye!" I called after them. *I'll come back and help you if I ever can.*

Once they got to the tree line, most of the boys slipped into the jungle. But Pierre stopped, staring at me dully. Unable to take the guilt of leaving him behind, I ducked inside the house.

My belongings only half filled the plastic basin. Inside was a hospital form I'd kept because my mother had once signed it, a cloth purse made from an old pair of pants and tied neatly with scrap rope, and a second shirt with a hundred-franc note hidden in the lining. I hefted the basin under the crook of my arm and got ready to leave.

My stomach was fluttery. Monsieur Tatagani's house had been a misery compared to the home I'd once had. But leaving it still felt like leaping from a cliff into a current.

I left the small amount of money I'd scrounged under Pierre's bed cloth. Prof had thousands — millions? — of francs, so the money would do Pierre a lot more good than it would me.

Monsieur Tatagani was seated on his couch as I left, staring at his check. I was tempted to leave without saying anything more to him, but felt I had to say some kind of good-bye, despite everything.

Having his house to come back to at night had kept me alive. I cleared my throat. "Monsieur —"

"Get out!" he thundered, snapping his head up, wounded fury on his face. I fled.

"Everything fine, Luc?" Prof asked when I returned. I nodded. I didn't want to talk about what had happened. I didn't even want to think about it.

I stared down at Prof's heavy valise and stretched my arms over my head, hoping my muscles would loosen in the morning sunshine. I'd seen plenty of ancient women trekking home from the fields with babies on their backs and huge bales of greens on their heads. If they could handle those, I could handle this bag. Couldn't I?

As Prof took the metal briefcase and started forward, Omar chattering on his shoulder, I heaved the valise to the top of my head. Once I'd gotten my balance, it wasn't such bad going, and the sunshine felt wonderful. I reminded myself that I would always have sunshine, no matter how my life changed.

We didn't have far to go. Prof stopped us outside of High Fashion Works of God, Franceville's fanciest store. I put the valise down and sat on top of it, preparing for a wait. Prof, already halfway inside, waved me through.

I timidly edged inside the store, stashing the valise in a corner. I'd studied the shelves from the outside many times before, but now I could see them up close. Rows and rows of treasures were lined on shiny brown shelves. Ties and tie pins; lace christening dresses; bottles of medicines in identical green glass bottles, each with its own cork stopper and hand-printed label. Omar scampered along an aisle, his tail knocking down a whole row of straw dolls.

The shopkeeper, a famously beautiful woman who wore lipstick and had her hair swooshed to one side like some boyfriend was pulling on it, smiled tightly at Prof and then frowned at me. I got ready to apologize for being there.

But Prof spoke first, his French suddenly more sophisticated. "My research assistant will need to be outfitted. Only first I must ask him a few questions."

He leaned into me. With the beautiful shopkeeper staring us down, I found it hard to meet Prof's eyes. "Do you own any shoes?" he asked.

I shook my head. I'd had shoes until a year before, when my feet had grown too large and I'd passed them along to another boy. I suspected I'd never fit into shoes ever again — my toes had splayed from being barefoot all the time. The littlest ones made sharp turns at the end of my foot.

"Then we'll need to get you shoes," Prof said. "Next: Do you have any worms?"

I nodded. I had seen the things crawling after I relieved myself. It was perfectly normal, though — all the boys had those.

"Do you have *the* worm?"

I shook my head. Missionary nuns had driven through on a bus last year and tested people for HIV. I went in and let them prick me because it was free and I got a cookie afterward. When I went back the next day, they told me I didn't have the virus. Then they wanted me to find God. But I said no because I didn't know how; besides, there was no cookie involved in that.

Prof turned back to the shopkeeper, who was still frowning, her disgust so big, it was almost funny. I thought it was just me, but her most severe looks were at Prof. They say the only person a Gabonese hates more than a European is an Arab. I hadn't thought that was true, but it certainly seemed to be the case for the beautiful shopkeeper of High Fashion Works of God. "My assistant has spoken," Prof said. "We need a pair of shoes and a set of boys' clothes and a bottle of anti-worm medication. The pill form, if you please, madame."

I left there with brand-new shoes slapping the ground and an exquisite green glass bottle in my pocket. My smile was as huge as the shopkeeper's frown had been. In one pocket I had another bottle, filched rubbing alcohol. I knew by now that treating a cut quickly was key to staying alive. The shopkeeper would never miss the bottle — and deserved what she got, anyway, for the nasty looks she'd given Prof.

Even though mud and garbage no longer squeezed up between my toes, my new shoes didn't make carrying the valise easier. They were hard and unforgiving, and my feet seemed to find a new edge inside them at every step. I was happy that Prof stopped us once we got to the edge of the road that headed into the interior. It was paved for only a short way before turning to dirt and mud, then led only to . . . green. For that reason, very few people took it, unless they were cutting down trees or escaping people.

In Gabon, we called the places men live the Outside and the jungle the Inside. Humans weren't supposed to go Inside.

"Now we wait for our ride," Prof said cheerfully, stroking the top of Omar's head.

I thought right then about running away. Now that I was free of Monsieur Tatagani, I could visit every village until I found my mother's family, even though I'd never met them. Maybe they would let me farm a small plot of land. The idea of four walls that gave onto a little garden, of people nearby who cared about me, was so wonderful that it hurt.

But I couldn't abandon Prof. Not yet. My side of our bargain was to split my destiny with this bizarre old man. I had betrayed him last night, and we both knew it, and yet he'd taken another chance on me, even paying my debt. He'd bought me clothes and shoes! I looked down at them proudly, taking in their neatly threaded seams, though they caused me such pain. I would help this professor until he was set up. Then I would leave.

We waited a long time by the side of the road, until Prof hailed a rattling lumber truck. He spoke to the driver for a while, then out came that floppy leather wallet and more traveler's checks. I would have done anything to have even one of those meaningful slips of paper, and he had so *many*. It nearly set my mind reeling, the scale of it, like I was a beetle and Prof was a mountain.

Within minutes we were sitting in the back of the truck, Prof's belongings mounded around us. The truck had no sides, so we held on to the thick rusty chains that would eventually be used to secure lumber on the return trip. Despite our best efforts, we bounced and swung as the truck rumbled forward.

Omar leaped from one side of the truck bed to the other, excited and squawking, sometimes disappearing under the vehicle to investigate its workings and then returning triumphantly, ranting and baring his teeth.

We faced out the rear. I'd never traveled on a vehicle before, and the wind blowing past felt as thrilling and upsetting as my freedom. I held my hand out over the side, let it be lifted by the too-fast air. Prof leaned against his valise and closed his eyes, the metal briefcase pinned securely between his knees.

"How did you get all that money?" I risked asking.

Prof groggily opened his eyes and looked down at his prized possession, as if surprised to see it there. "This? Nothing worth spending a thought on." Then he changed the subject. "I was advised by my fellow scientists that I would need an assistant. So this has worked out very well. You will be a great help to me, and to science. We will have a life with great purpose! Our mission is to set up camp in a part of the jungle with many chimpanzees. Most of my time will be used to make crucial notes and observations for the National Geographic Society, so I will need you to maintain the camp and help me keep us and the chimps safe. Your payment will be your food and the solution I've provided you for your impossible situation in Franceville. Not that you're in any position to refuse, but do you at least acknowledge my terms?"

A fat mantis whizzed through the air and landed on my arm, and I flicked it off into the hurtling wind. Prof was right. I was in no position to refuse. But he was forcing me into this choice all the same, and because of that, I figured I would feel no guilt when I abandoned him later. For now I nodded. I acknowledged his terms.

Tall trees rushed by on either side, as if fleeing the liana vines strewn between them. Shrieks of birds, monkeys, and insects filled my ears, even above the roar of the truck. "Why did you do it?" I asked. "You could have hired someone much more skilled than me with all that money."

Prof was silent for a moment, then chuckled. "A terrible man, that Monsieur Tatagani. I knew it the moment I met him. He deserves this."

"Deserves what?"

Prof pulled out his leather wallet and showed me a thick wad of those American traveler's checks. "See these? We make much better fake money in Cairo; he'd never seen a forgery that good."

"What you gave him wasn't *real*?" I asked, my insides dropping away.

Prof nodded and began chuckling again. "Trying to extort twenty thousand francs out of an AIDS orphan," he managed to get out. "That Monsieur Tatagani truly does deserve it."

I imagined Monsieur Tatagani arriving at the tax collector's that very moment, and pictured what would happen when they discovered the money was fake. He might be imprisoned. I was horrified by the thought of his fury. He'd cut the hands off that boy who'd run away, and this was much worse. I didn't feel like laughing. Not at all.

Our truck drew off the road to let another pass. As if frustrated at being confined, the machine thrummed angrily. "What about the cash in the case?" I sputtered. "Is that real?"

"Hmm . . ." Prof said. "Some of it!"

"You gave these loggers fake money, too?" I whispered, glancing nervously at the hulking men in the truck's cab.

"All in the name of science, Luc," Prof said. "All in the name of science. Besides, they should not be cutting down these trees. Look at it this way — they are donating their services in the name of chimpanzee conservation. It's time they helped endangered animals instead of destroying their habitats."

I lay on my side, feeling sick. A few things were clearer now. One, I could never return to Franceville — whether he had meant to or not, Prof had guaranteed my doom if I showed my face there again. Tatagani, if he was free (or the police, if he was not), would destroy me the moment he saw me. If he could, he would hunt us down. I had no doubt of that.

Two, Prof was far more clever — and dishonest — than I'd first thought.

And three, there was a reason he'd picked me to be his assistant: I was a lot like him.

# FOUR

Only an hour after we'd started, the truck was stuck in mud. I ripped down branches and placed them under the wheels for traction while the men pushed until the engine kicked and we all rushed to hop back on. Omar was calm, sitting with both hands on the truck bed as he watched us get splattered in red mud. Then, after ten minutes more of pitched driving, we were stuck again and had to push. The roads were so muddy they foamed, and it wasn't even the rainy season yet.

Each time we passed a village, a stray dog or two would get fascinated by us and trot along. Once we'd gone a few miles they'd give up and sit down, watching us leave. Then it was back to the usual scene: me staring over the side, Prof reading his religious book quietly, Omar talking to the wind, all accompanied by slurping wheels and the echoless screams of wild animals.

Around midday the truck eased over two boards laid over a steep ravine. The earth fell away, and I could no longer see any road over the side; it was like we had lost all our weight and begun to float. Soon after we'd returned to normal ground, we pulled over beside a fenced-in compound. Tall steel poles were capped by spotlights, creating a piece of Outside at their center. The loggers piled out and went inside the chain fence, where they were met by a trio of Chinese men.

Prof got out and prayed on his rug while I watched the men and wondered what they were talking about. It amazed me that these foreigners had come from a far-off land to get our *trees*. So much effort was going into harvesting something that took no work at all to make. I was proud of my people, that we were able to convince wealthy outsiders to come this far to give us money for wood. If we did this right, our whole country could be rich and none of us would have to work at all. Even if they took away all our trees, that would leave us more room for homes and farms. Fathers wouldn't have to go far away to work, then.

We'd no sooner left the logging camp than the truck stopped again. A boy, no older than me, had nailed to a tree various animals he'd hunted out of the woods. Back when Monsieur Tatagani had sent me on bushmeat runs, I'd caught similar animals: monkeys, antelope, porcupines.

The loggers got out and chose a couple of rock badgers. Prof went the cheaper route and selected a monkey for us, a skinny, furry body with an arrow wound in its side and astonished, broken eyes. He flung the corpse onto the truck's bed, and Omar prodded the body curiously. I'd eaten monkey often enough after a boy had a good hunting day, but it surprised me that Prof would choose one when there were other options. That he could care for his silver monkey and eat this brown one. Legs, arms, body, head, tail.

He saw my puzzled expression, but must not have read my thoughts right. "The loggers have their dinner, and we'll need something to eat, too," he said. "We'll be cooking tonight!"

My belly rumbled. Startled by the noise, Omar poked at me. I gave him a little tickle, and he ran in a circle, shrieking hysterically, then poked me again to start the game over.

Once we were under way I lay in the air-wet wood chips of the truck bed, head propped against my hand as I watched the greenery smudge by. Omar calmed down and lay next to me, uninterested in the monkey corpse, its tail twisting around his own.

Since we were on a bouncing truck, Prof skipped the rug and the kneeling and prayed by nodding his head to his chest and saying his words. Once he was finished he looked at me. "Your parents died of the worm, yes?"

I debated what to answer, and decided to go with the truth. "My mother did, yes, and my sister. But my father has been away on a job. He paves roads." I didn't mention that it had been years since anyone had heard from him. I didn't mention that every time Monsieur Tatagani overheard me talking about my father to the boys, he'd say that he was most definitely dead, because it must have been him who'd gotten my mother sick.

Prof returned to his book, which he called a Koran. He gave a small, tight smile and bowed his head.


The loggers pulled to the side before dusk. We cooked and ate dinner, then spread sleeping rolls in the truck bed. The nights weren't overly cool yet, but even so I was glad Omar chose to sleep draped over my neck, blocking the worst of the chill breezes. Prof drew a heavy canvas coat out of his bag and tucked it over his face, sleeping within the fabric like a bird under a wing.

Prof had the strangest habits. He refused to bathe, claiming he was going to wait until Friday. When I went to the stream and offered to rinse his galabia along with my clothes, he refused. And yet he was very fussy, and would only squat near running water so he could rinse himself afterward. He washed his mouth out every night with a soap made especially for teeth.

We woke to the sound of the truck's engines starting, and had barely gripped the lumber chains before we were rumbling forward again. I scrambled to get our bedrolls in hand before they tumbled from the truck.

It seemed we couldn't go more than one horizon length that

morning without passing a broken-down vehicle. Some had turned sideways in the red mud; some had simply stopped along easy stretches of dry road. Ours pressed along at its turtle pace, taking corners slower than I could have walked them on my hands, battering down thickets of bright green grass on either side as it squeezed by. Sometimes log trucks passed going the opposite direction, always empty. Prof told me that any trucks that were full of timber would be heading to Libreville, on the coast, so the logging companies could fill their boats.

There were no vehicles other than the trucks. Not even villages anymore. We were heading into an area where no one appeared to live except loggers.

And, if Prof was right, mock men. I wasn't sure what was more fearsome: the moneylender behind us, or the *kivili-chimpenze* ahead.


On the morning of the third day we finally came to a village — no more than a few dozen huts scattered along either side of the road. Chickens and goats and even a pig wandered past, easily sidestepping our pathetically slow truck. We'd arrived in Okondja on its market day, and what an assortment was spread out! Tidy pyramids of green oranges. Plastic bottles that had once contained water but were now filled with wild honey or red cooking oil the villagers had made from palm nuts. I'd rarely been able to afford meat, so my eyes naturally went past it to a pile of wrinkled passion fruit set out on a scrap of sacking. But Prof went right up to the oldest woman in the market and pointed to the town chickens. Soon the slowest one was wrung and plucked and frying in palm oil.

That evening we sat outside the huts and ate delicious fried chicken, the meat darker and tastier than any I'd ever chanced into in Franceville. "Wonderful, no?" Prof asked. "We need to store up energy."

I nodded vigorously, bits of crispy golden chicken skin on my fingers, more grateful to him with each morsel.

"How do you feel when you see wooden crates of chickens?" Prof asked. "When they're all crowded in together?"

I shrugged. I could see where he was leading, but since I had a chicken wing in my hand, it was hard to feel bad for the birds. You couldn't kill them and eat them and then wonder about their suffering. Besides, they clearly deserved some of the blame for tasting so amazingly good.

The next morning, when the loggers filed into the truck to begin the day's trek, Prof hung back by the market. None too excited to haul the massive valise back up onto the truck bed, I was happy to loaf around. When the truck's engines started, I ran to find Prof and tugged at the sleeve of his galabia. "Shouldn't we get going?"

"No," he said. "This is where we stay."

"Oh," I said. "We're living in this village?" I didn't like the idea — if we stayed put, Monsieur Tatagani would find us more easily.

"No. This is where we begin our safari."

I looked into the jungle all around us. The Inside. The road and the village were like skinny roots civilization had pushed here, but beyond it was only dense, wet wilderness. Why would even mock men want to live in there?

Prof laid an arm across my shoulders. "Do you know what *safari* means?" he asked.

I remembered the times I had heard the word used at the bar. "It is when Europeans come to see animals."

Prof shook his head. "It has nothing to do with animals. It is a Swahili word that means *journey*. It means a person is far away. That he cannot be reached."

I shrugged.

"We will be on safari," Prof muttered quietly, almost to himself, as he stared into the Inside. He removed his arm from my shoulder.

Around the marketplace were women toiling, children playing, men lounging. Above their chatter I heard not the hoots of the mock men, but the cooing of turtledoves. Their pretty call gave me hope that this safari might not be so terrible. It was impossible to be a street boy, after all, where there was no street. Here I was, a — what had Prof called it? — *research assistant.*

The loggers pushed the truck until the engine turned over enough to drive the wheels. After running alongside for a while, the village children gave up and returned to us. Prof and I sat among them, walled in by our mismatched possessions. The children played games around us, giggling at the strange Arab while he prayed.

The village houses had neatly swept walks, and designs were woven into their thatch, each roof unique. I picked out the home I'd have chosen, a small but impeccable room with a blue door and rolled palm fronds banding the roof to make a gutter. Once Prof had put away his rug, he asked the children which house was the chief's. They pointed to a hut the same size as the others, but with a roof of shiny corrugated metal. Prof patted the overhang approvingly.

There was no one inside, so we went around back, where the chief was seated with friends at a sagging plastic table. Prof greeted the chief while I stood off to one side with Omar, peering into the wilderness and waiting to be useful. (Well, I was peering; Omar was chewing at lice.) Prof joined their conversation and was soon gifting the chief with francs and a morsel of cold fried chicken. Then he began gesturing excitedly in the way that meant he could only be talking about his chimpanzees.

The village was on a hill, with views for miles around. Except for the skinny road, the jungle was unbroken. It made me shiver to look out at it. No one lived in there, except maybe a few Pygmies. Once Prof and I had gone a few miles in, we might be someplace no person had ever been.

A river rushed by somewhere under the canopy, and from the sound of it the water was moving fast; there were probably waterfalls within the steaming greenery. We'd be smart to listen for one as we trekked in, I figured, because where there was a waterfall there would be a pool at the bottom, which would mean constant fresh water. The kids who survived longest always had an eye on fresh water.

Prof must have been making some sort of deal with the chief, because more of his money came out. He beckoned me forward. "This is Luc," he said. "Once a month he will come back here and pick up food. I am paying for next month's resupply in advance now. We will need at least two large bags of rice and a jug of oil. When he comes he will deliver money for the next month, and the arrangement will continue. Will you agree to this?"

The chief nodded. While his friends wore traditional outfits, he was wearing a T-shirt with the shadow of a girl on it and some words in English beneath. It was one of the American shirts that arrived in Gabon every so often, pressed tight into ship containers full of discarded clothing. "Where are you heading?" he asked Prof. They were speaking French, even though the chief didn't seem too comfortable with the language.

Prof pulled out a map, and the fascinated village men clustered around it. As Prof ran his fingers along the brown lines that riddled the paper like pinworms, my mind raced. A month in the forest with Prof. If he turned out to be as cruel as Monsieur Tatagani, I could make my escape when he sent me back to the village for supplies.

While Prof was meeting with the chief, I heard a distant rumbling and joined the children running to the village's last hut to find out what was approaching.

*No, no,* I told my heart, *it isn't Monsieur Tatagani come to take my hands. He can't have found us yet.*

It was just another logging truck. I returned to outside the chief's hut and sat with my head bowed, undone by my sudden fear. Once Prof and I were in the jungle, there would be no one who could tell Monsieur Tatagani where we were. But here in Okondja, any person could go to Franceville and spread the gossip that would bring our doom.

*Come on, Prof, let's go!*

But he was still talking to the chief; I could hear him droning on about chimpanzees, about their different names. How the Baoulé call them the "beloved brother" of humans. That the Bété call them the "men returned from the forest."

I needed some way to distract myself from my fear, and since Prof and I were a team now, I figured I could take stock of what we had. The first thing I pulled out of the valise was Prof's passport. A man on the edge of town was watching me, and although that made me uneasy, I liked that he'd know what kinds of treasures a *research assistant* had access to.

A passport — what an amazing thing! I saw a page with a photo of Prof and lots of words and numbers. One line was just four digits. I'd learned my numbers and letters in village school, but it had been a long time since I'd needed them; I studied these so I could try them on the case's combination lock later.

When chairs scraped against the ground, I hurriedly jammed the passport into the valise. Once Prof finished showing where we were heading on his map, the chief shook his head.

"None of us go there," he said. "Because there *is* nothing there."

"That's precisely it!" Prof exclaimed.

The chief shook his head in resignation and gestured over to the man who had been staring at me. He was shorter than the other village men and wore scraps of leather instead of normal clothes. His nose was pierced by a piece of bone. "This man is from a tribe that lives Inside, and only came to Okondja today for our market. He would know where you are headed."

The chief spoke to the man in a native language I couldn't recognize.

The jungle hunter stared at the ground for a long time, but when he finally did look up I saw an unfriendly expression. The chief turned back to us. "You can start by crossing that field. You will find a stream on the other side that leads to a river. That is where your new canoe is docked."

"Our new canoe?" Prof asked.

"This man is willing to sell you his canoe for five hundred francs."

Prof agreed, and I was relieved to see him pay the hunter from the stash of real money. The chief brought out a bottle. "To celebrate," he said. When he poured the liquid into cups, I smelled what it was: banana beer. No one poured me any, and I would have refused it if they had. Even the smell reminded me of Monsieur Tatagani and made me sick with fear. Prof took a long gulp. He winced, but once he'd made it to the other side of the swallow he cheered loudly.

The chief waved his hand at the hunter. "Do you want him to come with you and help you carry that bag?"

Prof shook his head. "No. That is what Luc is for."

Prof's breath smelled like the banana beer, and every time I got a whiff of it my heart seized. I was glad there would be no more of that stuff where we were heading.

While we crossed the field, he whispered to me as I wheezed

away under his giant leather valise. "I would have taken that hunter's offer to guide us, but the National Geographic Society gave me a lead on where a group of chimpanzees is, and we don't want any hunters to find out. They are endangered animals, after all."

"So we won't follow his directions?" I asked, so instantly relieved that I dropped the valise.

"No." Prof chuckled, his hands on his hips. He waited for me to get the valise back up. "We are going to a place where no one can find us."

*Then we are safe from Monsieur Tatagani,* I thought. Soon, though, my relief was shaded with dread. *A place where no one can find us.*

As we approached the jungle line, I risked a glance back. The hunter was at the village edge, staring at us, his unslung bow tight in his hand.

I hurried after Prof.

At the river's edge Omar drew close, pulling off Prof's taqiyah and clutching it for security. Prof tried to get it back a couple of times but gave up, limping across muddy rocks while the monkey scampered behind.

Like the chief had promised, there was a canoe waiting for us.

"It's a nice one, isn't it?" Prof asked.

It was a beautiful pirogue, a massive tree whose insides had been scooped out to make a boat. And it had an outboard motor! "Won't that hunter miss his canoe?" I asked.

Prof shrugged. "Yes. But this way, even if he wanted to track us to the chimps, he couldn't follow fast enough. Chimpanzees are very valuable to hunters; the adults provide plenty of meat, and the infants can bring lots of money if he sells them to American medical labs. It's very good he doesn't know where we are going. Come on, into the boat."

The canoe was plenty large enough for all of our belongings. Prof sat at the prow, Omar on his shoulder. As I pushed off from the bank, my feet pressed so hard into the mud that I was up to my thighs in muck before the boat finally groaned forward. I hauled myself in, bringing with me a stream of mud that pooled at my feet. I rinsed my new shoes in the river water and set them out to dry on the spare seat.

It was my first time piloting a boat, though I didn't tell Prof that. At least he didn't expect me to know how to start the motor; he lurched to the back and leaned over me to yank the cord. The smell of him, the rough feel of his fingers over mine as he caught his balance on the side, strummed some old string in me, reminding me of once spending a week beside my father to re-thatch our roof.

After coughing out blue-gray, the engine puttered. I'd seen people navigate pirogues before, so I took the motor's handle and copied what I'd seen them do. I got along surprisingly okay — we only slammed into low-hanging branches twice. Small fish swam at the edges of the whirlpool behind the motor, churned bits of them rising to the surface as we went.

Prof directed us down one tributary and then another as the afternoon reddened. We took frequent breaks, passing Prof's canteen between us and refilling it from the clearest and fastest streams. All around us were tremendous kapok trees, their wide wings plunging into the soil. Only when my neck began to ache did I realize I'd been craning, nervous of the snakes camouflaged in their branches.

But there weren't too many animals to see. Not yet. Small crocodiles sunned on floating logs. Now and then a kingfisher soared across the river. Everywhere that wasn't water was in constant semi-darkness, but I did once see at the river's edge a forest bushbuck, smaller than a goat, impossibly pretty with her pale brown fur glowing in the sun reflecting off the water. She had a starburst of white spots on her forehead. When she saw us she bounded away, flashing the underside of her tail.

"Did you see that?" I asked Prof.

But he put a hand in the air to silence me. "Do you *hear* that?" he asked.

"No," I said.

But then I did. A drumming.

"Is it the hunter?" I blurted. As I said it I realized I'd been scanning for him along the waterline all day, convinced he was silently tracking us, bow at the ready.

"No!" Prof said joyfully. "Listen closer!"

I heard the drumming again. And a shriek.

"It's them," Prof said. "The chimpanzees. We're nearly home."

# PART TWO:

## MOCK MEN

# FIVE

Prof motioned us to shore late that afternoon. I tossed my shoes to the bank and hopped into the green-brown water to drag us to the side, disappearing up to my kneecaps in silky river clay. Omar used my head as a stepping-stone to bounce to land. As I knew he would, the moment he was onshore Prof had his broad map out and was tracing the brown pinworm lines with his finger, slowly pivoting around in a circle. He announced that we would be setting up camp in the narrow open space by the river and continuing our journey the next day.

Unaware of the green katydid walking its elegant legs across his chest, Prof opened his valise and took stock of his belongings. I'd seen them bit by bit, but here they were all together. I did a mental inventory as he spread them out.

"What else is in the metal briefcase, other than money?" I asked.

But Prof ignored me, delving deeper into his valise. The final thing out was a large complicated mess of waxed tan fabric.

Once we'd managed to get the tent stakes to stay put in the loose soil, I was pleased with the large peaked structure. It had an overhang that shaded a few feet of earth, and might even keep us dry once the rainy season started. I imagined Prof teaching me to read on our improvised porch, then shook the thought from my mind.

I was smiling until I swatted the evening's first mosquito. It was huge — the beast's smeared gore ran the length of my finger. "Aayi!" I cried out.

"Home," Prof said, resolutely ignoring me. "Well. Home for tonight."

I shook the canister of gas, heavy with sloshing fuel. Fire would be crucial for us. It would help keep away not only mosquitoes but also much larger predators, like vipers and leopards. The street boys kept a constant fire at the Franceville trash pit, adding anything flammable the moment we came across it, and it did wonders to keep rats away.

First I hunted for rocks and positioned them in a circle. Then I started rolling logs near. Most were too wet to catch fire that night, but I hoped they'd dry and eventually burn if I kept them close.

The fire itself I managed to start with the sparker and a kindling pile of fluffy palm threads. As they lit and I boiled water, I proudly realized that Prof might not have been that insane to choose me. Our first camp meal was simple: cups of rice that tasted of char. I threw the bugs I'd unearthed beneath the pit stones into the fire's edges, and we ate them once they'd crisped over, padding them in rice and rolling them in broad leaves. When the heads were plucked off, most of the guts came away, too, but the bugs were still bitter. They had a pleasant steamy crunch, though, and tasted of flame.

While Prof read his Koran after dinner, I rummaged through the nearby undergrowth to see what else might be edible — those leaves I'd recognized had greatly improved our dinner. Some shoots looked promising, and I found some half-rotten onions at the base of them, but I didn't recognize any other greens. I'd have to make finding some a priority; rice might keep us alive, but would quickly become boring.

Prof and I sat on a fallen log before the fire, looking across the narrow river and into the thick wilderness beyond. As the sun went down, the frogs and insects increased their noise, becoming almost too loud to talk over. Prof seemed to find the racket amusing. "We're not here to sleep easy, Luc!" he yelled.

The woods around Franceville and my old village had their dangers, but my helplessness had never felt as absolute as this. The streets of Franceville, too, had been full of threats. But at least I'd come to know and expect them; the unknowability of these new dangers made me worry I'd never manage to fall asleep.

The day's heat clung to the night air, so Prof and I decided to flatten the tent and lie on it beside the smoldering fire. While he went down to the river to wash his teeth, I lay on the canvas in the open air and watched the sun make its rapid red fall.

When Prof came back I saw his profile was studded with mosquitoes. But he was like me; the bites meant little to him anymore, wouldn't leave even a small mark in the morning. I'd fought and survived malaria once before, and they said God would not send that to you twice; I assumed Prof was the same.

Of course there were other things that could come across us in the night and easily kill us. Pythons, leopards, scorpions. But we would have to trust the fire to keep us safe from those.

Prof placed the plastic basin that had once contained Carine beside him. When he snapped his fingers Omar came right over, and Prof lifted him into it. The monkey looked confused for a moment, but then relaxed and lay inside, arms sprawled over the edges like a drunk man slumped outside the Léconi.

I wouldn't have ever thought it, but it had been easier to sleep crowded in with the boys, listening to Monsieur Tatagani fighting or seducing in the other room, than here, far from the street. Swaying palm fronds fringed the night sky like eyelashes. I watched them close and open their eyes. The moment the last sunshine disappeared, Prof shouted, "The light's gone out!"

I wanted to scold him for giving our location away to anyone listening, but he'd been so silly that I started giggling instead.

Almost as soon as our laughter had stopped, his breathing slowed, and I knew Prof had fallen asleep.

Somehow, despite the deafening music of the frogs and insects, despite the occasional tickle of an unknown bug crawling over my face, I fell asleep. It might have helped that Omar had decided to leave the basin and sleep curled against me, his hand in mine, just like Pierre might have done.


The next morning Omar was the first up, noisily picking through our stuff. Once he tired of that he explored the canopy, raining us with grubs and seeds. Grumbling, Prof and I got our belongings and packed up the tent. I was stepping into the canoe when I saw Prof back on his mat, reading from pages bound in raggedy leather.

"Is that another holy book?" I asked.

He chuckled. "Oh, no. Come here, I'll show you."

I sat next to him, and he showed me the cover. "No one has written a guide to Gabon," he said. "You are from one of the least populated countries on Earth, did you know that? Under a million people in a land the size of France."

I didn't understand — a million people sounded like more than could fit in the whole world.

He knocked the cover of the book. "This is the only guide I could find that has anything to say about Gabon. Written a hundred years ago by a German and translated into French. It's called a Baedeker. I could have read it in German, though, if I wanted to. Did I tell you I met the German chancellor, and that *she* is a woman?"

I knew I wasn't interested in German chancellors, whatever they were. "What does it say in there about Franceville? And is my old village in there?" I asked. It pained me that it would have taken me ages to read it for myself.

"Let's see," Prof said, flipping through. "Your village isn't in there. But Franceville . . ." He found the word and chortled. "It's called Francheville in this book, because that's what the city was originally named. It got shortened over time. It was supposed to be called 'City of the Free,' and now it's become 'City of the French.' Doesn't that tell you a lot about the whole region? Let's see, here we are. 'North of Francheville: One must exercise utmost caution, following the Ogooué out of Francheville, in the selection of one's companions. Generally speaking, the ilk departing the country's squalid eastern capital are interested less in experiencing the local life than with rushing across the countryside willy-nilly, keeping the curtains of their Transgabonais railway car tightly shut against the inquisitive trunks of forest elephants or the groping fingers of lowland gorillas.'"

Prof slammed the book closed and let out a hoot of laughter. "Isn't that amazing? The *tone*. But it's all we have to go on."

"Can you read it again?" I asked. I hadn't understood most of what Prof had said.

"What did you say?" Prof asked.

"Can you read it again?" I repeated, louder. I was eager to understand what this Mr. Baedeker had to say about my country.

"Of course I will," Prof said tenderly, giving my shoulder a squeeze. He repeated the passage, very slowly, and I understood more this time. I was smiling, too, because when Prof read he sounded like a nun giving a tour of a dump.

"Are you ready to move on, Luc?" Prof asked.

"Yes," I said.

We motored the pirogue up a quiet stream, sometimes having to drag the canoe through muddy reeds, but more often than not cutting easily through the dark water. Long, elegant birds lazily soared across our prow or let themselves be chased along corridors of tree and water, landing on a branch only to float forward again. I realized what a trek it would be to make my monthly voyages back for food — and how isolated we were. If I ever abandoned Prof, I would have to flee for days before I saw people again. Right then, I couldn't imagine doing that to him. But still the thoughts of leaving, and of being left, were like a Monsieur Tatagani that was always with me, bringing up everyone's doom even at my most peaceful moments.

Late that afternoon, Prof had me pull to the side. He spent a long time studying the map and his Baedeker. Then he clapped and pointed to the top of a shallow hill. "That's where our camp will be. Flat, high enough not to grow puddles in the rainy season, but not overly exposed. The National Geographic Society would approve."

It seemed like one more hill out of many to me, but I reminded myself that I did not have Prof's training.

Once we'd reached the top of the rise, we barely had time to set up the campsite before the sun fell off the sky. I'd have to save my exploration for the next day.

The next morning I woke before Prof did. Mustering my courage, I descended the hill and stepped into the jungle. Immediately the sunshine was gone and I was in a cool, vivid space. The leaves, which had been too washed out to really see before, were now small and lovely. Since they hushed the wind, I could hear so much around me: the rustling of ferns, the occasional drop of nuts, the hum of fat bees. There was no sign of any mock men. Or moneylenders.

Prof was still asleep when I returned, his taqiyah draped over his face to shade it from the morning sun streaming in through the tent wall. I kneeled over him and took in our spread-out belongings, the sum of our newly joined lives. Prof's leather wallet poked from the open valise, and beside it was the metal briefcase.

I figured if my survival was tied to Prof's, it was my right to find out as much as possible about him. I pulled the case into my lap. Remembering the four number symbols I had seen on Prof's passport, I matched them to the case's dials. 1-9-6-8. I waited for it to open.

But it wouldn't.

I was disappointed, and I was relieved.


I was far from the metal case when Prof woke up. He found me intent over the stove, boiling the rice we would eat throughout the day.

Prof patted me on my head while I inserted a stick through the rice froth and scraped the bottom of the pot so nothing burned. "You're a good little chef."

I grunted, not getting up from my squat. A feeling of pride had risen in me that felt strangely like anger.

I cut a glance to Prof as he dusted off a fallen trunk and sat, taking out a notebook and fussily blowing it free of dirt. He sampled each of his pencils on the inside cover before selecting one. Above the scribbles he wrote, in deliberate script, a short sequence of letters that I assumed was either his name or where we were.

When he looked up at me I quickly returned my focus to the pot of rice. "Do you know your letters?" Prof asked.

The hot murderous gratitude returned, and I didn't reply.

"Okay," Prof said. "I'll teach you once we've settled in." He coughed. "Even if it's only for my sake, so you can be more help to me." He pointed to his script. "This is my name the way an edu-cated person from Gabon would write it, or like a French person would. See? *Professor Abdul Mohammad, Primatology, University of Leipzig, Germany.* That's what those letters say."

"I know. I used to know how to read — I just haven't done it for a while," I said curtly. When Prof didn't respond, I stood and stretched to give my back a break from hunching over the pot. "What are you going to write in there?"

He let out a long breath. My question must have been harder than I'd thought. Omar had been sniffing around the tent, and sat in Prof's lap. Prof scratched behind his ears while he thought.

"What exactly has the National Geographic Society asked you to do?" I urged, giving the pot another stir and then, once I'd seen it was ready, scooping out rice. We only had the one tin bowl, so I figured I'd let Prof go first, then eat whatever portion remained.

Finally Prof spoke. "Once I find the chimps, I'm going to note every time I see one. I will number them. I will keep a record of their behaviors."

"Why?"

"Like us, chimpanzees know family and loneliness, victory and grief. They need our help to keep their homeland safe. And they are our closest relatives."

"Maybe they're *your* closest relatives," I snorted. "Not mine."

"What do you mean?" Prof asked.

I huffed in irritation. Why was he playing dumb? "Everyone knows the chimpanzee has a yellow face and is a cousin of the Arabs. Gorillas have black faces and they're cousins of black people."

"A fun theory," Prof said, "that also happens to be deeply disturbing and entirely untrue. Do you know that we are closer to chimps, and they to us, than either of us are to gorillas? That we humans are right in the thick of the tree of apes, not some distant branch?"

I shrugged. "You're the researcher. But I've always heard that the chimpanzees are people who stayed out after dark."

"Which is it? If both your theories are right, there would only be chimpanzees in the Middle East."

Prof turned back to his notebook, eyes twinkling. I instantly missed talking to him. "Haven't other people already done what you're trying to do?"

Prof narrowed his eyes. "Not here. Gabon has so many chimpanzees! Once I publish my book, people will come here to visit the famous chimpanzees of Professor Mohammad. They will spend money here to visit them. My work will benefit everyone in this country, including the apes."

"Is that what a janegoodall is? Someone who gets foreigners to take a safari?"

Prof passed me the empty bowl. I refilled it and handed it back, but he shook his finger and pointed to me, indicating that I should eat. I did, gladly. "Jane Goodall is a woman who lives with the chimpanzees in Tanzania, far from here. She has studied them for many years, and made people realize that although animals might not be quite as smart as people, their feelings are complicated and strong, and they are worthy of our respect and protection, even if they are not like us. Jane Goodall is white and English, though. And Dian Fossey, who made the highland gorillas famous, was white and American. I am *African*."

*No, you are an Arab*, I thought. But it wasn't a fight I knew enough about to win, so I nodded, picking rice bits from the edges of my lips and placing them on my tongue.

"Humans will break your heart," Prof said. "The same selfishness that makes so many of us hurt the ones we love makes our species hurt creatures that it admires. To hunt and destroy chimpanzees, like they would never do to us. Our treatment of animals is a great failure of our empathy."

Prof sighed, then continued. "I have written many articles. I have taught many students about chimpanzees. I have worked closely with Jane Goodall herself. But I have not undertaken my own study. Not until now."

"Do you have an expensive camera to take pictures?" I asked.

He shook his head. "The National Geographic Society will send someone to take photographs. I have told them precisely where we are heading, so they will know where to find us. I must have my study well under way before the photographer arrives, though. They don't want to pay someone to wait around while I search for chimpanzees, you understand." Prof stood. "I'm off to explore. Do you want to come with me?"

I shook my head. "I'm going to set up our camp some more. Then I will wash our clothes." I knew Prof didn't want his galabias cleaned — but I was in charge of the camp, and since neither of us wanted insect eggs hatching in his skin, I was going to wash our clothes whether he wanted me to or not.

As Prof left to explore, he kept glancing back — maybe he worried I'd try to escape to the pirogue. I wished I could tell him he had nothing to fear, but all the ways I could say that would make him suspect he *had* something to fear. I didn't know how to make someone trust me.

Once he was gone I unpegged the tent and shook it, pouring out twigs and curled-up caterpillars. I suspected that was the first of many thousands of times I'd be shaking the tent clean. I took our clothes down to the river and washed them, using up a precious sliver of soap to scrub the smelliest parts, the screams of mysterious animals all around me. I returned to the campsite and rigged up the nylon rope so I could hang our clothes to dry. I also suspended our food bag from it, so animals would find it hard to raid. Omar climbed a nearby tree, leaped to the bag, and perched on it. He didn't try to get to the food, just appeared to be enjoying his new nest.

I'd kept Prof's paper envelope of dried mint out of the food bag, and rummaged through it. Below the dried leaves I found what looked like fine black dirt at the bottom. Seeds. My mother had the best herb garden in our old village, and my father's cousins would often come by to snip a leaf here and there. When I was little I would follow her along the rows, watching her select which plants would go where, how far apart and how deep to plant the seeds.

I selected a patch of earth by our tent, near enough to the base of a tree to avoid the worst sun. I squatted and raked the soil with a stick so it softened, yanking up small roots and vines. I made a shallow trough, sprinkled the seeds in, and loosely patted the soil on top. Finally I filled our rice bowl with river water and wet the soil. Some bits of rice tumbled in, too, but I figured those would only help make the soil fertile.

If I didn't plant those seeds, Prof would eventually run out of leaves for his tea. Tending the mint was the only way I could think of to tell him he could count on me.

As the heat got stronger, I took a break by sitting in the sunshine. Omar joined me and gave happy gasps as I picked through his fur and scratched deep into the folds of skin behind his ears.

A branch snapped at the bottom of the hill, cracked by a creature larger than a bird or monkey. My thoughts went immediately to Monsieur Tatagani. I pulled the knife out of Prof's bag and brought it with me as I crept down the hill. Almost the very instant I left the campsite, a tiny wasp stung my face. I rolled it between my fingers and flicked away the plated yellow corpse, and when I looked up I realized the jungle had closed around me. I was surrounded by kapok trees, their thick wings flying into the soil. In some areas the ground was soft enough for my legs to sink up to the ankle, and in others there were rocky gullies wide enough that I could have sprinted along them.

As I was crawling over a slick mossy rock, I heard a shriek and saw crashing branches. The shriek repeated farther away, and then I saw the branches of the next tree over start swaying. Then it was the next tree, and the next, until I could see nothing.

Any medium-size animal could shake tree branches like that. But it wasn't any animal; I knew what I had heard.

It brought back memories of our village hut, of nesting within my mother's arms, eyes scrunched shut as the sun went down over our crops and the mock men began to shriek in the night.

I felt a terror unlike any I'd felt for years. And it was worse now: The last time I'd had this feeling, my mother had been around to protect me.

Gripping the knife tight, I waited for the chimpanzee to return. But it did not, so I began foraging. A little ways off the faint trail I found an old, bent tree, most of whose fruit had dropped and rotted. But a half dozen of them were not so worm-ridden that they couldn't be eaten. I piled the mangoes in my arms and started back to camp. I'd go in a circle, returning from the opposite direction.

The trees were vigorous and dense near the river, hunching in so tightly, I almost couldn't squeeze past. Two saplings with fresh slick bark grew especially close, and I climbed into their V and leaped down into a soft pile of fallen leaves on the other side.

I knew there was something wrong as soon as I landed; the motion of my fall continued even after I'd hit ground. I heard a crack and was back off my feet. I thought I was tumbling at first, just a hard sort of tumbling, until I saw that pile of leaves far below my head and realized I'd been hurtled into the air. A serpent was tight around my ankle, gripping and squeezing. The whirling jungle floor filled with stars.

Struggling against gravity, vision flashing, I pulled my gaze upward. A circle of vine was tight around my ankle.

My immediate, crazed thought was that I'd been attacked by a plant, that one of these trees was a meat-eater and was reeling me in. But then I saw the neat knot in the fibers, something only a human could pull off, and realized the truth: I'd been caught in a snare.

I was lucky that my fear of the mock men had made me clutch the knife so tightly; otherwise it would have dropped like my arm-load of mangoes. Straining, I reached up and had the swaying vine within arm's reach. Praying to miss my toes, I flailed out with the blade, aiming as high up the snare as I could. The knife bit, and when I didn't feel immediate pain I knew I'd hit vine and not foot. The snare held for a moment and then tore, sending me plummet-ing to the ground. I let the knife go this time, flinging it far and hoping I wouldn't impale myself at the bottom.

I hit the nest of leaves chest-first, my neck angled nearly flat against the ground. I breathed through the pain in my shoulders and spine, concentrating only on the rotten smell of the earth until the pain faded. Then I got to my feet, my first priority to recover the knife. Only once I had it did I examine my ankle. The snare had a neat, efficient knot, better than any I'd pulled off in my own hunting days. I kneeled down to cut it away and then paused, deciding I should keep it intact so I could try to replicate the knot later. I examined the sapling that had lent the snare such force. Even freed, it still arced in the shape of a C. The same style of knot attached the vine to it. The liana was bright green, which meant the vine couldn't have been cut more than a few days ago.

There had been humans nearby.

There might *still* be humans nearby.

Watching.

I slowly pivoted in the clearing, peering through the growth. My heart pounded as I waited to see fronds part and a man step through.

My foot was giving me pins and needles, so I flexed and pointed it to keep the blood flowing under the pressure of the snare. I'd sketch the knot into Prof's notebook before I finally undid it. I climbed back between the trees and down the trail, wading along the river's edge to return to the campsite.

I found Prof sitting beside our smoldering fire, Omar watching him sleepily from his food-bag perch, arms flung out like a dozy cat's. Prof was staring into his notebook, but nothing was written there. That Prof had found nothing to write down meant I had been the first one to catch a sign of a chimpanzee, and I brimmed with pleasure that I would be able to tell Prof that his mission had worked, that the mock men were here.

Then I frowned.

I would also have to tell him that they were being hunted.

# SIX

While Prof drank his tea the next morning, I examined the snare. Making it must have taken a lot of effort; it had an elegantly carved disc of wood at its center, with fasteners of the perfect thickness for the vine to slip through. But that work had paid off — I remembered how easily I'd been hoisted into the air, the amount of force the simple device had been able to muster. The snares spent their existences like I'd spent mine, announcing themselves only in the quietest moments.

The moment Prof had finished his mint tea, I eagerly led him toward the spot on the faint trail where I'd heard the chimpanzee scream and crash away. He pulled us short well before we got to the site. "Look," he said, grabbing my arm and whirling.

It was a dead body.

The skeleton dangled from a wrist, still striped with sinew and scraps of skin and straight black hair. At first I thought someone had hung a human skeleton from a tree to warn us. But then I realized it wasn't a human and that it hadn't been hung; it had been trapped. The liana vine was older and brown this time, but I recognized the snare's knots.

"Is that a mock man?" I whispered.

Prof nodded sadly. "Yes. It was a chimpanzee. Do you still have the knife on you?"

I nodded, then climbed the tree and cut the skeleton loose. It clattered to the ground, flies and maggots and scraps of skin falling from it. Some rotted tissue opened up at the center of the corpse, letting out a terrible smell. I tugged at Prof's sleeve. "We'll be sick! There's nothing you can do with the body."

Prof dry heaved for a moment, then approached the corpse. Clutching the vine, he dragged the skeleton to the river and hurled it in. We watched it disintegrate in the current. When Prof returned he had tears in his eyes. "It is illegal to hunt chimpanzees! They are endangered! And this hunter set a snare that he didn't return to. This chimpanzee probably took over a week to die from infection on its wrist. An exquisitely sensitive creature, with family and hopes, died a very painful, lonely death."

I imagined hanging by my wrist from a tree, crying alone. The pain spreading from my wrist to my arm, watching my body rot until I died of thirst. That was often how I'd seen snared animal corpses for sale in Franceville: One limb had rotted too much to eat and had been chopped off. Even if these mock men were monsters, no creature deserved to die that way.

"It is awful," I said.

"The irresponsibility of it," Prof said. "We will find this hunter!"

"Okay, Prof. Of course we will," I said quietly.

I thought Prof might want to return to camp after that, but he wordlessly pressed on.

Once we'd reached the clearing where I'd heard the chimpanzee, we stood still for a long time. Omar had followed us at a distance, emerging from the green and clutching my shirttail like Pierre once had; but he soon got bored, climbed a nearby tree, and nodded off. Prof was patient and still, staring into the foliage with intense focus. At points he rolled out his rug, kneeled, and prayed to his god. But even with the power of his prayers, no chimpanzees came.

"We must be very patient," he said in a hushed voice once he was back up, shaking soil from the rug. "The chimps are smart creatures, and clearly they are already being hunted by humans. Why should they trust *us*, who are also humans?"

Asking Prof to stay where he was, I returned to the mango tree. There I gathered up more of the wormy fruit. Inspecting the mangoes, pink grubs waving from between the plates of their cracked skins, I realized they might be too far gone to attract any mock men. I let them fall with a wet thud, wiped my hands on my pants, and shinnied up the trunk until I reached a couple of choice ripe mangoes still on the branches. I got bitten by some insects as I scaled the tree, and already had a raised rash from a vine that had broken my skin as I rolled across it, but I thought these delicious fruits would be worth it.

When I returned to Prof, he realized my intention right away and nodded toward the far side of the clearing. Once I'd laid the fruit there in a small pile and returned, we stood behind a tree and watched.

All was quiet. Omar woke and chirped down at us, as if asking what was supposed to happen.

"Mangoes are not native to Africa," Prof whispered. "Maybe the chimpanzees know this and do not like them."

"I bet the chimpanzees don't care where mangoes originally came from," I said. "They care that they taste very good."

But still — the fruit didn't seem to be working very well so far. All that happened was a red-brown snake wandered across them, flicked its tongue into the air, and then disappeared into the brush.

"What if the mock men decide *we* are tastier than the mangoes?" I asked. "What if something is watching, waiting for *us* to be eaten?"

Prof considered my words. "All the literature I have read indicates that chimpanzees will not eat us."

I gave him a long look, then returned my gaze to the mangoes. "Does *Jane Goodall* write books about —" I cut off.

The drumming was loud and purposeful, like a chief preparing his people for war. And it was getting louder.

I crouched as the noise approached, heart thudding. For many seconds in a row there would be no drumming, then it would start again, each time much closer than before. I pointed high when I realized nearby treetops had started trembling along with the thuds.

The shaking branches were no more than a dozen yards away. Alarmed, Prof clutched my forearm. Then all was still.

Until a mock man came into view.

He was low and muscular, stiff black hair messy over a tan face and pouting pink lips. Easing forward on all fours, he sniffed curiously at the pile of mangoes. When the chimp grunted, Omar bounded to the top of the highest tree. He was a smart monkey, choosing a thin branch where it would be impossible for the heavier animal to follow. The chimpanzee's attention snapped to the vervet. He stared at Omar for a few seconds, then brought his attention back to the fruit. Before taking any of the mangoes, he approached a nearby kapok, which he drummed by going into a half handstand and flailing his feet against it. It was a loud, impressive sound, and the chimpanzee paused to look at Omar, as if to see whether the monkey had been as awestruck as he ought to be. Making soft hooting sounds, the chimp drew nearer to the mangoes.

The chimpanzee was shorter than me, but his hands made deep indentations in the ground, so I knew he was heavy and strong. Though he mostly walked on all fours like a beast, occasionally he would stand on his two feet to look around. Then he'd go back to walking along the narrow forest path. The chimp seemed to have forgotten about the mangoes, and didn't appear to have anything else to do with himself. He sniffed a branch and grasped along it to pluck a single berry. His hairy black fingers drew the red treat close to his lips. There were more berries on the branch, but he didn't bother with them, instead plopping down in the grass, head resting on his joined palms. He looked like a boy kicked out of his home for the day, walking the streets and looking for trouble so he'd feel part of something.

I thought Prof might take his notebook out to make notes, but he was quietly watching the chimpanzee, face full of joy. He'd gone so long without blinking that tears were falling down his chin and dripping to the ground.

As he sat, the chimp held one of his feet to his nose and sniffed it; I saw that the bottom of his foot had no hair on it and was as brown-orange-pink as a person's.

He lay still for a minute or two, then unexpectedly took off at a run. When he tripped over the pile of mangoes, he skidded to a stop and peered at them. After scanning the scene like a burglar, he placed one in his mouth, easily biting through the tough skin. The others he piled into his arms. Then he hurried away.

"Come on," Prof said once the chimp was out of sight. "We're following." He took off down the path, moving surprisingly fast considering his limp. I trailed a safe distance behind, Omar bounding down from the tree and holding tight to my shoulder. We must have looked like nervous children trailing after Father.

Prof led us fast enough to keep the chimp in view, tracking the black figure against tangled flashes of green and brown. One time the chimpanzee halted and looked back at us, his black eyes meeting ours, but he didn't seem alarmed; he clutched his mangoes tighter and continued on. Eventually the chimp stopped in a clearing and began hooting. Prof and I froze at the opposite end, hiding ourselves in the greenery as best we could.

The chimp held still, his hoots softening. While we waited I idly kicked at one of the large flat tree wings — and it made no sound at all. The chimpanzee must have been incredibly strong to make that drumming noise.

I decided to call him Drummer.

There was an answering chimp cry nearby, and then Drummer shot out of the clearing. We rushed to follow, and when we peeked around the bend we saw him with more chimps: a female with an infant playing at her feet. I figured she was older, since her skin hung loose, with hairless patches. The infant seemed healthy, rolling around on the ground and insistently climbing up her mother to suckle, even though the old female kept casting her off.

For a while Drummer stood near the old mother, swaying, the stack of mangoes tight in his hands. Then he turned away from her, squatted, and began to chew through the mangoes. The female crossed in front of him. For a while she kneeled there, infant wrapped around her belly, and stared longingly at the mangoes. Drummer pivoted again so she was out of his view and continued to eat. Then the female lay on her back, arm flat out on the ground. While Drummer ignored her, she flicked her fingers against his back, trying to attract his attention.

I named her Beggar.

Once Drummer had finished his second mango, he placed his free hand, downturned, on top of Beggar's. She panted softly and cautiously reached for one of the remaining fruits. Drummer continued eating calmly as she pulled it and then the other mango away from him. She bit into the thick skin and peeled, rapidly eating one and then the other. As the peels dropped, the infant played with them, tossing them between her hands. When her lack of coordination made them fall, she got down from her mother's lap to retrieve them — kicking them farther away in the process. Then she returned and began to suckle.

I decided to name the infant Mango.

Drummer's attitude toward the old female was so dismissive yet respectful that I guessed he was no longer a child but not yet an adult; I suspected that he was even her son. Prof and I didn't dare speak and risk drawing attention, but I made mental notes of what I wanted to tell him so he could record them in his notebook. I wondered if this was a little family alone in the jungle, or if there were other chimpanzees nearby.

Prof refused to leave the trio all day, but at one point I got hungry, so Omar and I returned to the campsite. Some small, fat brown monkeys, like yams with arms and legs, were poking around our stuff. I chased them off. Omar scolded the intruders even louder than I, though never leaving the security of my shoulder. Once we were alone I cooked some more rice, indulging in salt this time to make the meal taste at least a little different from breakfast. Omar seemed to feel at home at the campsite; he climbed into the plastic basin and stayed there when I headed back to check on Prof.

Along the way I foraged more mangoes. We ate them in our hiding spot, watching Beggar and Drummer and Mango. The chimps were conscious of us, but didn't seem wary. Maybe they had already been around humans. I made a mental note to tell Prof that later: The hunter might have been someone the chimps already knew.

Prof's head bobbed as he ate his salted rice. We'd been in that clearing for hours, and squatting so long had worn on the old man — like all foreigners, he crouched on the balls of his feet, instead of on his heels as he should have done. I leaned in and risked whispering, "Do you want to head back to the campsite? I can stay here a while longer and remember everything I see."

Prof shook his head, then reconsidered and nodded. He must have seen I was upset to be alone, though, because he leaned down to look right in my eyes, hands squarely on my shoulders. "I know it's frightening out here. But if we lose track of the chimps we might not find any again for weeks. I need your help; do you think you can give it?"

I nodded solemnly. I didn't want to separate, but I owed Prof everything. If he wanted me to do this, I would. I pressed the knife into his hands. "You should have this. If that hunter or Monsieur Tatagani comes to me, I can run. You can't run from the campsite."

"Monsieur Tatagani? He doesn't know where we are, Luc," Prof said. But he did take the knife, and limped back toward the campsite. When he was gone I felt very much alone, even with the chimps so near. Once it was dark there would be no tracing my steps back to the campsite; whatever happened out here, I'd have to deal with it myself. I wedged myself between two baobab trees to feel safer.

As the afternoon wore dim, the chimps focused less on eating and more on relaxing. Beggar reclined at the base of a tree, arms behind her head and legs crossed. As soon as she was laid flat her eyes closed, as if she'd been waiting all day for this moment. Mango scrambled over her mother's torso, slapping her head. Throughout it all, Beggar resolutely scrunched her eyes shut. Even though I was only a few yards away, neither of them paid me any attention.

Drummer, though, was a different story. At one point a stream of army ants shifted routes so that they passed near my shoe, and when I'd finished shaking my foot clear, I looked up to see the young male a few feet away, hunched over his knuckles, the hairs on the back of his neck raised. He'd stalked over soundlessly and now stared at me, the glow of the fading afternoon sun rimming his hard shiny eyes with rust. He took a step forward, his eyes locked on mine. Then he took another.

I'd confronted aggressive dogs before. I knew that you weren't supposed to run from a violent animal. As this muscular creature crept toward me, teeth bared, all I could think was *hold still*, and all I could feel was *get away*.

I backed up, heedlessly stepping through the crust of a termite mound. I was sure the insects, plump with venom, were biting my ankles, but I couldn't feel them. I could only stare at the beast before me. I sensed our locked gazes were only making things worse, but I couldn't look away. Like I'd once done for Monsieur Tatagani, I had to learn as much as I could about his anger and how I might survive it.

Suddenly Drummer sprinted toward me, dragging his hands along the ground. Rocks and branches scattered before him, making a terrible noise. I sensed Beggar sitting up and heard Mango shrieking in fright even as all my thoughts turned to escape. As I leaped over a stream and into a thick stand of ferns, there was a rush of sound and a beating black wave. For a moment I thought another chimp was in front of me, that I'd been hunted and surrounded. But then it turned out to be a cluster of startled black birds, their underwings blurred arcs of white within black as they rose to the sky.

When I stumbled into the campsite I surprised Prof at his prayers; he leaped to his feet and blinked wildly while I doubled over and wheezed.

"What happened? What is it?!" he cried.

I tried to tell him, but the words wouldn't come out right. "One . . . of those chimps . . . charged me."

Prof nodded, suddenly calm. "I see. Is that him?"

I whirled and looked where Prof was pointing. There was Drummer, standing at the base of our hill. He steadily turned his gaze to me, then to Prof. Now that I'd run from him, his fury seemed to have drained. He was holding a hefty rock, which he hurled vaguely in our direction; it went far astray, but he still hooted triumphantly.

"Yes," I said. "That's him."

"We appear," Prof said, "to have met our neighbors."

# SEVEN

Drummer ran off as quickly as he'd come. Prof and I spent the evening telling each other our impressions of the chimps while I scrabbled together a dinner of rice and canned fish. We plopped into the tent as soon as we'd finished. Prof was too exhausted even to do his ritual teeth cleaning.

The next morning Prof headed back for the chimp clearing while I rinsed out the breakfast things. After my run-in with Drummer, I was more than happy to stay back. Burned rice kernels were steadily accumulating on the bottom of the pot no matter how hard I scrubbed or how long I soaked, and I found myself wishing that my mother were there so I could ask her how she cleaned out her big blackened pans at the end of the day. I remembered her scrap of steel wool and wanted even one small piece of it.

Once I'd shaken the tent clean I took down the clothes I'd hung to dry on the nylon rope — they were still a little wet, and would probably never be fully dry again until we were back Outside. Omar had continued to take to the plastic basin, sleeping curled at the bottom, but I was worried that being on the ground night after night was dangerous. So I ran the nylon through the rope handles and suspended the basin. He stared at it, suspicious of what I'd done with his home. "This is for you!" I scolded, finger wagging. "Don't be mad!" His little black face frowned back.

When I walked to the far side of the clearing, Omar nervously tailed me. I crossed back, and he continued to follow at my heels.

Giggling, I climbed a tree. Omar was so much faster that he climbed me as well, ending up at the nylon rope. Then he noticed the basin again, forgot all about me, and plopped inside. He was soon out again, but at least he knew where his basin was now. I headed back down the tree.

And froze.

There, beside the tent, was a hunter. He wore simple cloth shorts and no shirt, a small sack slung around his torso and an unstrung bow in his hand. From his waist were tied lengths of snare liana, their bright green coils as lovely as vipers.

He'd just stepped into our campsite and hadn't seen me yet. Heart pounding, I watched the man poke at our tent, prod the valise with a stick.

Then Omar saw him, shrieked, and leaped down from the tree. I got ready to jump down in case the hunter went after him. Looking around nervously — I guessed because he figured where there was vervet there was owner — he left.

When he passed right under the tree, I recognized him. It was the hunter from Okondja.

He'd followed us here and was heading toward Prof and the chimpanzees. As I left the campsite to tail the hunter, Omar's hand was unexpectedly in mine; maybe the outsider had made him nervous and eager to reinforce our bond. He could only make it so fast on two legs, though, so I was glad that when I paused with arms outstretched he bounded up and onto my shoulder.

The hunter was already out of sight. That was for the best. I didn't want to confront him; I just wanted to get to Prof as soon as possible so I could tell him the hunter was out there.

At night the jungle line was like a heavy curtain, but during the daytime it opened, revealing a world surprisingly still. Looking into the growth was like peeking into an abandoned house. The space inside was so heavy, the air so hot and thick, that it seemed nothing could ever move inside it. As I followed the sound of the hunter's movements, I was especially cautious to track my path. I made up a little song to help me memorize: "Rock, turn, fallen log, rock, turn, hole-in-ground." As I softly sang it, Omar made surprised chirping sounds and tugged on my hair.

Eventually I heard familiar shrieking and whirled to see branches shake high above. I'd found the chimpanzees a second time.

I backed behind a tree so I'd be more out of view. I didn't have to worry about Omar revealing us; at the sound of shrieking he went silent and rigid, gripping my ears.

A branch creaked and broke as a large male dropped into the clearing. Drummer had been intimidating; this one was fearsome. Thick patches of silver hair banded the sides of his face, and a gnarled ear looked like bites had been taken out of it. He sniffed the air, and as he did two other males dropped from the trees beside him. They were communicating with looks instead of noises. They were stalking.

All three chimps were focused on a patch of tied branches, high in a tree. When I squinted, I could see a black limb outstretched. It was a chimp up there, and these males were taking pains not to be seen or heard. I knew from my years in Franceville that a group of males traveling in secrecy didn't bode well for whoever was in that nest.

The males climbed nearby trees, perfectly silent except for the occasional creak of branches. The ape in the nest didn't move as they ascended, but as the older chimp with silver stripes on his face approached it, I saw a small head appear over the side. Mango.

As soon as she saw the males approaching, Mango cried out and began tugging at whoever was with her in the nest. There was a frozen moment, the males and the young female equally startled, then Silver Stripes lunged for her, the whole branch shaking. Mango was under his hand and then slipped away, abandoning the nest and dashing higher in the tree. The three males lunged toward her. They'd very cleverly surrounded her, I realized — one was in each tree she might have used as an escape route.

I almost cried out, but stopped myself in time. My warning wasn't necessary, anyway, as another black form shot across the clearing: Drummer.

The moment he showed up, the males leaped down from the trees and whirled on him instead. Hooting loudly, they thrashed around the clearing, pulling up rocks and mud and baring their teeth. In the face of it all, Drummer skidded to a stop and hooted gently, almost begging. Silver Stripes lunged, gnashing the air as he tried to get his arms around the smaller chimp's chest. Drummer managed to keep Silver Stripes at bay and wriggled free. Howling in fear, Drummer bolted from the clearing, the enemy males in pursuit.

I stood there panting, my pulse only slowly returning to normal, a terrified Omar wrapped tight as a bandage around my neck. Mango moaned from her spot in the tree. Standing on two feet, holding on to a branch for support, she stared after her departed brother, chirping worriedly. Then she went silent.

I startled when Mango suddenly flurried down the tree. She jumped the last few feet and tumbled, then regained her legs and stared up at me, a trembling finger in her mouth. After a moment's hesitation, she toddled over and pounded on my shin. Her finger had gotten cut during the scuffle, I saw, and was trickling blood. She shivered in fear, looking at me for help.

After deciding we were alone, I opened my arms and leaned down. The little ape's courage disappeared and she dashed behind the tree, emerging around the other side, sucking even harder on her finger. I assumed her mother was somewhere in the trees above us, and wondered why she hadn't come down in all the fighting.

I backed up to get a clearer look up the tree, Omar making anxious gasps in my ear. Mango toddled after me, arms out, but now I thought better of trying to pick her up; the last thing I needed was to set off Drummer or Beggar. I stared up at the bed of foliage, a comfy-looking mass of leaves with a black arm outflung. It was too far away for me to make out much, but I assumed I was seeing Mango's mother.

I squatted, hands open, and whispered soft nonsense to Mango. She watched me curiously, head tilted. Then she sat heavily on the ground and, suddenly bored, did a perfect somersault. She must have landed nearer to me than she'd planned, because she gave a surprised shriek when she looked up and found me only a foot away.

Beggar stirred and leaned over the side of the nest. Seeing me below, she hooted in panic and leaped out. Her coordination must have been off, though, because she missed her landing and rolled, falling off one branch and striking a few more on her way down, reaching for a hold and repeatedly missing until she managed to snag one long enough to slow her fall. She struck the ground on her shoulder. When she righted herself, she came toward me and Mango, teeth bared unconvincingly. Something was wrong. Beggar tilted as she moved, nearly toppling before she reached Mango. Her lower lip drooped and she breathed heavily; I'd seen enough sickness in humans to know this chimp was ill.

I held out my arms, open-palmed. "Don't worry, I'm not trying to hurt your daughter," I said.

Beggar huddled around Mango, who instantly clasped her arms about her. Mother leaned heavily against daughter, so much that Mango tried to squirm out. To ease their distress, I backed away.

The old mother calmed a little, though she still bared her teeth between moments of grooming and kissing her daughter. Mango accepted the attention, but she'd clearly become fascinated by me; she stared at me hungrily, like she'd decided I should become her big hairless pet as soon as we could manage it.

Beggar pushed herself off her haunches and began to crawl away. Mango wrapped herself around her mother's belly and tried to suckle, but Beggar dragged her daughter to her back, grunting in irritation, as if Mango were too old to ride under her belly anymore. Mango was having none of it; she held on so limply that as soon as her mother started moving she slid down her arm into the dirt. Mango's hurt finger was immediately in her mouth, and she gave me a sweet little smile as she rolled from side to side. Her mother again tried to place her on her back, but Mango let herself fall off again, this time with more flair, arms dramatically outflung. She tried to suckle, but nothing appeared to be coming out; she winced in a look of hungry frustration that I recognized well.

"Why did those other chimps attack you and your child, mother?" I asked. "Why won't they leave you alone?"

She turned, and I realized some of what was ailing her. From her backside emerged a shattered stump of wood barely visible above her skin, surrounded by dark clotted blood. A broken-off arrow. She'd been hunted.

I heard a distant thumping, and Beggar called out in response. I turned to go, but before I could get out of the clearing, Drummer appeared at the end of a short channel between the kapok trees, taking his slow and sulky time returning to his mother. When he saw me he bristled, arms out wide and fingers dancing madly. He beat his palms loudly against the ground. I told myself that this time I wouldn't run away. If I did, this mock man would decide once and for all that I was prey, and I'd be running from him forever. I crouched and prepared to defend myself.

Drummer started making more and more ruckus, shrieking and bounding. It was such an over-the-top show; maybe his pride had been wounded by the attack by Silver Stripes and the other males. He dredged heavy logs up from the mud and flung them about easily. Then he gripped one of the largest logs like a club and charged.

The hunter in the camp, the three males, and now this. It was too much. I ran.

This time Drummer was ready for me. He grunted, and then I heard a whoosh. The log caught me at the back of my knees, and I fell flat on my belly. The fall knocked the breath out of me, and my ribs stuttered as I tried to heave air in. The violence of the fall was enough to hurl Omar from my back and up around my neck. He gurgled — that sound, so unexpected from the monkey, doubled my shock.

Strong hands were around my neck, and then I was dragged to my feet. As soon as I was up, Drummer kicked me hard in the ribs. I fell again, my breath gone before it was fully back, intense pain shooting along my spine. I'd been kicked by Monsieur Tatagani plenty enough, and though his blows had been strong, this agony was far worse; I was worried less about my flesh than about my bones. Before I'd recovered, I was pulled back to my feet and kicked again. This time Drummer hit my gut, and my vision went white. What few wits I had left went to Omar, and I pivoted as best I could so I wouldn't crush him as I fell. If Drummer continued to beat me, there was little chance I'd be able to survive. And Omar would have no chance at all.

Drummer dragged me back to my feet. I cringed, but no blow came. His teeth were no longer bared, and he'd stopped shrieking. Something had made this less a matter of life and death than it had been a moment before. He tilted his head, staring at me.

I tilted my head, like his. Because I, too, had heard the strange noise.

It was Omar. The vervet was crying, his narrow little rib cage heaving against the back of my neck.

All I wanted to do was run, but I knew Drummer would chase me, and that he was far faster and far stronger. Slowly, so as not to excite him even more, I backed away. I dropped into a huddle and tugged Omar from around my neck to cradle him.

Tentatively, panting softly, Drummer reached a hand out to Omar. I nudged him away. He tried again, more insistent this time.

Drummer placed his face right next to Omar's and watched him, transfixed, tilting his head from one side to the other. His shoulders were low, almost submissive. His head bobbed as he made his soft grunts and reached a finger to Omar's cheek.

Then, quick as a blink, his other hand lashed out. He got his fingers around Omar and wrenched. I was instantly off my feet, surfing through the soil, and Omar squealed loudly, in a way I'd never heard before. The chimp had both hands around him, and I could feel the monkey's body stretch. Drummer's fierce yanks should easily have pried Omar from me, but he was fighting fiercely, twisting rapidly to prevent the chimp from getting a good hold.

Beggar joined in, shrieking as loudly as her son, a hand around Omar's ankle and tugging in another direction. I let go and yelled, but then Beggar had Omar in her hands and Drummer was yanking me through the clearing. I struck trees and stones as he dragged me along a dried-up streambed. I caught glimpses of Mango, clutching her mother as hard as she could and watching as Beggar tore at Omar.

There was banging, and instantly Drummer let go of me and jumped to the other side of the clearing, hooting and pounding. I lay on the ground and heaved air in and out against the wet soil, the smell of blood thick in my nostrils. I rolled over and looked up.

Prof was holding his metal briefcase and our cooking pot, slamming the two against each other, a furious leer on his face.

Drummer and Beggar barked at him from the other side of the clearing, wrapped tight around each other. Mango hid her face at her mother's breast.

There, making strange jerky movements in the center of the clearing, was Omar's body.

I got to my feet, and Prof jerked his head in the direction of camp. "Keep facing them, move slowly, and we'll retreat." He handed me the pot and case. "Make noise."

I banged the two together and backed away while Prof approached Omar's body. Gently, he kneeled and scooped up the silver form, holding it close to his chest.

We retreated. I kept up the noise, and though the chimps continued to howl and shriek at us, they were still cowering. We slowly returned to camp that way.

Once we were back, Prof and I hunched in the tent. He laid down Omar's body as I zipped the tent closed. The air was instantly hot, but I didn't care. Hands shaking, Prof examined Omar. "He's alive!" I said, surprised, when I saw the monkey's eyes dart beneath his lids.

Prof nodded. "But his shoulders are dislocated."

Omar's arms were at odd angles, and there were thick bands across one shoulder where the hair had rubbed away and the skin had risen and swelled. His eyes were closed, and his breathing was rapid; I guessed he'd passed out.

"Keep your hands on his torso, please," Prof said. "In case he wakes up."

I put my hands around Omar's chest, narrow as a bird's. His chin thrust out as if in defiance of the pain.

Prof steadied his hands on the monkey's shoulders, and then, with a popping sound, expertly snapped Omar's arms back into their sockets. Prof massaged the rest of Omar's body as he examined it. "I think he'll be okay."

I stared at Prof in awe.

"Are *you* going to be okay, Luc?" he asked, peering deep into my eyes.

I nodded, kneading my own neck and shoulders. I was faint, and I'd be sore tomorrow, but I wasn't seriously injured. "I heard the drumming and then the shrieking," Prof continued. "I ran to you as soon as I heard it."

I watched him tenderly arrange Omar's unconscious body on a bedroll, folding a handkerchief to make a pillow. I felt warmth at seeing the kindness, and something darker — a weird jealousy — that came out as accusation. "They nearly killed me and Omar," I said, my voice unexpectedly choking. "You told me chimps didn't hunt and kill! That they're better than people!"

Prof opened his hands wide. "I had no idea they would attack. I never would have knowingly let you be in danger." He cursed and unzipped the tent. "Can we open this a little? It's roasting in here, and after what's happened, I'd like to see if any chimps are approaching, thank you."

Now Prof dared to be irritated at me? I rolled through the opening and got to my feet, swiping sweat from my brow. Then I bent down and began to rummage through the valise. "There's a hunter here — do you realize that?" I yelled. "He was in our campsite!"

"What? What do you mean?" Prof laid a hand on my arm to get me to stop. I shrugged him off.

"The one setting the snares for the chimpanzees. The one selling bushmeat in Okondja. We're in his territory."

"He cannot hunt chimpanzees. It's illegal. We will stop him."

"We should *help* him! They're monsters."

"What are you looking for in the valise?" Prof asked calmly.

"The knife! The moment a chimp shows up here I'm going to kill it."

Prof watched me. "That is a very bad idea. A chimpanzee is not a bonobo or even a gorilla. They are aggressive. That knife isn't enough. And I haven't been sent here to kill endangered animals. Come, let's figure out together how to deal with the hunter."

I kicked the valise onto its side. Clothes and rice and cooking instruments went clanging and spilling. "If you won't keep us safe, I'm leaving!"

Prof stooped beside me, picking up our stray belongings, scooping spilled rice into his fingers and returning it to its burlap sack. "I don't think that's a good idea," he said. "But it's your decision. If you are going to try to wander your way back to the village without a boat, you should have some dinner first. And you should let me put some alcohol on those scrapes. Infection sets in easily in the jungle. Let me take care of you."

His attitude made me so angry that I turned hot. I yanked at the neck of my shirt. It infuriated me that he thought he could take care of me, and that if I accepted his care it meant I had to do whatever he wanted.

"You're cut along the bridge of your nose," Prof said gently. "It's pretty deep, and I don't think you even realize it yet. That's where we should start disinfecting."

I yelled at him, too furious to form words, and stormed around the clearing, kicking at tree trunks. But all the action caused a stream of blood to run down my face and into my mouth, and the taste of it stilled me. I huffed to the ground, cross-legged, while Prof rummaged the bottle of rubbing alcohol out of the valise. "Where is this from, anyway?" he asked. "I don't remember bringing it."

I stayed punishingly silent as he began to tend to my wound.

"Not talking to me, huh?" Prof said. He peered into my face, his eyes wrinkling, daring me to smile.

Finally I did, because what I had to say next would feel so good. "I stole it from that beautiful woman at High Fashion Works of God."

Prof guffawed. "She deserved it."

"She didn't like us very much."

"No, she didn't," Prof said. "No one seems to like us very much. Except each other."

I didn't know what to say to that.

After a few minutes of Prof cleaning my wounds, my anger faded a little. "Can we check on Omar?" I asked.

"Of course, Luc," Prof said. "That is a good idea."

Prof and I went back into the tent, and he cradled the unconscious monkey in his arms. I stroked the soft silver fur of the monkey's wrist. "It's going to be okay, right?" I asked softly. I was talking about Omar, but I think I also meant me. Prof nodded.

"How do you even know we're where we're supposed to be?" I pressed. "I mean, why have you dragged us *here*?"

Prof sighed. "There are many chimpanzees in this jungle. But I worked closely with a chimpanzee scholar who told me that Okondja village used to be the base of much logging. Foreigners built a road into the Inside, and many trees were cut down. There used to be many apes and monkeys in the forest, and they provided meat for many, many loggers. And then most of the trees were gone and the primates had died and the loggers left. It has been eighty years since then — long enough for the chimpanzees' numbers to grow back, and the forests, too. I hope that if I make people know them, then the wise president of your country will not allow more loggers to come in. That he might make this area a new national park. Gabon is very good about setting land aside for preserves, but less good when it sells that same land to logging companies."

"From his clothes, I think the hunter lives in this jungle," I said proudly. "He has a bow and snares, but no gun. No western clothes."

"Thank you for telling me," Prof said as he dabbed at a cut on my throat. "He's not the worst kind of hunter. Those have guns and can kill a troop of chimpanzees in minutes. But still — he should not be hunting chimpanzees. Every tribe has taboos against it. He knows that. We just have to remind him."

"Won't he starve?" I asked. "Doesn't he need these animals to eat and keep his family fed, too?"

"You mean *non-human* animals," Prof corrected. "Humans are animals, too, you know."

I huffed. Prof always chose the worst times to teach lessons.

"Most tribes eat very little meat," he said thoughtfully. "He's probably hunting to sell, at the village or in Franceville. You've seen the tribesmen in the market with their racks of meat, no?"

"Yes," I said. They always had much better catches than the songbirds and rodents boys like I could get. Only occasionally did you see someone selling a chimpanzee, though. I tried to remember if I'd ever seen this particular hunter in Franceville. I wasn't sure.

"He probably has a wide range," Prof said. "He doesn't have to hunt here. And he doesn't have to hunt chimpanzees."

Somehow I didn't think that would be so simple to this hunter.

Prof went to put more alcohol on my cuts, but I stayed his hand. He'd already used half the bottle; I wanted him to save some for if he was attacked, too.

My thoughts went to those loggers who had left eighty years ago. Prof said they'd run out of monkeys to eat, but I suspected that wasn't why they'd gone. I bet they'd left because the Inside would have killed them if they'd stayed. I'd learned that much today. The Inside would destroy you. It wasn't a question of if, but of how.

# EIGHT

Omar was walking around by morning, but couldn't climb with his wounded shoulders, so I didn't want to leave him alone. He spent most of his time safe in the air, curled up in Carine's old plastic basin. Sometimes I'd take it down to hold in my lap, rocking from side to side while he slept.

That night, while Prof prepared canned fish for dinner, I lay in the tent beside Omar, the muscles of my back protesting, still tight after Drummer's attack. I looked at the monkey and the drab bit of tent at the far side of him. When I closed my eyes I saw Drummer bearing down on me, teeth bared. Felt Omar pulled from me, his shoulders popping free. I stroked the vervet where he lay sleeping. I'd almost lost him. My body ached.

My quietness only made Prof more talkative. "So," he said as he came in, "I read in the Baedeker today that we should sleep with our legs apart. If a python gets into our tent, with our legs apart it will be harder to pass into his belly."

Was he joking? I couldn't tell. I stared deeper at Omar. There were so many ways to lose a person. So many ways to be lost to a person.

I whispered, "Why do you think Silver Stripes and the other chimps went after Drummer and Beggar and Mango? What could they possibly have done so wrong?"

"Luc," Prof said, his hand under my chin, "I'm sure they didn't do anything wrong. When a chimp group gets too large, it splits and the two sides go to war until one has been killed off. My suspicion is that those three are the last of their side."

*Poor Drummer. Poor Beggar. Poor Mango.*

Day crept away and the night deepened. Prof called, "The light's gone out!" but this time I didn't chuckle.

The tent made pinging sounds as insects and twigs dropped from the trees above. The spiders that chose to spend the night on its canvas — and there were many — made eight points of darkness on the moon-bright surface.

I thought Prof had fallen asleep, but then he spoke up. "Don't kill a chimpanzee," he said dozily. "Please. Don't ever. They're trying to survive, like you and me, like we've always been fighting to do."

I'd killed plenty of things that were fighting to survive — how else did anyone eat? But I understood what Prof was saying. The chimps were mock men, with family and hopes. I guessed that could make it different. "Was your life hard before?" I asked. "Your life Outside?"

Prof took a moment before answering. "Yes, but not in the same way as yours. You were *by* yourself. I was *not* myself."

I grunted and turned to face the tent wall. There was a thump and a scuffling sound as a tiny snake dropped onto the tent's roof and zigged away, scattering the spiders.

The next morning, Prof declared that he needed me to come with him to find the chimpanzees. I guessed he'd noticed that lurking around the campsite wasn't good for my mood.

He waited patiently while I rinsed the dishes and hoisted up the food. Despite my uneasy feeling, I was ready to go. Between chimps and hunters, maybe it *was* safer for us to be together, even if it meant leaving the campsite unattended. Omar couldn't climb to safety yet, so I carried him along in the plastic basin.

As we walked, I imagined ways to protect the camp. The best I could think of were snares — the hunter had proven that liana was strong enough to capture a chimp. I'd been practicing my knots until they were nearly as fine as the one I'd found, and imagined I could make a line of traps all around the camp's border.

The area below Beggar's nest was silent and dusky. Where Drummer's attack had overturned the soil, bright brown streaks crisscrossed the earth. "It doesn't look like the chimps are here anymore," I said.

Prof's only response was to point: Beggar's nest still sagged heavily. Though I couldn't see an outstretched hand or leg, a chimpanzee appeared to be inside. And sure enough, after a few minutes, a little head appeared. Mango pulled herself out and skittered down the trunk. The tree limb still sagged, so I assumed Beggar was in the nest. Mango toddled over to us, making squeaking sounds.

*Stay with your mother,* I thought.

"We can't let her come close," I said to Prof, my mind on Omar in the basin. But Mango stopped on her own. She kept on crying, but plopped down in the soil. Maybe she remembered the violence her brother had brought on. There was no sign of him, but there hadn't been before, either — until his arms had been wrapped around my chest.

"Something is wrong here," Prof said. "A little chimp should not come down from the nest without its mother."

It did seem strange.

Mango was sifting through her arm hair and idly inspecting (then eating) any bits of dirt she found. Periodically she looked up at the nest and squeaked for her mother, but didn't seem to be expecting any response. She went back to her arm.

"Chimps groom to form relationships," Prof said. "She's got no one to groom, so she's grooming herself."

Seeing her there, small and lost, laid concern over my fear. Pressing Omar's plastic basin into Prof's hands, I said, "Call out if you see Drummer coming."

Not wanting to give him time to stop me, I started climbing the tree beside the one with Beggar's nest.

It was a half-rotted Okoumé, its black bark slick with moss. As I pressed my fingers against the trunk, the wet outer layer squished into the layer of bugs and crunchy wood beneath. I gripped a low branch while I flailed a leg higher until it caught on the next branch up. After a few minutes of exertion, I was above the nest.

There Beggar was. Lying on her side, she had her hands pinned between her thighs, looking over the side of the nest with a serene but absent air, like she was watching herself from somewhere outside of her body. The old chimp was alive, but breathing shallowly. The body was all beast, but the eyes brought back thoughts of my mother in the hospital bed — how she, too, had once looked at me and seen nothing.

I crept along the branch. Beggar turned and watched me with her wide eyes, tilting her head to see me better. She let out a long sigh. If she was alarmed by me, she didn't have the energy to express it.

"What did that hunter do to you?" I murmured. Her branch was near enough to mine that I was able to transition over, sling my legs over the edge, and sit beside her. As I nervously stroked her forearm, she made wheezing sounds. Staring at my hand as I groomed, Beggar adjusted her legs so her arms came free. I picked up one of those old rough hands and held it. She lifted her head an inch, her chest shivered, then she let it rest back down into the bundled leaves.

I clenched her hand. Maybe she didn't care if she died alone, but it mattered to me.

I heard a rustling and small squeaks from below, then Mango's head appeared over the side of the nest. Before I could stop her, she was crawling over my lap to huddle in next to her mother. Her eyes on mine, she tugged at Beggar's lips and ears. When I didn't do anything to help, she gave up on me and tried to suckle. But she soon gave up on that, too. Mango perched on the skinny bit of space that remained at the nest's edge and lay on her side. Resigned and miserable, she propped her head up on a folded arm, fixing me with a stare that was complicated and lost. Up close, I could see that her hair was patchy in places, where she'd probably plucked it out by overgrooming. She burrowed, like she wanted to be closer to her mother than was possible, like she couldn't get enough heat from Beggar's body.

When I lifted her arm, Beggar grunted weakly in protest. I rolled Mango toward her mother, provoking some outraged squeaks of surprise, and then placed her mother's arm over her. Mango immediately quieted and tucked in, trying again for the nipple. She was shivering, I realized, even surrounded by her mother's body. I thought of the failed attempts at suckling I'd seen the other day and worried that Mango wasn't getting enough nourishment, that she would soon go the way of her mother.

For right now, I was glad that she and Beggar were together. I wished there were something I could do to keep things that way.

Prof whistled sharply from below.

Now that he'd alerted me to it, I could hear a distant drumming. My thoughts instantly on Omar, I scrambled down the tree. As I tumbled the final length to the ground, I looked up to see Mango had untangled herself from her mother and was staring over the edge of the nest, watching me hurry away.

We rushed from the clearing before Drummer arrived. Once we got back to camp, I held Omar tight in my arms and took a deep breath, ready to tell Prof what I had seen of Beggar and her wound. But before I could speak, he shook his head sternly and muttered something about "improper scientific method." Suddenly I was tearing up, and before I could even try to hide my tears, I was sobbing. I kneeled on the ground, head in my hands.

Once I was able, I looked up and saw Prof kneeling beside me, hands on his knees. "The old chimp mother is dying, Prof," I managed to get out. "She's never going to get back out of that nest, and we have no way of knowing why and no way of helping Mango."

"Many chimps have lived and died in this jungle without anyone knowing about it," Prof said.

I hated him for being so *reasonable*. But when I looked at his expression, I also saw something unexpected there: a broad, deep suffering that I realized had always been his. His sympathy was wider and calmer than mine, expansive enough to include the Inside and the Outside and everything in both. I found myself wondering, not for the first time, what Prof had been through before in his life to bring him here now.

"They're alone there," I said, tears leaving my voice. "Mango and Beggar. In that tree. They're all *alone*."

"Drummer is there by now," Prof said.

I was furious again. That he hadn't known what I'd meant by *alone*. That *I* hadn't known what I'd meant by *alone*. And I was furious, too, that I was crying, that I'd proven I could.

"You know," Prof said, whispering like he'd wandered into a private home and was worried about being overheard, "when you think about it, all survival stories that end happily are also family stories."


That evening especially, I wanted for us to be inside the tent, Omar, Prof, and me, zipped in before the jungle's night curtain drew shut. As I curled down in my bedroll, listening to the mutter-ing and cursing on the other side of the canvas as Prof made dinner, I was slammed by an unexpected memory of my mother's embrace and the calls I'd once heard of the mock men.

I was glad when Prof finally piled into the tent, cradling a heaping bowlful of rice. My mood lightened when I smelled how fragrant it was today, and I soon realized he'd made us a special treat by drizzling in white papaya sap and cooking it all down into a soft goo. We passed the bowl back and forth wordlessly. Now that Prof had come in and broken the memory of my mother, all I could think about was the clearing half a mile away, darkness fall-ing on a milk-hungry little ape pressed tight against her mother's breast, falling asleep to the sound of a slowing heart.

I was awakened not by the usual rising drone of the crickets, but by a strange call from Omar. It was like a siren, short blasts that seemed too loud for his small body. If I hadn't known his voice so well, I would have thought I was hearing a bird. I shuffled out of the tent and spotted him silhouetted in the dawn light, screeching from the highest point of our highest tree. I pivoted, trying in vain to see any danger. At least Omar had proven that his shoulders were well enough that he could climb from his basin to the heights of a tree.

Once Prof emerged from the tent, he raised the fire and steeped mint tea for breakfast. He said nothing while he sipped, but gave me sad, empathetic glances that bothered me to no end. I chewed the mint leaves from the bottom of the pot and paced while he finished his tea, prayed, and thumbed through his notes. As I approached the backside of the tent, a glimmering mist turned out to be a crowd of fat flies lifting into the air. I investigated, expecting to find a dead animal. But they'd been swarming a turd. Human-sized.

I was puzzled, since every child knew that you should only relieve yourself downstream of where you live. It couldn't have been from Prof, and it certainly hadn't been from me.

A warning from the hunter? Or from a chimp?

I dragged Prof near and showed him. He kneeled over the turd. "That's chimp feces if I ever saw them," he said. His face lit up. "This means they're not too scared to approach our camp anymore!"

He was *excited*. "It was probably Drummer," I said darkly.

Prof seemed upset that I'd spoiled his pleasure, but then his face softened. "Even if he wants to harm us, he won't be able to, do you understand? Because we will always protect each other, you and I."

I went to the valise, fished out the knife in its leather holster, and placed it in my pocket. Prof watched me disapprovingly, but I stared him down. "We're not going anywhere without a weapon. You should have brought us a machete, but this is the best we have."

Prof nodded resignedly. "Fine. We'll bring the knife with us. But only for defense."

The moment we emerged into the clearing, there was a blur of black and tan as something bolted toward me. I yelped as a creature clamped onto my shin, and I kicked out in fear until I saw it was Mango. When I stopped, she reached her arms to be picked up. They trembled; she looked even scrawnier than yesterday. I wanted to lift her up, but I was afraid Drummer was somewhere nearby and would attack. I made soothing coos as I scanned the clearing.

"Prof," I said as the old man shuffled near, "stay back here."

Either Beggar had died and been scavenged or she had been killed in her weakened state. Whatever had happened had been savage. Her body looked like it had been hurled under a tree, the throat gashed and the rib cage parted, blood painting wet trails on the ground around her, like some little red beasts had burst from her chest and scattered.

Something had tried to eat her. And the meal didn't seem to be finished. Her limbs were intact. "Prof," I said, "stay alert. And stay back!"

Mango was gripping my ankle so tightly that my foot tingled. I sensed Prof next to me and heard him gasp when he saw what I'd seen.

"What could have *done* that?" I breathed. "Is it the hunter?"

"Not him. He would have smoked the entire chimp to sell. But it's hard to know otherwise," Prof whispered. "Could have been vultures, or mandrills. I'd say a python, but a snake wouldn't cause that sort of damage. At least she was probably dead before this happened, or very soon into the attack."

Without really knowing what I was doing, I lifted Mango into my arms. The orphan pressed herself against me as I squeezed her tight. Beggar might have already been dead, but Mango had to have been very much awake when the scavenger had attacked. The little chimp kept moaning, pressing her face against my chest. I felt her reach under my shirt, trying to press her mouth to my nipples, looking for any source of comfort.

"It's important that we not hold them," Prof said.

"I know you don't want me to," I said. "But I'm doing it anyway."

There was a commotion at the far side of the clearing, and then I heard a familiar shrieking. Before I could move I saw Drummer's shape sprinting toward us, low to the ground. He'd be on Prof or me in a moment. I struggled to pull Mango off and get the knife out. But Mango fought hard to clasp me, shrieking the whole time. Her foot blocked the opening of my pocket.

As I tried to free myself, I shouted to Prof to go back to the campsite and was relieved to see him turn and speed away without hesitation. I widened my stance so Drummer would have to face me if he wanted to follow Prof along the narrow pathway. I could move fast, but knew Prof needed a head start with his limp.

I'd have expected Drummer to be upon me already. But he wasn't. He'd stopped halfway across the clearing.

He crouched over his mother's body, but she wasn't where his attention was focused. He looked up at the nest Beggar had once slept in, barking wildly. It took me a moment to realize what Drummer was seeing.

Over the far side of the bent branches was a large cat. It had a broad, heart-shaped face and a chest speckled with black spots. A leopard.

Whatever meat it had gnawed out from Beggar's body had been taken up to the nest to eat in privacy. The cat's mouth was stained pink, and as it licked its lips it growled low and loud, peering at Drummer. The leopard exited the nest, gracefully pouring its body down branches I had struggled to climb the day before. Yowling, it stopped directly above Drummer, who was pacing around the body of his mother, staring up at the predator.

The leopard clearly wasn't about to give Beggar's body up to Drummer, but it was intimidated enough to remain in the tree, continuing its soft keening. Then it abruptly quieted and looked away from the chimp, faking a lack of interest as it chewed a paw and then yawned widely. Its long teeth were yellow and sharp.

By now Mango had calmed enough to release me. At the sight of her brother, she was down from my chest and toddling across the ground toward him. The leopard snapped to attention when it saw the tiny ape struggling to make her way across the tangled ground.

We all froze, Mango squeaking in fear as she looked up at the cat, Drummer's mouth opening and closing in panic. I eased the knife out of my pocket and freed it from its sheath.

Drummer pulled himself up the tree with two powerful strokes and then was on the leopard. His strong arms grappled the cat's middle as he leaped off the branch, tumbling to the ground while wrapped around the yowling animal. One of the cat's paws hit the soil first, and as I saw dirt spray under sharp claws, I realized the other set had disappeared into the chimp's belly.

The leopard whirled and sank its teeth into Drummer's arm. The ape released, shrieked, and kicked out. The two faced off, circling each other. I took advantage of their absolute focus to creep over to Mango and tug her into my arms. Startled, she bit me on my hand, but I was able to hold on. She buried her head in the crook of my elbow.

Never turning his back on the leopard, Drummer grabbed his mother's ankle and started to drag the corpse away. Howling, the leopard pawed the air and lunged at Drummer, each time losing heart and pulling back before it made contact. Blood was flowing freely from the puncture wounds on Drummer's arm, but he seemed to take no notice as he hurled his free arm against the ground and hooted, trying to intimidate his enemy. The leopard was smaller, but with those teeth — I didn't know who would die in the fight, and hoped I wouldn't have to find out.

I backed from the clearing, Mango in my arms, moving slowly so I wouldn't draw the attention of the fighters. Nothing could keep me out of the leopard's keen hearing, though, and when I stepped on a crisp pile of leaves, its ears twitched. As the leopard snapped its attention to us, Drummer took advantage of the distraction to roll into it, tumbling with the cat. For a moment the leopard was a rag in Drummer's grasp, and then it twisted and fought back, again raking the chimp with its claws. I heard something that sounded like shredding cloth as Drummer's shrieks grew more frenzied. He released the leopard and rolled away. The cat pounced, missing Drummer's neck but sinking its teeth into his ear. A chunk of it parted under the leopard's jaws, and blood erupted from the chimp. He still had a hand on the leopard's tail, and with a grunt he swung the entire cat around his head. He bashed it once against the ground and then let go. The leopard bounced, thudding against a tree.

For a moment it was twisted and still. Then it got to its feet, gave a groggy shake to its head, and limped from the clearing.

Drummer didn't have enough energy to move. He sat where he was, panting and staring after the leopard. Blood streamed from his ear and from his belly wounds. One of his arms hung limply.

He tried to stay seated but fell over in the dirt, turning as he sprawled so that he could keep his sister and me in sight. I had the knife tight in my sweaty grip, ready to defend myself, but soon knew the chimp was too far gone to fight. Instead he lay on the ground, holding his arms out to Mango, palms up. His eyes were cloudy, but even on the verge of passing out he bore an expression of intense pain, anxiety, and sorrow. The ravaged body of his mother was only a few feet away. And his sister was in the arms of a strange creature.

I struggled to unlink Mango's hands from around my neck. She protested, but then I kneeled and turned her so she could see her brother. Mango got to her feet and toddled toward him. It took her a few seconds to get across the upturned clearing, but then she was finally in her brother's arms. He held her close, leaning heavily on his tiny sister. There, in that very position, he closed his eyes and passed out.

●　　　●　　　●

I crouched at the far side of the clearing for a long time. I had no fondness for Drummer, but Mango was another story — though she was unlikely to survive without her mother's milk, she would have no chance at all without her brother alive to protect her. Even if I couldn't imagine the wounded leopard returning anytime soon, the jungle had plenty of other scavengers that would make short work of a creature as critically wounded as Drummer.

It was hard to tell how much blood was flowing under his matted black hair. The wounds on his belly appeared to have clotted over, and though his gouged arm still shone wet, there was no longer enough blood to soak through and drip to the ground. I doubted any human could have survived what he'd been through.

Mango was wide-awake but nestled motionless under her brother's powerful chest, her eyes shining out. He must have been leaking blood on her, but apparently she preferred being under him to being apart. I understood.

Distant chimpanzees called as the afternoon waned, but the sounds never got too near. At one point, a graceful little bushbuck entered the clearing, nibbling at tender grasses. When she saw Drummer and Mango, she froze, one foreleg in midair, then bolted away.

Not too long after, I heard Prof making his slow, shuffling progress through the jungle. "What happened here?" he breathed.

"Drummer fought a leopard. I think he should survive, though," I whispered back. "The leopard, too. It fled."

"I went back, but you never followed. Why didn't you come to the campsite?" Prof said, voice trembling. "I was worried about you."

*You might have come back earlier,* I thought. "I can't leave them," I said. "Drummer is unconscious. If there is no one here to protect him, he and Mango will both be killed."

"*You* are in danger out here after dark. Come back with me now."

"There is a little time before sunset," I protested. "Give me that. I promise to return by then."

Prof sighed. "Fine. Come back before the bottom of the sun reaches the top of that tree. If you don't, then I will come back for you and you won't be allowed to say no. Besides, I have a surprise to show you at the campsite." He limped away.

Maybe the sound of our conversation, whispered though it was, triggered something in Drummer's sleeping mind. He opened his eyes and groggily propped himself up on his good arm. Startled, Mango sat up.

Drummer cried softly, wrestling with some great pain, but managed to press his weight up farther from the ground. Mango climbed onto his back, struggling to keep her grip on hair slick with blood.

The boy chimp staggered to the tree and, even with one arm hanging loose at his side, managed to muscle his way up. He and Mango rolled heavily into the same nest where Beggar had once lain. Exhaustedly, Drummer reached for more branches and bent them down, pinning them in place with his feet. He tucked in some nearby twigs, and then finally curled up. The nest hadn't been quite large enough for two before, but now he'd made it plenty big enough for himself and Mango.

A heaving sigh. Then all was still.

# NINE

I got Beggar's body back to the campsite by gripping her ankle and dragging, never looking back. I knew if I left the corpse in the clearing, more scavengers would come. Which would not be good for Drummer and Mango, huddled above in the Okoumé.

I had to have been making quite a racket as I passed through the jungle. The campsite was barely in sight when I heard Prof call out, "Stop, Luc!"

There, hanging from a snare at the edge of our campsite, was a man. The hunter. He pinwheeled his arms, trying to reach the ground. But he couldn't manage it, and each flailing movement set him rocking. He streamed out curses in his native language. Prof was calmly seated before him, hands on the galabia fabric pooled in his lap.

Seeing me, Prof stood and shifted around to the rear of the hunter, out of his view. He grimaced when he saw what I'd hauled in. "Is that Beggar's body?"

I nodded, eyes still fixed on the dangling man.

"You had a good idea," Prof said. "The hide might be useful. Bring it over."

My eyes never left the hunter. "Prof, did you set that trap?"

"You weren't the only one studying the snare you brought back," Prof said. "Come on; I've nearly got him there already. A little more terror."

Stunned, I emptied my hands and followed Prof nearer to the man. "Stay back," Prof warned. "You'll know if I need you." He took the knife from where I'd had it sheathed.

I did as I was told, and watched as Prof waved the knife in the hunter's face and began yelling. The man started sobbing, reaching out for Prof and failing each time. But Prof was getting more and more enraged, his air-slashes increasingly wild, nearly connecting with the man's flailing arms.

"Let him go!" I yelled. "He understands!"

Prof took a moment and then, breathing heavily, held the knife out to me, handle-first. "Can you cut him down?" he asked.

I took the knife between my teeth and climbed the nearest tree. The hunter peered up fearfully as I sawed away at the liana. His weight shredded the vine sooner than I'd have thought, and he fell against Beggar's body. Shrieking in horror, he pushed back from the dead chimp and sped from the clearing, plucking his bow from the ground as he went. Prof and I stared at each other, stunned, as the hunter's screams gradually receded.

Prof smiled triumphantly. "That should be the last time we see him. There are limits to what humans are allowed to do to survive. He crossed them."

I didn't agree that survival ever had limits, but for Prof's sake, I stayed quiet. I wanted to say that he had been very foolish, that the hunter might one day get his revenge, using that swift and silent bow. Prof had gambled both of our lives to save chimps. We could be the hunted ones now.

Prof looked down at Beggar's body and sighed with a sadness that seemed centuries old.

When Prof came out of our tent the next morning, I shook the empty gas canister at him accusingly. "We're out. It's fire or nothing now."

He smiled kindly at me, like I was being a silly child.

"When was the last time you had a home?" he asked.

"Why are you asking this now?" I snapped. Having to depend on fire for our cooking wouldn't be funny at all when it rained.

Prof stared into his tea. It steamed his cheeks, giving him a ghostly sheen. "I suppose because Mango and Drummer have lost the final piece of their home. And your cooking made me feel for a moment that this campsite was a home." He chortled. "A strange one, of course."

I took a moment before answering. "I'm not exactly sure when I last had a home. A few years ago. I was nine when we had to sell our house and come to Franceville. Not since then."

"Would you like one?"

I couldn't stop my irritation. "What are you talking about? Of course I'd like one!"

"What if I could help you with that?" Prof asked, slowly and calmly.

I concentrated on the tea. Green flecks swirled down and rose up as they got hotter and hotter. Maybe I wasn't actually irritated. "What do you mean?" I asked cautiously.

"You agreed to come here with me, and I couldn't do my study without you. But I am not a slave master. If you stay here with me for a year, then I will give you some money that you could use to buy a small house and a farm. Would you like that?"

"Fake money, you mean," I scoffed.

Prof laughed. "Yes, fake money. But you're a smart boy. You could change it in one city and then settle somewhere else. Have you ever imagined what you would do with money?"

I stopped stirring and looked into his small brown eyes. "Of course I have. I'd invite the orphan boys to settle with me. No one should have to live with Monsieur Tatagani. We would find a place to live far from Franceville. We'd buy an ox. We would plant peanuts and peppers and grain for chickens."

"A year, then," Prof said. He sounded almost wistful. "Stay with me for a year, through one dry and one rainy season, and it's yours."

I examined his expression to see if he was tricking me, but he was serious. A grin spread over my face, so wide it almost hurt. "Okay. Yes."

I wouldn't have to deceive Prof to get what I needed. Even though I didn't think I'd have betrayed him, I was surprised by how good it felt to know so for sure. I hummed as I stirred the teakettle.

"This is good," Prof said as I served him more tea. "I will be very glad to have you here with me."

"What about *you*?" I asked. "When was the last time that you had a home?"

Prof looked shocked. "What makes you think I don't have a home?"

"You are here with me in the jungle. You don't have a wife, or a job to go to. I thought . . . I thought we were the same that way."

"I suppose you're right. I'm homeless, too." Prof sighed, as if he'd just discovered something about himself. "I am much older than you. My first family rejected me, and that weighed down my heart. And the new family I tried to create for myself couldn't handle that weight. So I've had no choice but to give up on people. We've both been let down by humans, Luc. That's one way we're the same."

"I haven't given up hope on people," I said quietly. "So we're not the same that way."

Prof gulped his tea — it had to have burned his throat as it went down — and started stuffing papers and notes into his bag. I stood, surprised that I mattered enough to be able to hurt him. "Why did your family —"

"You've given me plenty to think about today, Luc, while I watch the chimpanzees. Let's continue this conversation later. I'm going to try to find the other group, the one led by that male with the silver stripes. Would you check on Drummer and Mango?"

I nodded, stunned, as Prof hobbled out of the campsite. As he departed, it hit me — what he'd promised to give me, the home he'd offered. "Thank you! Thank you!" I yelled after him, repeating it well after he'd disappeared into the tree line.


Drummer and Mango remained in the nest that day, and I spent every hour I could spare sitting below them. Sometimes Omar was around to distract me, and other times I'd find ways to keep my hands busy, more often than not by slicing off hard manioc skins with our dulling knife, stopping to peer up at the nest if I heard any rustle from above. Otherwise I had my new dreams to occupy me. I pictured a garden, rows of sweet potato and maize sprouting thick green leaves during my first rainy season; a pretty young wife drawn to my prosperous farm.

While Drummer and Mango were laid up, Prof began adventuring farther afield, getting up at dawn to search for the males I'd seen, returning to pick me up from the chimp clearing before night fell. Each evening he was full of stories — of a group of mongooses he surprised as they rooted for insects, a troop of red-tailed monkeys that rained him with nuts, and a tree that had the precise odor of rotting meat.

He also found more chimpanzees.

He'd creep up on three or four at a time, taking a few notes before they scattered. All told, he thought he'd seen ten or twenty different chimps, among them Silver Stripes. He was surprised that our trio had been so easy to meet, when the others were so fast and suspicious, but I suspected Beggar's injury might have had a lot to do with it.

Omar was turning into a great help in my foraging — he was getting more courageous about the jungle, wandering from the campsite for many hours at a time before returning with a rounded belly and a satisfied expression. Only a few yards from the clearing I discovered him eating a broad and spiny green fruit that, once opened, revealed sweet-sour flesh. I'd only started collecting pieces of that fruit when he left the clearing in the other direction and returned munching broad leaves. Lettuce! From then on, Prof and I began every meal with salad and finished with tart fruit.

I cleaned Beggar's hide as best I could, then draped it to dry on a mangrove island in the center of the river. Weeks from now, when flies had picked it clean and the rainy season was upon us, I could retrieve the hide and use it for warmth.

No matter what I was doing, though, my thoughts weren't ever far from Mango and Drummer. It was hard to get a good view of the high nest through the tree's thick foliage, and sometimes I could see no signs of life from it at all. Each time that happened I feared Drummer had died and Mango had left. But then the next day I'd relax when I saw an outflung limb or a tuft of hair as Drummer rolled into a more comfortable position.

Drummer could survive a few days without food so long as his wounds didn't kill him. Mango, though, hadn't been getting much milk from Beggar for a while, and now was getting none. I had no idea how young chimps worked, if she would be able to eat solid food at her age. But it was her only hope.

I arranged a chimp meal in the center of the clearing, right below the nest. Laying flat a lettuce leaf, I placed three bananas at the center, two mangoes on top, and beside them a half shell from one of the new fruits, which I'd filled with pulpy juice. Something there would have to tempt Mango.

For two days, nothing did. What my delicious meal did do, though, was attract every other creature in Gabon. Almost immediately I was waving away flies, then using a stick to churn up streams of determined ants. I fended off spiny caterpillars, mantises, small green snakes, even a trio of parrots. The pretty bushbuck with the starburst on her forehead even visited once — she licked the fruit shell, spotted me, froze, then scampered off, little white tail bobbing. By day three, the beautiful meal I'd laid out was crawling with flies, even though I'd replaced the fruit and juice.

Omar came with me as I replaced the juice a third time, and while I squeezed the fruit between my fingers he leaped off my shoulder and went exploring again. He found a stick bug and soon had it crackling between his jaws, swallowing only with some work, brittle legs flailing against his black lips. I guessed he liked the taste of it, since he was soon off searching for another. His hunt brought him alongside the chimp nest, and he unwarily began picking through the ferns and bent branches at its edge. I watched, worried but curious, as Mango popped her head out from the foliage and shrieked. Omar tittered hysterically and ran a few tight circles on the branch before hurtling down the tree and onto my shoulder.

Mango watched Omar flee her. Then her focus wandered and she finally noticed me and my chimp picnic. I made soothing sounds I remembered from Beggar — a sort of drawn-out breathy panting — and laid my chest toward the ground, palms upturned. After a few minutes I was satisfied to hear a scrambling from above, then a plop and a grunt. I confirmed Mango was approaching when Omar promptly ran away with his arms flailing, yelling his head off in outrage as he disappeared from the clearing.

I risked looking up. Mango was circling me and the food, making a mournful hooting sound. Eventually she selected a banana, chewed thoughtfully on one end, and put it down. She'd neglected to peel the fruit, and I would have done it myself if I hadn't been afraid she'd run away when I moved. Mango got interested in the giant lettuce leaf, bouncing her palms against the edge. Then she yanked it and the fruit went rolling away. The juice that I'd portioned into the half shell spilled, most seeping into the soil and the rest collecting along the valley of the leaf. Mango tasted the sweet liquid, then started lapping furiously. Once it was gone she ate the leaf, barely chewing as she scarfed it down.

I guessed I'd found my answer for whether she could eat real food. I cut away the peel of a mango and offered the flesh to her. She watched curiously, waiting for it to do something. Realizing it was juice that had attracted her more than solid food, I pinned the mango between my palms and squeezed. Goo appeared along the seams of my fingers and dribbled off my pinkies. Mango was instantly there, sucking the sugary fluid away, her teeth sharp against my finger. When I opened my hands she squished the remaining pulp into her mouth, yellow-orange smearing her cheeks and neck.

I sliced open another mango and she ate it the same way, scarfing it the moment I'd lowered it to her level. Then she downed the last one. She slowed by the end, resting back and farting long and loud. I was tempted to try to play with her, but before I could I heard stirring in the nest above. Drummer rolled over conspicuously, two times in a row, and I thought I saw his black eyes open and peer down at us. Mango bounded back up the tree, taking a flying leap onto her brother's belly like it was a soft bed and not the body of a suffering sibling.

By the time I was back to camp I had just enough time to prepare dinner before Prof returned. He bubbled about every detail of his day as he ate, ending with the chance sighting of a forest elephant — he was excited to have seen it uprooting soil with its tusks and chewing down the onion bulbs it had unearthed. Prof didn't ask what had happened in my day, maybe because he assumed there had been nothing but cleaning and cooking. I didn't tell him about feeding Mango because I didn't want him to tell me I couldn't do it again.

The following dawn I found it hard to get out of my bedroll. I listened to Prof scraping the remains of last night's dinner out of the pot, smacking the morsels down and gulping his river-water mint tea before setting off to make his observations. I listened for the sounds of his slow limping exit to fade, then rolled out of the tent.

Unhitching the food-bag line, I lowered it to the ground, Omar leaping out of the plastic basin. I'd rummage out some more mangoes, I figured, then go about replenishing our stock this afternoon. The ones that remained at the bottom were bruised and mushy, but I figured that was good, since what Mango seemed to like most was juice. I arranged the mangoes in the crook of my arm as best I could —

I saw movement at the edge of my vision and raised my head, terrified the hunter had sneaked in, that the next thing I'd hear would be the creak of a drawing bow.

There, on the other side of the campfire, was Mango.

She was frozen on all fours, watching me nervously, mouth opening and closing. I immediately squatted, making myself as small as possible. Mango's shoulders slackened, but otherwise she stayed still. She made more of her mournful *hoo-hoo* sounds, scanning for her mother.

I carved deep into a mango. The leathery shell came away in two halves, and I held the fragrant, gooey core out in my open palm. Mango watched me intently, her eyes never leaving the bruised golden sludge in my fingers.

I lowered my hand and waited for long moments, neck beginning to ache. Finally Mango came forward and delicately placed her fingertips, one by one, over the slick fruit flesh. She was careful not to touch my fingers where they held the fruit — but she clearly wasn't aware of what she was doing with the other hand, which she was using to grip my thigh for balance. Once she'd eaten all the peeled mango, she plucked a second fruit I'd peeled and scampered away to the edge of the site, where Drummer was waiting.

I'd had no idea he'd been there, watching us.

The chimp looked terrible; his face, usually a deep leathery tan, was delicate white, almost as colorless as the Europeans at the Franceville bar. Three wide scabs banded his torso, and the wound on his arm still glistened. He cradled it in the other limb and idly sucked at the bleeding wrist. Swaying on two feet, he watched Mango and me with eyes that shone with alertness. Mango scampered to her brother, food in hand. As soon as she was within arm's reach, he gave a fierce bark and cuffed her hard on the head, enough to send her sprawling into the dirt. Mango squealed and pulled herself up the nearest tree.

Drummer plucked the peeled mango, now covered in a layer of dirt, and swallowed the flesh. He looked at me, as if waiting for me to provide another, while Mango cried pitifully from the tree above.

I knew animals were more dangerous when wounded, but Drummer still seemed very weak, and I wasn't about to flee my own campsite. Drawing the knife, I shouted, "That food was for your sister! Get out of here! I'll kill you!"

I kept yelling, to keep noise coming out. It was having an effect: Drummer reared, repulsed, like I was spraying him with water. He started backing from the clearing, still barking, but more quietly now. Then, with a crashing of foliage, he disappeared into a thicket and was gone.

Mango squeaked in panic and fear. Again I lay low, palms upturned, a piece of fruit in hand. But when Mango descended, she turned not toward me, but toward her brother. She bounded into the thicket after him, making little chirping cries.

I lobbed two mangoes and a banana deep into the brush, hoping she would pick them up on her way. I had no way of knowing if she stopped to eat them, and I certainly wasn't going to head into the thick underbrush to find out.

"Kor-kor," I whispered, a Fang expression meaning *may your days be long*. My mother used to say it to our cousins whenever they left our house.

Prof looked even more drawn and ancient when he returned that evening. Broad patches of his blue galabia were purple with sweat. When he reached the top of our hill, he slumped on the sitting log. I brewed a tea and served him sliced banana and snails, boiled after I discovered them lined up on the trunk of a nearby tree.

"I got so very near them today," he said, panting. His eyes gleamed in an oily way that made me nervous for his health. "I have found a hill from which I can watch the chimpanzees in peace. They can see me, but they don't seem to mind! I think they have become more habituated to my presence. Perhaps in a day or two you will come with me to watch. They split into small groups during the day and begin to come together in the evening. Perhaps for safety. That is my theory."

"I would like that. To go with you there . . ." I said. My voice trailed off.

"What is it?" Prof asked.

"Drummer and Mango appeared in the camp today," I said. "I think they're hungry. It makes me worried."

"How did they seem?" Prof asked, surprised. "Did you feel like you were in danger?"

I shook my head. "Drummer seems too weak to be a threat. And Mango wants to eat something, but I think her brother is taking all the food they come across."

Prof rubbed his hands in excitement. "Male chimpanzees are very dominant. I've seen them beat the females. Mango is lucky not to have been hurt — perhaps she is too young for Drummer to use his full force on her, and he knows that."

"I think she might not survive without a mother," I said glumly.

Prof took a long sip of mint tea.

I got worried he was about to tell me never to feed Mango, so I found something to ask. "What happened to Omar's hands?"

"His what?" Prof asked.

"His hands," I said. "They have scars up and down them."

"I adopted Omar when I was in South Africa," Prof said. "From a rescue sanctuary. Vervets treat utility poles like trees, jumping between them. Omar's mother must have jumped on one with exposed wire. She died, and they found Omar holding on to her charred body. He'd gotten terribly burned; they were worried they'd have to take off his hands. But he recovered. And I adopted him."

We looked at Omar, the back of his head just visible over the edge of his basin as he dozed. "Poor Omar," I said.

Prof nodded.

"They should put something on top of the wires," I ventured, "so that monkeys don't get electrocuted."

Prof sucked in his breath, which made his eyes crinkle. "Yes! That's precisely right, Luc. And it's what they're actually doing! A cheap and very effective corrective. I bet that if you'd continued in school, you'd have been top of your class."

I didn't like that last part — I had scored very well on my primaries before leaving the village, and being reminded of it was like learning a stolen treasure had been more valuable than I'd thought. But I mouthed Prof's compliment to myself as I cleared up the dinner bowl and straightened the campsite.

As I was falling asleep that night I decided I'd set a fish head aside for Omar after I made breakfast the next morning.

The next day I told Prof that I wouldn't go see the new chimpanzees because I was guarding the campsite, but I was really hoping to see Mango again. I didn't stray far from the tent that morning, just refilling our water and cutting a red-flecked wild pineapple from the center of a sharp bush to serve after dinner. As I was carrying it back to camp, I saw one tree after another shake, nuts and twigs and insects falling, until the one with our food bag was trembling. Two branches parted, and Mango emerged. She made panting hoots, then descended the food-bag rope and dropped to the ground near me.

In doing so, she startled Omar, who had been sunning himself on the tent fabric. He shrieked; she shrieked. She soon stopped, but Omar kept screaming as he ran a complete circuit around the site, stopping only after he'd run up my back and onto the top of my head. Mango stared at him, a finger in her mouth and love on her face.

After taking a good look around and seeing no sign of Drummer, I pulled Omar from my back and set him down. He squawked and cringed, but all Mango did was turn around and crouch, presenting herself to him. Confused, Omar reached forward and gave Mango's bottom a hesitant tap. She wiggled in response. Then Omar gave it a slap, and Mango turned around, grinning as she reached out and clasped Omar's tail. He wrenched it free, shrieked, and ran up a nearby tree, scolding. Once he'd calmed down, he pretended to fall asleep, but I saw him cut glances at Mango. In no time he couldn't resist going back down and the two were playing.

Once they'd tired out, I got Mango to eat a leaf and some of the wild pineapple, followed by a banana. After she'd eaten she was back into the trees, bounding after Omar. When she'd tired of playing she headed out, staring back mournfully every few paces.

Prof returned earlier than usual, looking even more tired than the day before. As I started making dinner, he mopped his brow sluggishly and let out a low, long sigh. When he brought the rag away from his face, something struck him and his features lit up. "I haven't told you the day's news yet: They're nearer!" he said. "The chimps are foraging closer and closer. Our campsite wasn't a bad choice after all — I knew it! The chimpanzees wander according to which trees are fruiting, and the coming rainy season must be tempting them to pass near. They're under a half hour's walk away. You know the high hill, away from the river? You can see them well from there." He got to his feet. "Come and look. It will take only a minute."

I wanted him to rest, but Prof insisted. We had to clamber over ground that was slick with mud and tangled with vines, and Prof needed frequent breaks. Once we were on the hilltop he pointed to the next forested valley over.

I watched a muscular chimp pass through the canopy. With short legs and a broad back, she gracefully swung hand over hand between trees. I watched her approach a clearing where, thanks to a tree that had recently fallen and ripped down much of the canopy, I could see all the way to the jungle floor. A cluster of chimps was squatting around a termite mound. "They're eating them," Prof explained, "by using grass!"

But I wasn't interested in the group, because I'd spied Mango. Many feet away from the other chimps, she sat with her foot in her hand, kissing her toes one by one. Her eyes drooped, her lips full and sad. I watched her pluck up her courage and work her way over to a chimp with an infant suckling at her breast, slinking sideways, as if moving strangely would prevent her from being recognized. She squatted next to the mother, watching the grass blade dip in and emerge from the mound and disappear into her mouth, I guessed with succulent termites wriggling along it. The mother resolutely ignored Mango, concentrating on her work. Mango lay out on the ground, hand upturned, in a now-familiar begging pose. When the mother continued to ignore her, Mango inched forward, waving her fingertips.

As the mother ate strand after strand of termites, licking them off the grass with her bright pink tongue, Mango wriggled ever closer. Finally she dared tug on the mother's arm to get her attention. The big female whirled and barked, hair standing on end. Mango scurried away, flailing her arms in fear. She hunched over at a distance from the group, feet clutched in her hands, rolling herself small. She looked as miserable as a creature could be.

She must have sat in the path of the riled termites, though, because suddenly she howled and jumped, swatting at her butt. Having experienced firsthand the termites' powerful jaws, I knew what pain Mango was in. Softly panting, she dusted herself off and slinked away. For as long as I could, I tracked her movements from the hilltop. Trees quivered as she climbed and jumped from branch to branch, heading in our direction. Eventually she appeared at the base of our hill, no more than fifty feet away.

I couldn't resist. I waved.

She saw me but didn't react, her eyes moving right past me. Whatever she was looking for, I wasn't it.

Mango wove between the trees, cheeping. Then she squealed in glee and was back in view, her arms held out wide as she ran toward a distant black shape.

Drummer. He'd been so still that again I hadn't noticed him

hunched at the base of a tree, not a hundred feet from our position, coolly monitoring us. Mango tried to climb his legs to rest on his back, but he pushed her off and bared his teeth. She panted in submission and moved away, hunching down. Drummer had no focus to spare for her.

I nudged Prof and pointed at the chimp. Prof shook his head in incomprehension; didn't he understand we could be in danger? "Are you okay?" I asked.

He nodded. "Don't worry about Drummer — he still looks very weak. And don't worry about me, either — I just need to rest a little. I do think I'll skip dinner tonight, though. I don't feel very well. But we should head back so you can eat."

Prof leaned heavily on my arm as we shuffled back to camp. I had a moment's memory of my mom in the same position during her last week alive, of supporting her as she floated to the clinic window. A crepey, dusty hand on my arm. I looked down at Prof's hand and was relieved to see it brown and shining with health, even though covered in bites and rashes.

As we headed home, I kept us as far as I could from Drummer. When we were forced to come within a dozen feet of him I trained my eyes on the chimp, alert to any sign of attack. But he still looked exhausted, slumped at the base of a tree. The scabs on his torso must have kept reopening; their edges were slick. No wonder he wasn't foraging with the rest of the group. His ravaged body told me he was no threat. But the cool eyes that watched us so intently said he was.

# TEN

The next morning, I was woken up by waves of heat radiating through the tent wall. I'd slept in very late; it had to be midmorning. Prof was sleeping on his back, his face still as death.

Heart pounding, I gave his shoulders a gentle shake. A grim smile stole across his features, and he turned toward me. The skin around his temples was flaky and mottled, almost like mold. "My boy, I *will* get up. Only not yet. Today I intend to sleep late for once."

"Yes! Okay, Prof, of course you can," I said, relieved.

I unzipped the tent fly and rolled out into the sunshine.

Immediately, there was a black flurry. I'd surprised Drummer, who was only a few feet away, examining our smoldering fire. He had one of the blackened fire-pit stones in his hands, and heaved it at me. It whooshed by my ear. If his aim had been better, he might have crushed my skull.

I watched in shock as Drummer chewed on one of my dirty shirts. He had the armpit in his mouth while he investigated the fire.

Why hadn't I kept the knife beside me? I'd left it in the valise, and that was on the other side of the chimp. *Idiot!*

Drummer hurled his body against the ground and barked, setting my terrified brain sputtering. I eased forward, arms outstretched. The hulking chimp kept feinting at me but not charging — I figured he was building his courage before attacking. The best I could come up with was this: If Drummer surged forward I would grip his head to stop him from biting me. I might survive the fists, but not the teeth.

He had my shirt out of his mouth and into his hand, whipping it against the ground in his fury. I screamed Prof's name as the chimp and I circled each other, and heard rustling from the tent in response. I scanned for something that would make a loud bang.

I stepped sideways, reached my fingers against the handle of the metal case, and grabbed. I flung it, not at Drummer, but at the dewy cooking pot, sending it clattering off its drying stone. Instantly Drummer darted backward, teeth bared in fear. I maneuvered to the pot, picked it up, and banged it against the case time and again, the combination dial rattling. Drummer hurtled into the jungle, shrieking his head off, one of my only three shirts streaming from his fist like a flag.

When Prof staggered out of the tent, blinking into the sunlight, he found me hunting down our scattered possessions. "What *was* all that noise?" he asked.

I picked up the metal case and hurled it at Prof. He managed to catch it, stunned. "Drummer! Was in our campsite! While we were sleeping! Eating my shirt!"

Prof placed the case neatly down on the ground, closed his eyes, and eased his jaw from side to side with his hand, as if he couldn't feel it and wanted to make sure it still worked. "That's probably about salt. Apes love the taste, and it's hard to find in the jungle. Your dried sweat had plenty of it."

While he avoided my gaze, I watched him weigh how best to deal with my rage. He spoke slowly, hands out. "It's not good that a chimp was in our campsite. You're right to be scared. Where is he now?"

"He hated the noise I made, so he ran away."

"Very smart of you." Shielding his eyes, Prof glanced up at the morning sun. "Glad that's over. Now I'm going down to the river to wash my face."

Somehow, the sheer unexpectedness of it — *Sorry, Luc, that you were almost killed by a chimp monster . . . now it's time to wash my face!* — brought a jagged grin to my lips. "You? Wash something more than your teeth?"

Prof nodded dazedly.

I peered at him. "Are you sure you're okay?"

He narrowed his eyes in irritation. "Yes, yes! Stop worrying. I'm having trouble waking up today, that's all."

I passed him the metal case and our ladle. "Bring these and make noise if you see any chimpanzees. I'll come help."

"Those won't be necessary," Prof said.

"Bring them," I said sternly. Muttering, he took the case and the ladle and headed away. I watched Prof lumber down the hill, and turned back to the campsite only once he was out of sight. Then I set about gathering the clothes strewn around the clearing, rearranging the pit, rebuilding the fire that had nearly gone out.

I heard a splash. The pit stone I'd been holding tumbled from my fingers. "Prof?" I shouted. "Are you okay?"

All I heard in return was a strangled cry.

I raced to the bottom of the hill, burst through the tree line, and jumped across the narrow brown ravine. I found Prof lying half in and half out of the river. His galabia was soaked, and he'd lost one of his shoes to the river. I rushed over and kneeled beside him, cradling his head in my lap while the river tugged at my clothes. He was breathing shallowly, his eyes pressed shut. "What's the matter?" I cried out. But he didn't answer.

He'd lost his taqiyah, I realized. It would have been far downstream by then. I brushed his wet dark hair back from his forehead, placed my hands on either side of his skull, and squeezed a little, I guess to try to surprise him into opening his eyes. It had once worked on my mother in the hospital.

Prof kept breathing, but his eyes didn't open for many long minutes. I didn't cry, but only because my upset was too new. I listened to his slow breathing and tugged on his collar, willing him to wake up. Slowly, he opened his eyes and squinted over my shoulder. "My boy. I don't feel so well. In fact, I think I am sick today."

"What do I do?" I moaned, worrying my hands together.

"I need to rest. And drink tea as much as I can. Would you make a big kettleful? I will be fine by tomorrow; I am sure of it."

I staggered to my feet; since my hands were still on Prof's collar, he came halfway up with me. "First we need to get you out of the water. Can you stand?"

Prof grimaced. "I'm not sure. Or, yes, I know I can. I'll need your help, that's all I meant." Turning onto his front, he tugged at rocks, trying to drag himself out of the water. But he kept failing; the mud at the bank was streaked where his every handhold had tumbled free.

"I've got you," I said, unsure that I did. I kneeled behind Prof's shoulders and placed my hands under his armpits. His body felt not very different from Beggar's corpse. "You're going to be okay," I said as I tugged.

Though Prof wasn't heavy, the thick fabric of his galabia had been soaked through by the river water. It was impossible to get enough traction in the mud to lift him, even with High Fashion Works of God shoes under my feet. I skidded half into the river myself, scrambled out, and tried again. I'd learned not to touch the vines because of their many hidden thorns, but this time I carefully set my fingers between their large spines and gripped Prof's collar with the other hand.

His galabia rode high around his shoulders, but stayed on him well enough that I was able to haul him out of the water. Once

I'd heaved us fully onto the jungle floor, I was able to support myself enough to get Prof to his feet. When I did I spotted his taqiyah — it hadn't gotten lost down the river after all — and joy wet my eyes. Before we began the trek to the campsite, I reached down, grasped the muddy taqiyah, and stuffed it into his pocket. "There you are, Prof. You didn't lose your silly hat. You're going to be fine."

He was moaning softly, but able to support some of his own weight as I led us back. The exertion was mind-bending, almost as difficult as my white-hot struggle to carry Prof's valise from the bar that first day. It took much of my concentration to stay upright, but I'd eaten better Inside than I ever had Outside, and some of my mind stayed my own as I strained.

Prof sighed something that sounded like "I'm sorry," followed by words in Arabic.

Once we'd arrived at the campsite, I propped Prof against the sitting log as I arranged the tent. Placing our bedrolls one on top of the other to make his rest more comfortable, I leaned him forward and peeled off his galabia, laying it flat on the rock outside so it could dry. He had one other clean garment in the valise, and I was tempted to put that dry one on him. But whatever he was suffering from seemed severe, and fever sweats would probably be coming soon. Better to keep that galabia dry so he could wear it after they'd passed.

I used my spare shirt to pat Prof dry as best I could, though nothing quite like dry existed Inside. I lined his slender old body straight on the bedrolls, folded a spare galabia, then wrapped my sheet around it and placed the makeshift pillow under his head.

I tucked a sheet around him, my core trembly but my hands sure. That was when I noticed the broad wound along his side, from ribs down to hips. The skin was unbroken, but underneath was red and purple, like a giant bruise. He was bleeding under the skin. Maybe he'd fallen. Or maybe he'd been struck. "What happened, Prof?" I whispered.

The man in the tent had his eyes closed, and I knew he would be sleeping for many hours or days before he became Prof again. If he ever became Prof again. I rolled out of the tent and zipped it shut. It was a beautiful day, with sun so strong it survived the trip through the trees' broad leaves and struck the brown river blue. The canopy was a katydid green, the jungle floor decked with clean circles and triangles of sunlight. It was almost as though the Inside was saying to me: *Yes, I will take everything. You will wind up alone here. But it will be beautiful. Once you and I are all alone — and you have always known this would happen, haven't you? — there will still be beauty.*

Omar waited at the tent flap, knitting his fingers. He was so vital, so *alive*, that his presence helped keep me from breaking apart. Omar had watched as I'd placed Prof on his bedroll, and now sat beside me on the sitting log. The monkey had gotten some sort of blister on a toe, probably from getting too curious about the campfire embers after we'd gone to bed. He picked at it dispassionately, flicking his eyes toward the tent every few seconds. As we sat together, he blinked his little eyes into the rare pleasure of direct sunlight. His head nodded, and he looked about to fall asleep. I nudged closer to him to feel his warmth and noticed little crusts dotting his eyelashes. As he fought sleep, I reached out and clasped his monkey hand in mine. The tendons running along the back were fine and straight in my palm. His little fingernails were perfectly formed, and so similar to my own.

We sat that way for hours of the afternoon, the monkey secure enough in my presence to fall asleep in the open. I felt strangely calmed by this perfectly formed hand in my own, so like my sister's had been, except for its velvet.

•   •   •

I listened all that afternoon for a sign of Drummer or Mango or any of the other chimps. But there was nothing. I retrieved the case and ladle from the riverbank, then paced the campsite. Occasional coughs brought me into the tent, but each time I found Prof unconscious on his side, his wound still angry under the surface of his skin. I took his sheet out in the sun to dry after he'd sweated through it, replacing it as soon as I found him shivering. I suspected there was more than the wound plaguing him. I knew mosquitoes in Gabon brought jungle illnesses that he'd probably never been exposed to back in Egypt, with names like dengue or malaria or yellow fever that were probably important to doctors but all amounted to the same thing. He had what my mom would have called *coup de lune*. Moonsickness.

As the sun began its swift descent, I slung up the food bag, and Omar took up his usual nighttime position in his basin, chirping worriedly. My first thought on settling in to sleep was that Prof hadn't brushed his teeth yet. I bit back the flood of dark feelings that followed as I lay next to him on the bare tent floor.

"The light's gone out!" I whispered. There was no answer.

I heard nothing all restless night but the usual animal screams. Come morning, Prof was still in a deep fever sleep, his snoring strong enough to set a sheet corner flapping.

The campsite was as I'd left it the night before, the cooking pot cold and dewy on wood gone black and wet. One ember remained, and I was heartened that I wouldn't have to light a new fire. I sat at the edge of the pit and fed the ember some twigs.

As I tromped around the campsite hunting for wood, I wished again we had a machete, that I could cut logs instead of having to find them. Once I was done, I settled in to cook and eat my first breakfast without Prof. Then I heard the tent unzip. Whirling around, I saw him unsteady at the entrance, blinking in the sunshine. "Lovely morning, isn't it?" he croaked.

"You're awake!" I jumped to my feet.

"Just," he said, smiling thinly. "I'm not up for staying on my feet, but it feels like I've breathed all the air in that tent forty times over by now. Help me over to the sitting log?"

I supported Prof around his slender shoulders and guided him to our spot. Making happy clicking sounds, Omar descended from the trees and curled into his master's lap. Prof sat back, eyes closed, and I could see pleasure pass visibly over his face. I resented his joy, even as I was glad to see him able to feel it. "Was this your plan the whole time?" I accused. "Dying out here in the jungle?"

After a while his eyes opened and looked through me. "I am so sorry," he said slowly, "to have brought you into this. I did not plan to get malaria, no. But if I have to die, I am content that it's here. This feels more like home than my home ever did. I had thought you might feel the same."

"But I'm just a boy," I said. "I didn't ask for any of this." I pressed the palms of my hands against my eyes.

Prof's arm was around my shoulders. The skin against the back of my neck felt hot and clammy, and I realized with a start that just because Prof was awake it didn't necessarily mean he was getting better. "People keep leaving you, don't they? It was not your mother's fault. It is rotten chance. A rotten time in history to live in. Your father was off building roads most of the time, you said? He probably brought the worm back. And, unlike you, your sister was breastfeeding after he'd infected your mother. That is how I imagine it went."

I stared at the ground, blinking. Why was he talking about my family?

Prof let out a guttering sigh. "We can try so hard, but in some basic way we're bound by how we're raised. There's no escaping it.

We can love someone and want to be open to the feeling, but fail because our hearts got wired one way long before we knew it was happening. We can break our own hearts because of what our souls believe."

I understood his words, but had no idea exactly who he was referring to.

Prof shook his head, a sign he wanted to change the subject. "I should not be sick," he said. "Not now. Allah would not want it. Once I've recovered, let me take care of camp so you don't have to worry about it. We can pause the study for as long as we need. Let me take care of you, instead."

I shook my head. "That wound you have along your side. What is that from?"

Prof looked surprised, then pulled up his galabia to inspect the broad bruise. "This? I got too close to Silver Stripes. He warned me away from his family. It wasn't his fault. You can't blame him."

"I think you're hurt and moonsick, Prof. And I don't know how to help you."

"You're taking care of me," Prof said after a moment. I hadn't thought about it that way, but he was right: I was taking care of him. The realization was an ache. I wouldn't trade it away, but having someone to care for made me feel heavy.

"Would you bring me my notebook?" Prof asked. I did, and watched pages flip. "How are our supplies?"

"We have a third of our rice left," I reported. "The bottom layer is probably rotted, but I've been too afraid to find out for sure. I will make myself look later this morning. We are out of dried meat and have one can of fish. No more dried mint leaves. Maybe I can find us some in the wild." The surprise at myself, that I cared enough about Prof to scramble across the jungle to forage mint for him, brought me back to the verge of confused tears.

"I should send you to the village for more supplies —" Prof started.

"No. You need watching over," I said.

Prof looked relieved. "If we don't go back to the village, do you think we could feed ourselves? It would mean figuring out a source of protein, probably river fish. We should look at the back of the Baedeker — it does give some rough guidelines for eating. What we're allowed and not allowed to eat can't have changed that much in a hundred years, can it? Between that and fruit and roots, do you think we could survive?"

I thought about it. "Yes."

Prof let out a long breath. His voice was husky, I realized, for more reasons than being sick. "I was sure that I would only have you for a month. That the moment I sent you on that boat to the village, you would pocket the money and vanish."

"I —"

"Let me finish, please. It's true that I'd rather not send you away. Because I would like you to care for me, yes, but also because I don't want to tempt you to leave forever. It would be a long journey there and back, with plenty of time to think, plenty of time for you to choose against me."

I had to tell him the truth before my heart retreated. "I did want to. Before. I wanted to escape with your case. But I don't anymore. I'm not going to run away, I promise."

He nodded. "Thank you for telling me. I trust you. But I still want you to stay near. Is that okay? I'm very sick," Prof said, laughing wetly, "and I'm afraid it's making me vulnerable."

I understood. "Don't leave me and Omar, Prof," I said.

"Don't you worry, Luc," he said. "Professor Abdul Mohammad doesn't give up on anything easily. But right now, he might need to sleep."

I managed to get him to drink a ladleful of water before going back into the tent. I left the zipper open, with only the mosquito netting down so it wouldn't get too stifling inside. "Don't kill a chimpanzee," he said sternly before he nodded off.

I didn't reply. I would defend us if I had to.

Agitated, I paced around to the back of our tent, where the mint I'd planted weeks before had sprouted in the wet, dark soil. They were further along than I'd thought; I wouldn't have to forage far for mint after all. I selected some plump watery leaves, choosing only the largest so the small ones sprouting beneath would have space to grow. Then I heated some water and made a cup of mint tea.

When I went into the tent, the scent of urine wafted out. I tried to get Prof to rouse enough to drink the tea, but every time I'd try to wake him he'd mumble for a few seconds, then pass back out.

I peeled Prof's moist, smelly galabia off him and replaced it with his dry one. Having gotten him into the best shape I could, I sat out on the sitting log and drank his tea. I spent that day near the campsite, foraging and frequently checking in on Prof. That night there were glowworms on the branches, specks of bright light that emerged ahead of the stars.

Night dropped further, and my thoughts were on spirits and things past until I realized Omar must have eaten one of the glowworms from his perch in the plastic basin; bright goo dangled from his chin.

"Prof," I called, chuckling, "you have to come out and see this." But there was no motion from the tent.

I shinnied up one of the trees and selected a leaf with a glowworm suckered to it. The light dangled like a lure. I carefully walked the leaf over to the tent. Inside was the smell and warmth of recycled breath. I tucked the leaf into the seam where the main stake joined the mosquito netting, and the solitary glowworm continued to shine above us. "Look," I said, nudging Prof. "Some-one left the lights on."

I lay down beside him and hoped for rest. The mock men shrieked somewhere distant as they did the same. I didn't have much faith that I'd ever fall asleep. I lay still, as motionless as Prof, and watched the single star above us, the one inside our tent.

# ELEVEN

At some point during the night Prof got up enough energy to leave the tent. At the sound of the zipper I was instantly alert, and lay there until I heard him stop peeing. When he came back in, I fastened the mosquito netting after him and busied myself killing the bloodsuckers that had managed to get in. He left the flashlight on, clutched to his chest, and in the artificial glow his face had an inhuman sheen to it, like the flesh of a cut melon. He suddenly sat up on his bedroll, panting stale and foul air.

"Are you okay?" I asked.

Prof shone the flashlight at the side of his bedroll. He'd brought the metal case into the tent. "I want you to know a secret," he said. "Remember these numbers: One. Nine. Seven. One."

"What are they?" I asked. But I knew exactly why he was telling me four numbers, and it made me queasy.

"Remember them."

"I don't need those numbers," I said, my voice quavering. "Don't give them to me."

"You'll remember them," Prof said.

I wanted to tell him he wouldn't die, but for the moment I couldn't speak.

"If I die . . ." Prof continued, his flashlight trained on the case. His voice was hushed; I didn't know if it was from faintness or if he was afraid of attracting the attention of whatever beasts were outside. "I want you to take Omar into your care. He is not a wild animal and can't live out here alone. Put him in your sister's basin and take him in the pirogue back to the village. The money that remains, both fake and real, is yours. Don't spend counterfeit money at the same place more than once. You'll have to keep moving. But it's enough to give you a start somewhere. You're such a smart boy — you'll find a way."

"Don't say this," I finally said. "I'm not leaving here because you're not dying. You need to rest, Prof. That's all."

He clicked out the light. A minute later, he said, "I'll stay up for a little longer. I'll watch over until you fall asleep."

I knew Prof needed his sleep more than I needed mine, but what he was offering was what I most wanted. "Thank you, Prof," I said.

"Of course," he said. "Of course, Luc."


It was still nighttime, but I was unexpectedly awake, skin pricking with fear.

The noise that had woken me had been lost in the waking, but I was rigid at attention, focused on the jungle sounds. I heard the rush and sway of the trees, watched our glowworm's lure make lazy circular motions as breezes rocked the tent. I was sharply aware of how thin the canvas walls were compared to the strength of the Inside's night creatures. It was an armor as hopeless as skin.

A bird whistled, and the noise sounded so perfectly birdlike. I imagined the hunter signaling to a companion, the two fanning out, fitting a poison arrow to a bowstring. . . .

Then I heard another sound and instantly knew it was the one that had woken me. A mournful *hoo-hoo*. In my confused state, I first thought it was Carine, back to life and reaching for my mother. But then I realized I was hearing Mango. Nearby. Suffering.

It had been days since I'd seen her, and I hadn't given the lonely little ape much thought since Prof had become sick. But now, listening to her cry, she was all I could think about. In the jungle dark, anything that wasn't a predator knew to stay hidden and silent. But Mango had come to me, and was risking death to call for help.

The crying got louder. "Stop!" I called out. "Please stop!"

She stopped for a moment. Then she continued her sad *hoo-hoo*.

There was something I needed, beside me. And something that needed me, out there in the jungle. I had to choose one of them.

*Come back.* That was to Prof.

*I'm coming for you.* That was to Mango.

I took the flashlight from Prof's side, then unzipped the tent and crept to the fire. Remembering the gray-faced, desperate Drummer who had so recently appeared at the campsite, and the man we had chased from his own hunting ground, I pulled the knife out of the valise. Light in one hand and weapon in the other, I crept toward the sound of sadness.

Mango's cries were coming from high up; she must have managed to make herself a nest. I tentatively stepped through the jungle, sticking to trails I knew as the fire's glow diminished behind me. I cast the flashlight's beam up through the canopy, unnerved by how often a pair of unknowable red circles reflected back.

I finally located the tree I thought was Mango's. I whispered her name.

The sad moaning stopped for a moment, then picked up again. "Mango!" I said louder.

This time I saw her little head appear over the side of a nest. I kneeled and beckoned her. She made curious hoots and gripped the side of the tree. I could see her judging the distance, trying to figure out the best way down.

I continued encouraging her, making cooing sounds and what I thought were friendly hoots. But then a sound caused my attention to whip back to where I'd come from. I sprung to my feet, the knife tight in my hand.

A screech had come from the campsite. From Omar. It was a call I'd heard only once before, when Beggar had been attacked.

I punched at my head. "No. No, no, no!"

I left Mango hooting behind me as I leaped across the ravine and raced back up the hill. The flashlight cut shaky triangles across the jungle floor. "Prof!" I yelled. *"Prof!"*

When I arrived at the campsite, I found Omar on the ground, jumping and making the same intense screech over and over. When he stared into the flashlight, his eyes were flat and red.

The tent fly was open and flapping. I realized, with a tremor in my chest, that I'd left it that way when I'd gone to help Mango. The tent's central pole was bent, and the top sagged. Like something powerful had charged it.

Yelling nonsense, I whirled around, the knife outstretched. As I did, I saw, on the far side of the site, palm fronds shaking as someone or something crashed into the brush.

"Hey!" I yelled, whirling the flashlight in a wide circle. "Come back!"

Heart slamming, I brandished the knife in one hand as I opened the tent farther.

The bottom corner of the flap was wet with blood. I pushed it back farther and used the flashlight to check inside.

Long moments thudded by as I looked over every inch of the tent floor, waiting for comprehension to arrive. Bedroll. Tent wall. Bedroll. Tent wall.

No one was inside.

How could that be possible?

Home was empty.

Prof was gone.

# TWELVE

I flung our bedding into the clearing, ripped the whole crooked tent off its stakes and shook it, fabric flapping. No Prof. He wasn't anywhere in the campsite. I chased off into the brush in the direction I'd seen the shaking branches.

I gripped the flashlight in two hands, but I'd dropped the knife while I was searching the tent, and that mistake was all I could think of — other than Prof. I didn't have time to go back for it, and if I found Drummer with the old man in his grasp, wouldn't the hungry chimpanzee fight for his meal? How could I hope to wrestle him back? I cursed myself as I hurtled through the undergrowth; I should have killed that monster when I'd had the chance.

All this time my pulse thudded through my veins like it meant to break out, and Omar's strange wailing was still in my ears. As I hurtled farther into the jungle darkness, the alarm call grew distant but no less present in my mind.

I slammed through blade-sharp ferns. Eventually the thicket gave way to a steep muddy slope, which I toppled down, only coming to a stop by gripping a tree at the bottom and swinging around, crumpling to my knees. The flashlight rattled off down the ravine, a bobbing orange glow rolling to the foot of a tree. I was being foolish, I knew — I would never be able to save Prof if I killed myself in the process.

I held still and listened, my hearing trained on every small sound. Stirred by my sudden entrance, the jungle was a noisy riot, full of the screams of birds, the relentless hums of crickets, and the humanlike screeches of the frogs. I wasn't going to get any clues by listening. I wasn't a chimp.

Which meant Prof was gone.

I gloomily retrieved the flashlight and stumbled back to camp. I did a circuit of the site, shining the flashlight in every direction. There was no further clue to what had happened to Prof.

He had already been near death from his wound and his moonsickness; he couldn't survive an attack that had produced as much blood as was left on the tent flap.

Before my knees gave out and dropped me where I stood, I went down by the river and kneeled in the dirt. My head rested heavily in my hands, the flashlight's plastic pressing painfully into my forehead.

After he'd been wounded, Drummer had lain helpless in that nest for days. I could have killed him at any moment, by any method, at my leisure. I could have consumed him, like any predator would.

But I'd shown mercy.

And now I was sure he'd killed Prof.

The day was well under way when I woke; morning sun had set one side of the tent glowing. I stared at the bright fabric for a while, then my eyes moved to the husk of the dead glowworm somehow still curled up against the post. Finally I allowed myself to look at Prof's empty half of the tent.

The void was an instant horror; I was immediately out of the opening and into the daylight. I nearly tumbled over poor Omar, who was sitting right up at the tent's edge. He peeked in and then up at me, squeaked, and ran up to my shoulder. I stroked his foot as I stared out over the campsite.

We were alone.

Stocky sparrows fought for space in the treetops. Downy flies fluffed in the open air. I heard the distant calls of chimpanzees. None of these animals meant anything to me, but the amount of activity in this vibrant clearing was proof of life, of the plenty of life. It was a cold comfort, like trying to trick a belly full of lime rinds into thinking it's had a full meal.

How would I survive alone? It had been the question of my life, and I was still no closer to an answer.

I started packing up. The damaged tent went down easily, and I wadded it into the valise. Omar watched nervously as I wedged in his plastic basin. I couldn't bear to look at Prof's bedding and spare clothes, so I kicked them behind a rock. Everything he and I had shared, everything that was now mine only, was packed within minutes. I ran a hand over my sopping brow and sat on our log. The bags were neatly lined up beside me, like I was waiting for the ten o'clock Transgabonais to Libreville.

I had all the money and whatever else was inside the metal case. I could get in the pirogue and make my way back to Okondja. Then I could hail a logger truck and take the first steps toward making a home somewhere.

But that would mean leaving Prof. Even though he was almost certainly dead, I didn't want to abandon him. What if he wandered out of the wilderness soon, limping and smiling?

I couldn't leave. Not yet. I would have to give him a day or two to come back to me.

I lowered my head. Omar left the valise to sit beside me, leaning his skinny torso against my hip. His delicate hand rested on my knee. I let the sunlight ache into me while I idly scratched at Omar's fur. He made satisfied groans. That seemed like a small victory inside my torment.

By this time in the morning, Prof would have gone down to the river to brush his teeth. I had never wanted to before, but this morning I plucked his odd little brush and the sleeve of tooth soap from the valise and went down to the water's edge. It was a job that had to be done — and since Prof couldn't do it anymore, I would. I scrubbed my teeth — a weird chemical sensation that I found unpleasant — then rinsed. The breeze was cool against my gums, like all the windows of my mouth had been left open.

It would take a few trips to get everything to the pirogue. If I wanted to get going today, I'd have to get started.

In my misery, I was convinced I was staying at the same time as I was convinced I was leaving. I sat still on the log. Where would I go? Monsieur Tatagani would destroy me if I returned to Franceville. My father's family had banished us out of shame after they'd decided he'd died of the worm. I'd have to head somewhere new, and in the meantime hope no one would take advantage of a boy traveling alone, that I wouldn't have everything taken from me as soon as my journey began.

But there were *people* out there.

In the midst of my sorrow, in the rapid turn of my anger and grief about the loss of Prof, I couldn't get Mango's sad cries out of my head. Alone in her nest, she'd said something I'd long ago lost the ability to say without embarrassment or anger.

She'd said, *I am lonely.*

I wondered why she wasn't making those sounds anymore. Had she, too, not survived the night?

I wrapped my fingers around the valise's handles, ready to heave it to my back. Omar sat beside me expectantly, waiting for Prof to return and determine our future.

Sighing, I let go of the valise and headed back to the tree where I'd last heard Mango. *This doesn't mean I'm staying,* I told myself. *The mock men will kill me, too, if I stay. If they don't, the Inside will find another way to destroy me. I know this.*

But even if her kind would be the ones to end my life, I had to know if Mango was okay. Nothing remained in the world for me to care about but her and Omar.

There was no sound from the tree. When I climbed it, I found the nest empty. She would probably be back in it at night, I figured.

By then it was close enough to midday that I figured I'd have some lunch at the campsite. By the time I'd cleaned up, it was afternoon. *It's too late in the day to start out now. Best to wait until tomorrow to leave. I'll just have to give Prof until then to return.*

After dinner, I lined up everything metal around the tent. The pot, bowl, ladle, old cans, anything that would clatter if a chimp or a leopard or a hunter knocked it. I brought Omar into the tent to sleep next to me, for his safety and my sanity, and he curled up at my feet.

Like back in Monsieur Tatagani's dress-curtained room, falling asleep and shutting out the world came more easily than I'd expected. As I finally started to nod off I had a terrible vision: that Prof would return and trip over an old tin fish can and be scared.

Darkness, even with open eyes. *What is that noise?*

I slapped at my face and quickly got out the knife. There it was again: a grinding sound. I went to wake Prof, but my hand contacted the tent floor and my heart seized.

The noise grew more fevered, desperate and scrambling. It sounded like my sorrow had become a beast, clawing through the campsite. There was something else familiar to it, too, though I couldn't exactly place it. This was a Franceville noise, not a jungle one — it sounded like a metal tool hitting wood, like construction. Beneath it there was also a scurrying sound, branches cracking and gravel flying.

Then I heard a clang of metal on metal. The thing had tripped my alarm.

Which meant it was right outside the tent.

I could wait and be taken like Prof or I could face my tormentor. I gripped the knife and ripped open the tent. Standing crazily before the moonlight and the glowworms, I spun, arms outstretched. "Who are you?!" I yelled.

The clanging seemed to come from two places at once. The earliest fear of my life, that a mock man would come in the night and take me or the one I loved, had arrived. The enemy was right here. And I couldn't see him.

Pulse thudding, I whirled and peered uselessly into the murky tree line. There was movement on the side of the campsite that led to the river, but I couldn't tell if it was from tree or beast. And always beneath was that same sound: metal thumping wood, something heavy being dragged.

After adding a log to the fire to intimidate any wild animals, I fished the flashlight out of the tent and clicked it on. Its jungle-corroded bulb glowed weakly. Small creatures stared back at me from the trees, their eyes perfect circles of red and silver.

An unexpected flurry, then Omar scurried up onto my shoulder. I felt sick with concern. Sick at being so concerned. "Please be okay," I called to Prof.

But Prof wasn't there. Instead I was alone with the beast in the jungle that had destroyed him.

The clearing was newly quiet, except for the hushed sway of the trees. My metal items were scattered, and I carefully set them back up. After a watchful hour, I got back in the tent and zipped it closed. I didn't fall asleep again that night.

•    •    •

"Prof is dead." I said it aloud as soon as I woke and then kept saying it, hoping the words would start to feel automatic. I knew no one but Omar heard me, but I desperately wanted someone to know what had happened. I didn't want to be the only person to own Prof's death. I wished I remembered enough of my letters to use Prof's pencils, that I could make a line across the end of his notes and write beneath:

*Professor Abdul Mohammad is dead.*

Years and years from now, some explorer might find that notebook and know. Then our having lived would feel like it had mattered. My mother and Carine and Prof and I wouldn't have grown from nothing only to become meat that others could eat and that could in turn be eaten by wild dogs or beetles or worms. Or chimpanzees.

I'd been the one to take care of Prof, and I hadn't kept him safe. No other feeling existed on the same scale, except one: The intensity of my grief had kept it at a distance before, but now a sensation rushed over me, dotted my temples with sweat, and squared my shoulders. Anger.

Once I'd uncovered rage, I felt alive again. Blisteringly, painfully alive. After breakfast I took out the knife and began to sharpen it until the point was fine enough to write bloodscript on flesh. Then my gaze turned to the dull green wall of the jungle line.

In my heightened, unreasoning state, I now saw it clearly: a bright brown track of upturned soil, leading from the clearing toward the river. Where something had been dragged.

This explained the sounds from last night.

Without another thought, I headed out into the private spaces between the thick green fronds. As I stalked through the trees I wondered if this was what it would feel like to be a mock man, to be so part of the Inside that I had no awareness of separation. The way I felt, I could climb to the top of the nearest tree without feeling, could fall without fear, could hunt without mercy, like the mock men I'd imagined as a child.

Because Prof had been killed.

The bloody flap insisted on that.

It looked like someone had chained a truck tire to a buffalo and set it charging; there were no footsteps, just a fat line of tan clay where the jungle floor had been roughed away. When I came to a fallen log blocking the path, there was evidence of a struggle — mussed dirt for a ways around, then two lines carved out of the bark where whatever was being dragged had been hauled over with great effort.

The tracks soon left the trail and dove into the thickets and interlocking trunks of the deep jungle. Normally it would be impassable, but enough plants had been uprooted that I had space to follow. I found myself in a thicker, darker jungle than I had known so far. Fat mushrooms grew on every available surface. A bright salamander darted away from me, disappearing into the fog hugging the jungle floor.

One of those mushrooms had been broken in the onslaught, its pure white insides glowing in the faint light of the jungle interior. Something was smeared on it. A dark red liquid, like blood.

Prof's?

More lines had been scored in the bark of a fallen tree, and to follow them I had to work hard to climb it, the mossy bark slick under my fingers. Finally I made it to the top and could look over to the other side.

There lay a crumpled dark-haired figure, on his back, staring up at me in exhaustion and fear.

It wasn't Prof.

It was Drummer.

# PART THREE:

## Family

# THIRTEEN

Drummer's gaze didn't waver for many seconds. At first I feared he was dead, that fate had taken my revenge for me. But then his eyes stopped gleaming for a moment as he blinked. His chest rose and fell while he took a deep breath, staring at me the whole time. His fingers twitched. So did mine.

I held the knife out in front of me, but otherwise remained still atop the fallen tree. There was no rush — this mock man wasn't going anywhere.

Before, Drummer had seemed all bulk and black hair. Now, with him on his back, I was seeing his vulnerable parts, the ones his body usually worked so hard to keep hidden: surprisingly long legs with delicate ankles and knees, toes pointed gracefully, like a heeled lady's; belly muscular but soft, too; skin glowing white wherever the hair parted.

I eased off the tree, dropping into a crouch. When the chimp still didn't react, I stepped nearer.

Drummer tried to prop himself up on his elbows. But he didn't have the energy for even that; his head lolled back to the ground. He looked away from me and made soft panting sounds, his muddy hair quivering.

A half-moon of rusty teeth had bitten into Drummer's leg, right under the kneecap. The line of metal clenched the limb with enough strength that the trap's smile joined at the corners. In the middle, the fat teeth had embedded deep enough to disappear entirely.

Drummer watched me as I crept closer. I stood beside his head, knife still tight in my hand. He appeared to have dragged half the jungle with him; mud caked his hair, pasting leaves and twigs. A network of scratches overlaid his tan face.

Blood pulsed beneath the skin of his neck. His mouth gaped, exposing his teeth, a maize mix of black and yellow and white. I couldn't help but imagine those same teeth biting into Prof's belly.

The knife shook as I aimed it, point down.

Drummer turned his face away so he didn't have to watch his punishment, like the boy thief in Franceville had when Monsieur Tatagani had come for his hands.

I kneeled and brought the knife to Drummer's throat. His blood was pulsing so intensely — if I held the knife there, it seemed the artery would open itself against the blade and he would kill himself.

Drummer let out a long sigh, either giving up or passing out. His eyes didn't have any white to them anymore, just glistening black. But I saw the pupils widen and narrow, his focus darting as tension coursed through him. Despite my best efforts, my thoughts went from revenge to what this mighty creature must have been through. Who knew how far he'd dragged this jaw trap before arriving at our tent. He'd hauled it over two fallen trees, at least, as he tried to outrun his mysterious and merciless predator.

I squatted so I could examine the trap more closely. Its grin was forced shut by heavy bolted springs at each joint. There had to be some release, I realized, so the hunters could remove their meat and reuse the trap. Drummer panted and shivered as I cautiously ran a hand over the edges of the metal, looking for a trip. I wasn't able to find anything, and my hand came back shiny with the chimp's blood.

I rocked back on my heels and squatted heavily, head in my hands. What was I doing? Why figure out how to release Drummer if what I wanted most in the world was for him to die?

I looked into the eyes of the monster my childhood self had feared so much. Tan ears stuck out far from his head, making him look almost comical. His brow was heavy over his eyes, slick with perspiration.

I put the knife down to free my hand and continued investigating the trap. After fumbling for a while, I found what I was looking for — latches entwined within the coils of the springs. They didn't have much give, but I hoped that if I managed to trip them both at once, the jaw would release. In order to get a thumb against each at the same time, I had to lift Drummer's good leg onto my shoulder. He watched me take his ankle in my hands and rest it against my neck. His leg was solid with muscle and loose with exhaustion. I teased my thumbs against the trap's mechanism, debating what to do with the creature Prof wanted so much to protect. The creature that might have killed him.

There was a rustle in a nearby thicket and I whirled to my feet, Drummer groaning as his leg dropped to the ground. I brandished the knife.

Ferns parted and a small figure emerged, her little hands curled nervously around two fronds.

"Oh." I sighed. "Oh, no."

Mango squeaked and managed a step forward before her courage failed and sent her scurrying back into the thicket. Her face emerged from between two fronds, only her sunken eyes and patchy forehead visible as she peered at her brother and me.

*Oh, little sister.*

She made my decision for me. I pressed the latches at the same time and, with a grinding of tired metal, the mechanism clicked.

The trap didn't spring open, but the jaws now had some give. I gripped the bloody metal, then thought better of it — who knew what would happen to me if I cut myself and my blood mingled with a mock man's. Mango was all serious attention as I pulled down a branch and wedged it between the trap's jaws.

When I stepped on the branch, the trap quivered and eased open. It made a sucking, wet noise as it parted from around Drummer's leg.

As I forced the branch closer to the earth, the trap finally clicked open and held. Without meaning to, I'd reset it. Very carefully, I took Drummer's leg in my hands, lacing my fingers into his bloodslick hair to get the best grip. He watched with an intense expression combining fear and hatred, staring me down like I was an extension of the trap.

Taking a deep breath and holding it, I tried to lift Drummer's leg free of the teeth. Ignoring as best I could the blood that flowed out around my fingers, I focused on getting the leg clear of the trap without dropping it back onto the trigger.

Soon after I'd freed him, Drummer began to scream. It was a high-pitched and shattering sound, as familiar and alien as a shrieking parrot. The chimp's arms thrashed, and I had to tumble backward to avoid getting struck. He screamed so much that his throat cramped, his mouth open but only strangled sounds coming out.

Dodging the chimp's flailing arms, I lined his gouged leg up along the ground. Then I dragged the trap off to one side. I was barely able to budge the contraption, and marveled at Drummer's strength to have heaved it through the jungle. I wanted to hang the evil device from a tree so that Mango wouldn't accidentally step on it, but I realized I didn't need to worry; she had attention only for her brother. She barely blinked as she watched him from the security of the bushes.

Drummer had gone into a fetal position, pressing his eyes shut as blood welled from his leg. He was pumping a fresh pool of it onto the ground, overlaying the blood that had already clotted on the leaves. I couldn't imagine he had that much more left. I ripped a large frond from a waxy yam plant and pressed it against his wound. Blood soon seeped between its edges, so I added another and then another. I yanked a vine down from a tree, careful to choose a young one whose thorns were soft, and tied it tightly around the fronds. It wasn't as good as a real bandage, but it might help stem the blood flow.

My anger at Drummer was becoming confusion. I was *saving* him. I kicked at his good leg. It jerked, but he didn't otherwise react.

Infection was what crept in and stole a life. Especially Inside, any wound could fester, and the rot would spread to the rest of the body. Drummer was already filthy with mud. He'd have been better off recuperating in a nest, but I had no way to get him up to one. I could bathe him as best I could, but his wounds were already filthy, brown swirling with the red.

I didn't have any rubbing alcohol left, any useful medicines, anything.

Except. There was one thing I could rig up, something my mother had once done for my father.

Mango had crept forward to sit at her brother's side. She wrapped around his arm, looking at his face and making her mournful sounds. "Mango, I'll be back," I said. Her attention didn't leave her brother for even a moment. I might as well not have existed.

I started scaling the fallen tree to get back to camp, then stopped. The steel trap was still nearby, and the thought of Mango's little body crushed within its jaws was too much to bear. I gripped the trap's chain, took a moment to collect my strength, and began to drag, relieved when it knocked a branch and snapped tight as it went. Taking pains to keep clear of the rusty hinges, I managed to maneuver it through the ferns, taking the long way to the other side of the fallen tree. After a moment's rest, I heaved it the remaining yards to the river. I tugged it into the water and watched it sink into the depths.

As I climbed the hill to the campsite, a wave of fatigue came over me. It had been a long day after a sleepless night, and would grow far longer before it was over.

And here I was, back at the campsite.

Our belongings were neatly stacked beside the sitting log, right where I'd left them. Before my heart failed me, I rummaged through the valise until I'd located our cylinder of precious salt and Prof's teakettle. I took them under my arm, as well as my food bag full of fruit, and sped away.

Drummer had passed out right where I'd left him. Mango was sitting on his chest, anxiously plucking at her brother's hair. When she saw me she made a fearful grin that looked like a gash spread across her face, but she didn't run away. She stayed near when I kneeled beside Drummer, and studied me as I shook salt into the water. Already chunked by the humidity, the salt instantly vanished. I peeled a stick until it was clean and green, then stirred the water until I felt nothing solid. After untying and parting the yam fronds, I held the kettle over Drummer's wound. Then, slowly, I began to drip.

Before he'd left to pave a distant road and never returned, my father had once come home injured. A truck had taken a corner too wide while he was walking beside it, and a scrap of metal had sliced open his arm. I was only small at the time, but remembered following as my mother helped him to the village doctor, who smoked the wound with burning grass. But my mother had her own techniques, which she had learned from her mother. I had stood on a chair to get a better view as she laid my father flat on the table and dribbled salt water into his wound. She had done so tirelessly for two days. After she'd finished, though the wound was deep and ragged, it did not become infected and my father did not die.

So I did the same now for Drummer. I even made the same cooing sounds, though those were for the sake of Mango, who was shaking with nerves as she watched me attend to her brother.

It was for the best that Drummer was passed out, as I remembered well my father's groans from the stinging salt water.

Mango poked at the kettle, then stopped after I repeatedly batted her hand away. Shooting me cautious glances, she eased into my lap. She was light on my thighs, smelled like damp hair and wild animal. With my free hand, I gave her wet little head a pat and said, "Settle in, Mango. This is going to take a while."


For the first few hours I was on edge, waiting for Drummer to regain consciousness and wondering what he — or I — might do once he did. Gradually I calmed: His good leg would sometimes twitch, but otherwise there was little sign of activity. He was deep in slumber, maybe even a coma.

I continued the salt drip all that day, switching arms whenever one got tired, only occasionally taking a break to forage or pee or check on Omar, and drenching the wound with extra salt water when I returned.

As the afternoon wore dim, I considered what I'd do come evening. The idea of making a solitary trek to the tent made me sick with lonely sadness. Once there I'd . . . what? Do a quick rice boil if I had the energy, another session of that chemical cleaning of my teeth that felt like a conversation with Prof . . . but then? Say good night to Omar and settle in to that tent alone, take in the lingering scent of blood and moonsickness? I couldn't imagine it. More than anything, I feared having enough free space for my thoughts to stay on Prof.

Mango relaxed more and more into my lap, reveling in our closeness. Sometimes she would raise her long arms and loop them around my neck, still facing her brother. She'd idly tug on my hair, hoping to improvise a game. Whenever I was still for too long while operating the drip, she would bounce in my lap to get my attention, amused when the salt water sloshed onto her brother. At least I assumed it was amusement; only her bottom teeth showed, and she made raspy sounds as she pouted.

I decided to gather what belongings I could in one trip to the campsite, including Omar's basin so I could tempt him to relocate, and then spend the night with Drummer and Mango. When I put the kettle down and stood up, Mango tumbled out of my lap and stared up at me in shock. She promptly climbed up to ride on my back, her legs a tight hoop around my waist. She was a lot heavier than Omar, who was so light that I could sometimes forget he was even on me.

As I started to climb the fallen tree, Mango scrambled down from my back and returned to her brother, draping herself over his chest. She glared at me, reproachful that I would dare leave her again. "Stay here; that's fine," I said. "I'll be back soon. Guard your brother for a few minutes, okay?"

When I returned with the tent and food, I found Drummer in the same position, Mango wrapped tight around his shoulders as she dozed. I cleared enough ground to pitch the tent in the lee of the fallen tree. I couldn't get the structure to its full length, but I got enough of it stretched over the roots for its sides to rise and serve as protection for us all. Omar perched on the fallen log, nervously flicking his gaze from Drummer to

Mango while I looped a sturdy branch through the handles of the plastic basin. He then took his usual spot inside and soon fell asleep.

I had enough time left to speed back to the old campsite one last time, racing against the failing twilight while I fetched the metal briefcase and valise. It didn't feel as heavy as it once had, both because we'd used up so many of the supplies and because the muscles of my arms and shoulders had thickened. Before I left the campsite for the last time, I gave it a long look.

*Good night, Prof. The light's gone out.*

Then it was back to the chimps.

This spot was much more thickly shaded by trees than the previous campsite had been, and once night fell the dark was nearly absolute. As I sat there in the off-blackness, listening to crashing sounds and screeches as the night predators began their hunts, I realized how risky it was for Mango and Drummer to be out in the open in their helpless state.

I unzipped the tent and crept to Drummer, arms outstretched in the darkness. Heart quaking, I located his good leg and took it in hand. I had no way of knowing if he was awake, and had to choke back the image of the powerful male baring his teeth at me. But he made no movement: Drummer was still unconscious. By gripping the hair of his meaty shoulders I was able to lug him over the roots and into the tent. I felt a small hand tug my pant leg as Mango joined us.

I used up some precious battery to power the flashlight long enough to get all of us positioned. Mango had wedged herself between her brother and the tent's edge and was staring at me, eyes gleaming electric orange. I decided to take the opportunity of Drummer's unconsciousness to examine his wound, steeling myself to find patches of rot.

The injury was laid over his marks from the leopard attack, making layers of crisscrossed red wounds.

But no black, and no green.

Relieved, I clicked off the flashlight.

I had hoped to stay awake the whole night to treat Drummer, but I must have fallen asleep on the job. The kettle had fallen over, wetting Mango and me and half the tent with salt water. I cursed and set it upright.

Then I yelped.

Strong black fingers had wrapped around my forearm.

When I yelled, Drummer averted his eyes. His hand stayed on me, though. The fingers began to move, passing through the sparse hair on my forearm.

He was grooming me. As best he could groom a human.

I remembered Prof once telling me how the chimpanzees groomed to determine authority. That it happened mostly between males, to establish partnerships.

I held still, marveling at the rough touch. Drummer's head lay against the wet fabric of the tent floor, as if he were in too much pain to budge any part of his body but the fingers. He was willing to suffer moving his hand, though. For me. To establish a friend-ship with *me*.

"Drummer," I said, "I may hate you, but I've decided Prof wouldn't want me to kill you. You don't have to groom me."

I cautiously lifted Drummer's hand and laid it on the canvas floor. Kettle in hand, I left the tent and headed down to the river. There I refilled it and poured in more precious salt. I let myself be stingier with it now, as Drummer's wound seemed to be healing well and our supply was more than half gone. Back by the tent, I lowered the plastic basin, dumping Omar and getting a loud scolding in the process, then pulled out some black bananas. When I went back inside, Drummer was instantly grooming me, kneading my pant leg.

I began the salt drip, and though Drummer scrunched his eyes at the sting, he did nothing to stop me.

That afternoon Drummer allowed me to turn him over so I could examine his other side. I was heartened to see the back of his leg in better shape than the front; the saltwater spill the night before might have been a disguised blessing.

I decided to scale back the saltwater drip even more, both to conserve salt and to give me a break from my hospital memories. I stepped out of the tent, Mango tight on my back. We surprised Omar, who had been sunning on a nearby branch; at the sight of Mango he shot up a tree. The little chimp squealed in joy when she saw her playmate and was soon chasing him through the branches. Up and down they went, all around the tent.

While they played, the metal case gleamed at me. I remembered the numbers Prof had told me. But I wouldn't open it yet. Instead I went into the valise and pulled out his bent notebook and a pencil.

He'd made meticulous columns of numbers and letters. I had no idea what the Arabic script meant, but some of the scribbles were in a column by themselves, and in them I saw numbers.

I arranged myself beside the river, cooling my feet and taking occasional drinks of water, then turned to the next blank page. Gripping Prof's unfamiliar pencil in my fist, I drew a shaky line across, and an X to indicate I was taking over. Then I painstakingly drew a little drum to represent Drummer, like this:

Then I drew a body of a chimp and made a mark where Drummer's injury was, along with a sketch of the jaw trap.

Because I wanted her included, I drew a picture of Mango, too. She had broken off from chasing Omar and was staring at me with such a calm, curious expression that I wanted to preserve it:

Then beside it I made one short line to indicate that this was the first day of my observations. I really didn't know what information Prof had been writing down, but for his sake I wanted to find some small way to continue his work. If I met more chimpanzees I figured I'd assign each a picture and draw simple images of what they did. I looked proudly at my first entry and imagined how it would feel to fill a whole page, someday a whole notebook.

I shut the book, smoothed my hands over the cover, and toyed with the spirals at the edge.

I wanted to live inside that book.

Which is how I knew I was staying.

I'd stay to continue Prof's work, the life's labor that had been so important to him. And I'd stay because no one was waiting for me anywhere else in the world, but here were Mango and Omar.

I went back into the tent and gave Drummer a fresh saltwater drip. I couldn't resist staring at the metal case, right outside the opening, and before I knew it I had tugged it onto my lap. I turned the dials to make *one, nine, seven, one* from left to right. I startled when the case clicked open. I hadn't expected it to work.

But it did.

# FOURTEEN

Right as the lid sprang open, a termite flew into the tent and landed on my forearm. Without thinking, I used my lips to mop the powerful insect up from between my hairs, felt it crunch satisfyingly between my teeth.

I creaked the lid open. There on top were the francs I'd seen long ago when Prof had convinced Monsieur Tatagani to let me go. I placed them carefully to one side.

I chewed on my lip. This was not the treasure I'd imagined.

Letters and photographs, all neatly bound in a pair of leather shoelaces. Some were in Arabic, but some others I could try to read. I would attempt it later. For now, though, I turned to the photographs.

They were soft and wrinkle-backed, some folded many times over. The topmost ones were black-and-white, while the ones on the bottom were color.

The first photo was of a family, parents and two girls and a little boy who I recognized as Prof from his knobby knees and crafty smile. The woman was shrouded in black, only her eyes exposed, and though she had a hand on a daughter's shoulder, she stood apart from the father. He was a man dressed in a galabia and taqiyah like Prof, though his stern face was worlds away from his son's excited expression. Prof stood apart from his family.

There were more photos of him as a child, looking strange and happy and separate. Then I came to a color photo of Prof as a young man, standing in front of a set of rough red buildings, surrounded in grass that had been clipped short, like hair. Prof looked tall and healthy, and though he still had his taqiyah on, he was also wearing a leather jacket with many zippers. Another young man was sitting next to him, smoking a cigarette. He also looked like an Arab, but he wore neither a galabia nor a taqiyah.

There were more pictures of Prof and the young Arab-not-Arab, lying on a beach on matching towels, then in a zoo . . . in front of chimpanzees! Then they were with a different, thicker ape, what I thought was a gorilla, asleep on a metal table. The Arab-not-Arab was in a white coat, and I figured he was an ape doctor. Prof looked very proud to be beside him. I started to think of the young man as Monsieur Baedeker, since he and Prof always appeared to be traveling.

Then the photos were back to family, and Prof had his galabia on again. Prof seemed above the crowd somehow, like he was at once part of everything and nothing. In one picture Prof was wearing a fancier galabia with gold trim, standing next to a kind-looking woman, and there were flowers in the background. Prof's family was lined up on one side, and I assumed it was her family on the other. It looked like a wedding.

Soon after, the pictures got more formal. Prof was smoking a water pipe in almost every picture, and his wife was often at the other side of the group.

Many photos went by without any sign of Monsieur Baedeker.

A wind came up outside the tent and the air turned even more moist, the sky stirring lazily, like gray soup. I didn't think it would rain yet, but all the same I realized the rainy season would soon arrive. I zipped up the tent and settled in to examine the remaining photographs in peace. Drummer was softly snoring beside me, and I found the sound comforting.

Prof went from looking young to looking old. And then Monsieur Baedeker appeared again. Earlier he had looked as skinny and impish as Prof, but now he looked solid, T-shirt tight over his muscles. In their first photo back together they were standing in front of a small car in a tall, bright city. The sky was night, but there were so many lamps on the street that it also looked like day. Monsieur Baedeker and Prof pointed at the sign of a shop. Something must have been funny about it, because they were laughing. It was amazing to see Prof's expression — he'd gone back to being an excited young man. He was really *looking* at Monsieur Baedeker. He wasn't just watching his own life anymore.

It was strange to see the two men together again, with Prof still wearing his galabia. There was one more picture of the two of them, in a big hall with indoor cafés and people waiting with luggage. There were planes out the window — it was an airport. The photo must have been taken by Prof, because it was only of Monsieur Baedeker staring into the distance. Something had attracted his attention — something that wasn't Prof.

I turned to the next photo, then flipped to the next and through to the end. I returned to the airport photo. That was it. Monsieur Baedeker never appeared again.

Neither did Prof's wife, or the rest of his family.

Prof was alone in every picture from then on. The strangers in the photographs went from Europeans to Arabs to normal Africans. Toward the end, the scenery started to look like Gabon, and I thought I recognized the facial features of Fang people. I was watching Prof work his way down into my life.

Then the pictures were over.

I flipped through the photographs again. And again.

The feeling of closeness I'd grown to feel for Prof was now clearer. I felt like I knew something, too, about Monsieur Baedeker — that I knew Prof's sisters a lot less, and his wife even less than that.

Prof had lived more than forty years, I told myself. That was a good long life, more than most of us could hope for.

I wished I could hang the photos up around my tent, that they wouldn't be ruined by moisture or bugs or apes if I left them out, that I wouldn't ever have to lock them away in the case.

The wind died down suddenly and as quickly started up again, rippling the tent fabric. I crept nearer to Drummer and lay alongside him.

I was glad to have seen the photographs of the chimps and the gorilla, since they meant Prof hadn't been lying to me about his research. All the same, I had expected to have seen a picture of Prof in a classroom with the devoted students that he'd said attended his lectures.

I knew more about Prof now, but I also had a better sense of what I did not know. I wished he could be here to tell me the truth, and realizing he never could was what upset me most.

The tent's fabric sighed beside me, and I barely managed to dodge Drummer's arm as he flung it in his sleep. The limb was wet with sweat; the wind had died and the sun had broken through the cloud cover to heat our tent. Tentatively, I reached out and touched my skinny fingertip to one of Drummer's rough ones. He woke and recoiled. I touched my fingertip to his again. This time he let it stay.

Feeling a little better, I unzipped the tent and rolled out to enjoy the sunshine.

I was only a few paces away when I realized there was motion inside the tent, growing in intensity until the whole thing was shaking. It listed to one side as I saw Drummer fall against the canvas. Then he appeared at the opening and emerged on three limbs, keeping his wounded leg high and tight next to his body.

He hopped toward me and, groaning softly, sat a wary distance away. He kept his hurt leg out of the dirt by resting it against the opposite knee. Lengthy scabs traced the limb, hard red and purple and yellow circling his calf. But I was relieved to see there was no green and no black other than dried blood — no sign of rot.

At the sight of her brother, Mango dropped from the tree where she had been playing with Omar. The vervet scolded the sudden loss of his playmate, anger and longing mixing on his tiny face. Mango approached Drummer, then did one of her neat little somersaults that landed her against her brother's good leg. She crawled up him and looped her arms around his neck. Then she peered at me and squeaked in the way I knew meant she was hungry.

I shrugged back. There were two sets of eyes on me then: Drummer peered at me with a guarded air, with as much desperation as his sister.

They were both hungry.

I stood. Daylight was already starting to wane, and if I wanted to keep us from starving that night, I would have to act fast. Weeks ago I'd seen the chimpanzees eating nuts from a gere tree not far from where we were. If there were any left, I would gather enough so that we could sleep; I'd forage more thoroughly tomorrow.

When I stepped away Drummer jerked in surprise, tumbling into the tent and scattering Prof's letters. I set about collecting them, Drummer wincing as I nudged him to one side to retrieve the ones under his butt. I arranged everything carefully in the metal case, flipping the numbers away from *one-nine-seven-one* so that it wouldn't open again unless I wanted it to.


The next morning, Omar stayed behind while Mango and Drummer joined me foraging. The little chimp was tight on my back while Drummer easily kept pace beside me, even on only three legs. He held the wounded leg tight against his hip, as if it were tied in place.

When we found nothing to eat, the hunger in my belly turned from an ache to a stab. As the day turned to afternoon, I picked a smooth stone from the riverside and placed it on my tongue. It was a trick I'd learned in my Franceville days; sucking on a stone kept hunger more distant.

It wasn't just food I had to worry about; I also needed to start a fire to keep predators away.

Drummer was still unable to climb trees — I once caught him standing wistfully at the base of a trunk, gazing upward, a vine slack in his hand. That evening he reluctantly made a bed for himself in the lee of a tree, assembling fronds against the ground, arranging and rearranging them, as though if only he perfected the nest he and it would magically be high up. Once he'd slumped into his ground bed, Mango draped herself over him.

Apparently the chimps didn't want to sleep in the tent if they didn't have to. So I brought it near them, hemming in their spot to keep them safer, bade them good night, and entered the tent. I listened to the apes' breath as my own slowed, could hear Omar's chirps as he settled into the basin. Hunger turned my breath foul. I smacked my tongue around my bitter mouth as I waited to fall asleep.

Drummer and Mango were still dozing the following morning as I went off in a light-headed search for food. Nothing was fruiting, though. Fear seizing me, I wandered from dry tree to dry tree in a panicked daze, the river stone gummy in my mouth.

Then I heard a humming behind me. I turned to see Drummer at the far side of the clearing, a gloppy honeycomb dangling from his mouth, his eyes scrunched as bees swarmed him. Hopping on one leg, he bit down heartily, chunks of molten honeycomb falling from either side of his mouth, a cloud of bees rising. Mango shrieked in glee and scampered over, taking a piece of the fallen honeycomb into her mouth, heedlessly chewing through bees and honey. Keeping an eye on Drummer to make sure I wasn't crossing some line, I did the same. The honeycomb was heavy in my hand, dripping with sweet goo. Inside the glossy yellow were tiny wriggling larva and adult bees struggling to free themselves. I quickly took the piece into my mouth and chewed before anything within could emerge and sting me.

That sun-warm liquid gold with crunchy bits inside was the most delicious treat I'd ever tasted.

Drummer looked very pleased with himself as we chewed through the honeycomb. Maybe he'd sensed that these bees were ill or weak, or that they were the stingless kind; for whatever reason we ate without getting stung, and the survivors eventually buzzed away.

As we settled into nap positions I noticed a piece of honeycomb stuck to Drummer's wounded leg. I gently pulled it off and held it out to Omar, who squeaked in pleasure and gobbled the morsel down. Once he'd finished that last bit, he climbed back to his basin. When I returned to Drummer, I saw he'd been watching us. He lifted his wounded leg to his lips, and kissed it. I patted him on the top of his head. He startled, then calmed and nodded. He patted his own head. So I patted it again. He patted himself. I patted him again. He grunted contentedly.

I would miss having someone to be angry at. But the companionship was nice. As was the honey.

# FIFTEEN

Within a week, Drummer's leg was no longer oozing fluid and his scabs had hardened tightly enough to his body that they no longer broke off and re-formed. He was still holding the limb high in the air, and might never use it again. But I was proud of him for healing so well only one week into a major injury, so I marked the occasion in the notebook like this:

Once he'd started feeling better, he improvised a way to climb: Drummer would hoist his way up a tree using only his arms, his good leg tapping the trunk for balance. Once high in a fruiting tree he'd munch away, sending down volleys of food that Mango and I would run around collecting. Some of the gloom that had attached to him lifted, too, and I'd catch him expressing feelings I hadn't seen in him for a while: a stare-at-the-sky boredom, a kick-at-this-snake boredom, a can-I-crush-a-plum-pit boredom. I was glad to see it in each version, since I figured you had to be at least a little healthy to be bored.

As he got more mobile, I followed him and discovered more foods that I could eat. The youngest green tentacles of the saba liana vines could be eaten. Drummer would strip the bark with his teeth and chew at the bright stringy interior, the fibers making wet cracking sounds as he wolfed them down. My teeth weren't strong enough to get me inside any but the youngest and slenderest off-shoots, but I enjoyed the addition to my diet. It tasted a little bitter, like celery, but also greenly sweet, like sugarcane, which Drummer found a patch of a ways upriver.

He would range as best he could during the day, Mango always near his side. Sometimes I'd follow them, but as Drummer increasingly took to the trees I'd sometimes have to turn back and wait for them at the tent.

There, I'd make notes or thumb through Prof's Baedeker, even though many of the words resisted me. I wouldn't ever be alone for long before Drummer and Mango came by. I would have thought chimpanzees toiled all day to survive, but these two didn't forage for more than a few hours at a time. The rest was lounging, and Drummer and Mango seemed to prefer doing that with me.

I was amazed that Drummer could be so tolerant of his sister's presence and so blind to her at the same time. He'd sit on his haunches, stripping bark from liana, and she would lean against him, tongue between her teeth as she concentrated on her own vine, watching his movements and carefully mimicking them. Then, after hunching down to concentrate on a particularly difficult vine, she would look up and find her brother gone. She'd stand on two feet and pivot, making concerned squeaks. He'd have lurched away without her, and even with only three usable limbs would soon have wandered too far for her to catch up on her smaller feet. So she'd fall back on her second-choice companion — me. She'd crouch in the dirt nearby as I sketched in the notebook or sharpened my knife. At times like that Mango's sorrow at being left out was so present and full — an unfiltered version of a feeling I'd long ago learned hurt less when it was walled away.

Her brother troubles worsened at night. Sometimes Drummer's

nests would be leafy and full and low in the tree, so Mango could manage the trip up to join him. Other times she wasn't as lucky.

When she couldn't be with Drummer one night, Mango made her own nest for the first time. It was directly beneath her brother's, though dozens of feet lower. She struggled to make the wiry branches stay down; no sooner had she gotten one under a foot and started reaching for another than the first sprang back, as often as not slapping her in the face. When she did finally manage to make a nest, it was a slippery, leafless thing, and looked as comfortable a resting place as a ladder.

Mango's plight was on my mind all the next afternoon as I cut more sugarcane. By the time I returned to the tent, I'd decided what I wanted to do. First I lowered the plastic basin and emptied it, ignoring Omar's outraged chatter. Mango looked at her own body in amazement as I placed her inside. All that showed out the top were a few wispy hairs and one tan little ear. Once she'd managed to get her head over the side, her expression was stunned and entranced.

I threw the rope over a low branch and took the free end into my hand. Cautiously, I pulled. Once the slack was gone, the plastic basin began to rise. Mango made pleased panting sounds at this new game, staring at the ground as she twirled. I lifted her to the level of a branch about ten feet up, then tied off the end. She sat in the basin, pleased, for at least half an hour. Then, bored, she easily scrambled out and onto the branch.

But my goal had been accomplished: I'd gotten her used to traveling in the basin.

Shortly before sunset Drummer took to his favorite tree and climbed to the highest branches. He often picked that same spot, and I wondered if it was because from there he could see the sunset. His body was framed in golden light as he stared at the glowing horizon. Mango tried to follow him, and as usual got only partway up the tree before she had to climb back down in defeat. This time, though, I held out the plastic basin and called her name. She remembered the game, bounded over, and got in.

I hoisted her into the air. Her little fingers gripped the edge tightly as she watched the jungle floor recede. The basin crashed against various branches as it ascended, the bumps only making her more and more thrilled. My arms were shaking with exertion by the time I got her to the top, the nylon rope drawing nicks of blood from my fingers. Alerted by his sister's squeals, Drummer sat up just in time to see her hop onto his face. The nest was only barely big enough for one, and so Mango sat directly on him, poking out of the nest like a peanut half on a bowl of rice.

All was silent for a few moments, until I heard Drummer give an exasperated grunt. There was a flurry of motion as he reached for more branches and expertly broadened the nest. Then all was silent. I restored the plastic basin to its normal position, and Omar huffily returned to his home.

As far as I could tell, we all slept well that night. The next morning, when Drummer got up early to seek out food, his movements woke Mango as well; she hitched a ride on his back all the way down the tree and then toddled off after him. When he returned hours later she was still tight on him, face turned so her cheek pressed as close as possible to her brother's warmth.


During the first weeks of his injury, Drummer was content to stay isolated with Mango and me. But as he got healthier, he seemed to start craving the company of other chimpanzees. Whenever he'd hear their distant calls, he'd bound to the top of the nearest tree and peer around, making calls of his own.

One morning the cries of the other chimpanzees were closer than they'd been for weeks. Drummer started demonstrating, ripping down a branch and lurching up and down the game trails with it. Hooting aggressively, he bounded from the campsite, tripping only once over his lame leg. Luckily for Mango, she'd already been clinging to his back and got a free ride.

I lay back, half in the tent and half out, and waited for Drummer and Mango to return.

They didn't.

The day's urgent brightness snapped off as quickly as an electric light, the patches of sun on the leafy ground flickering to black. I fed the fire more wood and kept telling myself I'd wait a few more minutes before retreating into the tent, give them more time to prove they hadn't abandoned me.

Maybe because he sensed my distress, Omar didn't take his usual position in the plastic basin that night, instead remaining on the ground so he could drape over my knees while I drank my evening mint tea. He relaxed as I stroked his silver fur, even raising one arm and then the other so I could better groom his armpits. His movements were a little stiff; I realized Omar might not be a young monkey anymore. As I finally washed my teeth and prepared for bed, he seemed to want to enter the tent with me, darting in and out. I decided to keep him outside, knowing he'd bother me all night if I let him in.

I lay and listened for any sign that Drummer and Mango were back. At one point I heard a loud rustling, thought of my chimps, and threw open the tent. The night was still and moist. Two liquid eyes stared back at me, and it took me a moment to realize it wasn't Mango; I'd surprised the bushbuck with the starburst spots. She bounded away, and the campsite was again motionless. I closed the tent and tried to sleep.

I wanted to be content for Drummer and Mango, that they'd gone back to the other chimpanzees where they belonged, but the feeling wouldn't come. Clouds rolled in that night and extended the moonlight's glow. For the first time since I'd arrived in the jungle, rain fell, big drops that pinged the canvas like pellets. I knew from experience that was only a warning of the deluges coming in the following weeks.

I opened the tent in case Omar wanted to come in from the rain, but the drops were finished as soon as I called to him, and he stayed up in the basin. I zipped the tent shut and lay back down. "The light's gone out," I whispered.


The waiting — the sadness — was exhausting, and the next day I was asleep before the sun went down.

That night raindrops again fell against the canvas, plunking loudly enough to wake me. As soon as I came to, my mind was racing and I knew that, even though it was the middle of the night, I wasn't going to fall back asleep.

*What am I doing in the jungle?* I asked myself. *Why do I stay?*

The world on the other side of the tent wall felt so solid and unchanging. I couldn't bear to open the tent and remind myself of the emptiness outside. But there was no everyday world that waited for me somewhere else.

This *was* my everyday world, and it would remain empty unless I did something to fill it.

I was startled by a noise. It wasn't raindrops this time. My heart seized as I recognized distant drumming against kapok trees.

I didn't even try to fall asleep after that. I sat up in the tent, rigid with excitement, and waited for the Inside to become light enough that I could set out.

As soon as morning broke, I sharpened the knife against a

rock and tucked a photo of Prof into my pants pocket. I ate a full breakfast of my last remaining scraps of cooked rice, the last can of preserved fish, and some strips of dried dragon fruit.

"Don't wait up," I said to a bewildered Omar as he stared after me. "I'll be home after dark."

Then I headed deeper Inside.

# SIXTEEN

As I crept through the overgrowth, I remembered Prof's warnings about staying a lengthy distance from the chimps, remembered how careful he'd been to observe them only from the next hillside. I would have to be very cautious if I didn't want them to run.

Or attack.

I stopped frequently — sometimes it was to listen for chimp calls and scan for predators, but other times my heart raced with panic and I needed a moment to calm down. I was used to Drummer and Mango, but the rest of the chimps were still mock men.

There were plenty of other dangers to fear, worse than surprising a chimp: thick muscular snakes or thin venomous ones; bird-eating spiders fast as rats; leopards and golden cats; a porcupine or a buffalo; other animals I hadn't come across yet but knew lived in Gabon's jungles, like gorillas and forest elephants and hippopotamuses. My knife would be a pitiful weapon against any of them . . . or against a hunter returning for revenge.

I finally heard what I was hoping for: chimps. Some calls were high-pitched, others low and throaty, and all came from the river's left fork. I started down it, keeping tight to the edge.

The mangroves along the shore grew so dense that it was impossible to pass any way but through them, and to move forward I had to clamber between their slippery stalks. Fat water crickets scattered as I wedged forward. Each time I thought I was stuck, each time I feared there was going to be no more room for me to pass, the jungle unexpectedly opened.

The river coursed between two boulders and then tumbled away, and I figured from the crashing sound below that I'd reached a waterfall. I crept forward, hiding behind one of the boulders, and cautiously peered over the top.

After cascading a dozen feet, the water tumbled into a lagoon. Whatever stone was beneath made the water appear almost purple instead of its normal tea color. Red and yellow flowers bordered the edge, and the soil beneath them looked loose. It meant that the trees couldn't huddle around the lagoon, so the water's surface had the rare luxury of full sunlight. It lit the depths all the way to the bottom, where fat fish, long as eels, darted in the sun-mottled water.

I wanted to lie in those soft, short flowers and feel that light on my face. This nestled clearing would make a perfect home. Water was right on hand, and many of the plants had tender yellow-green — probably edible — buds. Because of the lack of trees, I'd have more warning when predators came near.

I started scanning for a good spot to pitch the tent. Above the waterfall the vegetation was too dense, but below — my eyes followed the waterline and saw that the immediate shore was too narrow, but around the bend the river widened and burbled beside what looked like another tidy little clearing.

My mind filled with fantasies. I imagined the little house I might build in that clearing, starting with four walls of mud baked onto logs, like in my old village. I'd make thatch from the dried fronds of various oil palms, using old and stringy ones to give the roof structure, and overlaying young and bushy pieces to keep the bugs out. I'd carve a well into the stump out front and collect rainwater there. I'd sow a small garden in the black soil.

Even as my mind was spinning stories, I was pulling dead fronds from a nearby tree, pressing them together and twisting twine around the stalks to make a broom. I would need one to sweep my stoop each morning.

Once I realized what I was doing, I cast the bundle down in disgust.

As if to prove how stupid I'd been, a shaggy black form dropped from a tree and walked right across my home site. Silver Stripes. He swaggered through on all fours and plopped down right where I'd imagined my hut. He yawned, exposing long, sharp canine teeth. It was like the Inside had heard my dream of something beyond survival and sent this mock man to punish my ambition.

As I watched, the grizzled old male swaggered to the lagoon's edge and dangled his feet in the water. He was soon followed by two more males, full-size adults without the silver hair. Even though they were larger than Silver Stripes, they deferred to him, making nervous hoots before settling in.

I watched from my hiding place above the waterfall as, one by one, more chimps plopped down along the edges of the lagoon. This spot was as attractive to them as it was to me.

I scanned the face of each arriving chimp, but there was no Drummer and no Mango.

I watched the mothers the most. One had a very little boy she held close to her chest, sometimes letting him play with the males but fetching him the moment they bared their teeth or bristled their hair. When her infant toddled near Silver Stripes she hurried over, head bowed in submission, and plucked him away. She took her son to the far side of the lagoon, kissing the baby's neck and caressing him like he'd been returned from the dead.

Another mother seemed to be having a harder time of it. Her daughter never seemed able to find a good position on her body, and frequently slid off into the grass, reminding me of Mango with Beggar. After this mother got sidetracked by a bush crawling with snackable worms, her child wandered far. When the infant plopped into Silver Stripes's lap, he bared his teeth. It was only when her daughter shrieked that Bad Mother snapped her head up from her snacking. When she didn't see her child nearby, she ran in tight circles, moaning. Then she located her daughter, cringing as Silver Stripes loomed over her. In Bad Mother's rush to reach her child, she didn't crouch as low as Good Mother had, and Silver Stripes was immediately on her, giving her savage kicks in the ribs. To defend her mother, the daughter lashed out with her tiny fists. By the time Bad Mother managed to get her daughter and herself safely away to a treetop, she was bleeding in a few places. Her daughter had escaped being crushed by Silver Stripes, but only barely. The attack and the retreat had happened in under a minute.

Everything went back to normal. Not long after, Bad Mother and Silver Stripes calmly passed near each other like he hadn't attacked her. He even tapped her open palm graciously when she laid it out to be touched.

My stomach corded and tensed in a way familiar from my Franceville days. I hadn't eaten since breakfast and hadn't brought any food from my supplies. Even if they were edible, the buds nearby weren't plentiful enough to fill my belly. If I didn't want to risk fainting, I'd have to head back to the tent soon. I was reluctant to leave — going a third day without seeing Mango might break my heart.

I took advantage of the stream to strip off my clothes and give myself a rinse. After emerging from the water, I picked up my shirt and pants, debating whether it was worth dressing for my trip back. The only real use for clothing was preventing mosquito bites, and I'd stopped noticing those long ago. I decided to walk back to the tent naked except for the shoes on my feet. Happy with my decision, I turned and started on my way — only to come face-to-face with Drummer.

He and Mango must have crept up under the concealing roar of the waterfall. I was so startled to see them that I dropped my clothes. My tattered shirt and pants fell into the current and, quick as fish, were swept over the fall.

Intimidated by Drummer's expressionless face, I gave up on the clothes and froze. I realized that, though Drummer and Mango were focused on me, they weren't showing any fear or concern. They'd approached me like any chimp would approach another. Like something fearful and puzzling, sure, but also something . . . accepted. Maybe even useful. They'd approached like I was family.

I kneeled where I was, opening my palms along the ground like I'd seen Bad Mother do, and after a moment's hesitation Mango bounded into my lap. Drummer approached more cautiously and sat beside me. He faced my back and tried to groom me, but soon gave up; I guess the process was too boring when there wasn't much hair to trap tasty bugs. Even though it was a hot day, the breeze rising from the waterfall made me shiver and I hugged Mango for warmth. She seemed to enjoy the crush, sighing happily.

With Mango's wet little head tucked under my chin, I finally crept back to the waterfall to see if I could spy where my clothes had gone. I eased my head over the side of the rocks to scan the lagoon. No sign of my shirt and pants.

Another head appeared next to mine. Drummer had adopted my exact stance, peering over the other rock. He'd glance at me occasionally and adjust his position, as if by mimicking me perfectly he'd gain some clue as to what we were supposed to be doing. It made me smile, his bare butt next to my bare butt, both of us standing on the tops of our toes to see as much as we could of the chimp scene below.

Bad Mother and her daughter had wandered away, but Good Mother was still there. Still around, too, were Silver Stripes and the other males. When two of the males greeted each other by clasping hands, Drummer got so excited, he made a loud bark. I ducked behind the rock, hoping no chimp had spied me, and watched Drummer jump to the dangling tree nearby and climb hand over foot down its vines. Once he reached the males, he grabbed the thickest loose vine he could and whipped it around his head as an introduction, balancing on his good leg. He looked expectantly in my direction — apparently I was supposed to have joined him.

Some of the males had been crinkling leaves in their hands and sponging nectar from large flowers. After watching Drummer's efforts for a second, they calmly returned to their work. Drummer, infuriated, whipped the vine even more and charged. He'd neglected to notice, though, that the vine was still attached to the tree, and before he made it to the males, he reached its limit and jerked backward, popping into the air and landing on his back.

The other chimps stared at him for a moment. Then one calmly placed a leaf in his mouth, and another followed. They turned back to their snack.

Drummer stayed on his back. He massaged his hobbled leg and stared into the gray sky. Could a chimp feel embarrassment? Certainly chimps seemed very aware of who liked whom, and being aware of yourself seemed like an important piece of that.

Soon after Drummer's pitiful entrance, the males wandered away from the lagoon. Drummer watched them leave, only getting up once they were gone. Silver Stripes unexpectedly reappeared, though, and Drummer was caught by surprise when the elder male charged him, his hair standing on end to look bigger. Silver Stripes made an impressive ruckus, barking and flipping large rocks as he went. Drummer hooted and fled, but not fast enough. Silver Stripes cuffed him across the head, sending him falling onto his bad leg and then sliding into the water. Immediately, Drummer was flailing and splashing.

Prof once told me that chimpanzees couldn't swim because they didn't have enough fat in their bodies to help them float. Drummer was in shallow enough water that all he had to do was stand, but in his terror he was making everything worse, sputtering and hurling himself about like a bad actor. Terrified I'd lose him like I'd lost Prof, I pressed Mango into a nearby bush, dove off the rock, and splashed into the water.

I hadn't swum since leaving my village, but I knew I could at least do better than Drummer. Within two strokes I had his torso under an arm and had started dragging him to shore. He was flailing so wildly that his heels kept striking my thigh, making great shuddering blows right on my bone. I heard shrieking from Silver Stripes and made sure to tug Drummer far from where he was. As I kneeled in the mud, I spotted the elder chimp racing back and forth along the far shore and barking furiously.

I managed to get my backside against the muddy bank, then collapsed. Once we were on land, Drummer went limp, falling flat open on top of me.

I'd brought us to shore on a stretch of mud near the waterfall with a narrow inlet in either direction. The males had raced back into the area to join Silver Stripes, and they were all only a dozen feet away, making their terrifying shrieks and showing every intention of tearing me apart. But they couldn't reach me without entering the water, and that seemed like something they were unwilling to do. Which was why I was still alive.

Eventually Drummer got his hands under him, nearly pressing the breath out of me in the process, and rolled onto his side. He winced as he lifted his wounded leg into the air. "You nearly died there, friend," I whispered as I cupped water and rinsed his wound. "*We* nearly died."

With Drummer and me noiseless and nearly still, the males eventually bored of their angry protests. Now that the surprise of my entrance was over, they'd probably realized I was as little a threat as Drummer. We were just orphans of extinct tribes.

The lame chimp was on his side, facing me but avoiding my eyes. His breathing had returned to normal, but he seemed unwilling to move or do anything beyond glumly stare into the rocks at the bank. "No one's giving you a break, are they?" I asked.

Once the males were gone, Mango plopped down beside us. "Ready to go home to our old spot?" I asked. "Can you convince your big brother to join us?"

Mango clung to my neck as I crossed the water and worked my way up the waterfall ravine and over the boulder. Drummer sulkily followed behind. I was glad to have him and Mango back, but also uneasy. These two might have been willing to follow me back to camp that night, but I assumed from their long absence that this lagoon, and this chimpanzee troop, was where they really wanted to be. I'd keep losing them if being with me meant not being near their own kind.

And I'd lost half my clothes. I was down to one shirt and one pair of pants from here on out unless I figured out how to make some new ones.

Losing those clothes should have been the important thing, but all I could think about was Drummer's brutal rejection by Silver Stripes. I shared the sting. As we silently dropped into our dark, narrow gulley, chosen only because it was where Drummer had been trapped by some old human torture device, I realized that I, too, wanted for us to be able to consider the lagoon home.

I just had to figure out how.

•   •   •

I didn't need to lift Mango up to Drummer's nest by the plastic
basin anymore; she made sure she was stuck on her brother as soon
as the afternoon waned, so he had no choice but to take her with
him up to their favorite nesting spot. Drummer made his nest
fresh every night, and I never understood why until I started finding little red bumps on my skin each morning. They'd always fade
during the day, but when the number of itchy morning sores kept
increasing, I realized my bedroll had become home to some invis-
ible insect. I tried dunking it in the river and drying it in the sun,
but it was no help. The pests had moved in, and planned to stay
and multiply.

Infestation was the destiny of everything I owned, I was sure.
Already there were fine furry speckles on the waistband of my
pants, and my shirt smelled like the underside of a rock. I could
live without the clothes — already I only wore the shirt for "special occasions," namely foraging in prickles — but what I most
dreaded was the day I'd find rot set into my tent. It was an old
sturdy thing made of waxed canvas, and its ancient thickness had
done it well so far — even when wind pressed sharp branches
against it, the fabric didn't tear. I could do without the rest of my
belongings, but the tent and the fire were why I'd stayed alive this
long. Fear of losing the tent only made me lust more for the lagoon;
in that sunny spot I had a chance of drying it out thoroughly
before the rainy season was upon us.

While I inspected my tent, Drummer moped. He'd spend
hours at a time on his back, clutching his scarred leg to his chest
and staring up at the patch of sky, as if asking what he'd done to
deserve his fate. Then the mood would pass and he'd be soaring
through the canopy, panting happily. I wondered how his rejection

by the troop was affecting him, if a chimp could feel something like wounded pride.

Mango spent much of her days chasing Omar. Though she was stronger, he was faster, and they made a good match. If he hadn't had the liability of a tail, she'd never catch him. But I always knew when she'd succeeded by the indignant vervet howl that would resound through the jungle. Once she did have her monkey she'd hug him tight to her chest, petting Omar so fiercely, his little black head bobbed. He'd squirm to get away, which only led her to hold him tighter. After a while she'd get distracted and set him down and he'd escape into the trees. The chase would begin all over again, raining dead leaves and startled praying mantises into the clearing.

While Mango seemed to enjoy our shared life, Drummer withdrew more and more. Whenever a distant chimp call sounded, he'd find the nearest kapok and thump it, craning to listen for any response. There never was one. Newly depressed, he'd give up on drumming and massage his scar, ignoring Mango even when she pounced on him.

A week or so after his confrontation with the males, Drummer left one morning and hadn't returned by nightfall. Mango spent the short twilight pacing the clearing and moaning. Omar perched as close as he dared on a nearby tree and lobbed sticks, trying to get Mango to play. She was having none of it. It wasn't safe for her to be alone in the dark, so I called to her from the edge of my tent. When she wouldn't come, I tried to pick her up. She bit me on my arm, hard enough to draw blood, and I dropped her. "Fine," I said. "Have it your way."

I listened to her making mournful *hoo-hoos* for her brother during the night, though not as loudly as she'd done before. Come morning I saw she'd selected a low tree and made herself a nest, and not a half-bad one; there was a thin layer of bark on top of twined branches, moss dangling at the edges. But she clearly hadn't slept much; she was groggy and lethargic, and wouldn't have found herself anything to eat if I hadn't fed her some slices of soaked yam, placing them right in front of her mouth until she bit in. We'd been very lucky that she hadn't gotten sick, scraping by with an inconstant brother and an incompetent human.

The longer Drummer remained unhappy and outside the troop, the longer Mango, too, would stay on the outskirts. If this continued for too long, her future looked grim.

Males clearly held the power among chimps, so I figured Drummer was Mango's best hope of survival. But he was too small and too crippled to exert any influence, and had no mother left to secure a place for him and Mango, like I'd watched Good Mother do for her son.

The solution was simple, and impossible: I'd have to make Drummer more dominant. But I was far weaker than any of the chimps. Silver Stripes would easily kill me if he treated me as roughly as he'd treated Drummer.

My thoughts went to the knife. But Drummer would never be able to learn how to use it. And even with the weapon, I was no match for an adult chimp.

There was one time I'd seen a chimpanzee intimidated by a human, of course. Drummer himself had been the one to show me, when Prof had rescued Omar and me by making a loud noise. It was probably the same reason the males presented, dragging branches and screaming and splashing rocks into the lagoon.

Noise mattered to chimps. A lot.

And I had something that could make a noise like nothing else in the jungle.

Prof's box of secrets might save us yet.

# SEVENTEEN

I began my preparations to get Drummer — all of us — some family. Realizing I might not be able to forage much once my plan was underway, I spent a couple of days collecting food and fuel. Prof's dream of our being able to fish came true when I caught three catfish by heaving a log into a quiet side pool of the river, rolling it toward the bank until I'd trapped the unlucky animals and could pluck them out of the mud at leisure. I roasted the fish on a dome of green sticks and ate them right away, as even cooked meat would go bad within hours. The heads went to Omar and Mango.

Prof had read to me from the Baedeker that one of the only foods that could last more than a few days Inside was yam, so I thinly sliced and rinsed some. The same thing that made the roots so sharp and sour before soaking probably kept them safe from rot; they remained bright and crispy for hours.

Mango kept near my side as I prepared the slices, baring her teeth when I batted her hand away from the still-toxic yam. "Not yet," I said. "Tomorrow." Maybe chimps were immune to the mild poison of the wild yam, which left my throat numb if I ate it too quickly, but I didn't want to risk it.

The next day I nestled the swollen food bag into the plastic basin and brought it upriver to the waterfall, Mango tight on my bare back. Then I went back and lugged the case and a few supplies from the valise. Omar tailed me, passing from tree to tree and chattering. As we approached the waterfall he encountered a troop of mangabey monkeys in the treetops, whose greetings he snobbishly ignored.

I hid my belongings in the rotted-out trunk of a nearby tree and sat behind a rock to wait. Though there were no chimps around the lagoon, I could hear nearby calls.

I stared into the clear water, my mind again drifting to fantasies about the pleasant hut I would someday build in the soft grassy clearing. I was lost in thought until I sensed something near me.

A big chimp was no more than a foot away. I was already scrambling backward before I recognized him and stopped. "Drummer, you have to stop sneaking up like that!"

He wasted only a moment on me before returning his gaze to the lagoon, his eyes filled with a nervous sadness. I tentatively laid a hand on his back. "It's okay," I said. "We're going to figure this out."

His upset was clear in every aspect of him: his anxious face, his hunched shoulders, his toes worrying one another. My grooming did little to improve his spirits. I crept to the rotted-out tree and pulled out the metal briefcase. Drummer's mouth crinkled in worry when he saw it, so I set it down and continued to groom him until he calmed. He returned his attention to the lagoon.

He became all attention and bristling hair when I tapped my fingernails against the metal. Drummer crouched, teeth bared, until his curiosity got the better of his fear. He brought his head close to my fingers and peered at them as I repeated the unfamiliar noise. Finally he cautiously experimented with putting one of his fingers between mine and the case, and jerked with surprise when my finger hit his and failed to make a sound.

Mango tried to get into the game, reaching down from my back to put her hand between mine and the case, but Drummer batted her away and continued to scrutinize me. When he placed his fingers below mine, I hit harder, so it was his rough nails making the noise.

Then I stopped. Drummer peered at his hand, the case, and me. Then he started rapping his own fingers over the case. He did so softly at first, frequently pausing to assess the noises he'd made. Then louder. His hands wandered to the case's handle, and he yanked it from my hand.

Drummer clutched the case to his chest, waiting for it to make its thrilling noise, and only then remembered he needed his fingers to do it. Maybe not the most brilliant of chimps, Drummer. He strummed the case like a musician, fingers running down the ridged metal.

"Eventually you can use it to impress the guys down below there," I told him.

As if he'd understood me, Drummer hurtled over the waterfall before I even finished the sentence, case in his hand. I was glad I'd thought to switch Prof's letters and money into the valise back at camp before beginning our plan.

Mango climbed up me to get in a good viewing position. I peered over the boulder in time to see Drummer make a spectacular entrance, landing with one foot in the water and the lame limb secure on muddy ground. He held the case above his head and slapped it as it hung in the air.

The chimps in the clearing scattered, shrieking their heads off. Mothers grabbed for infants, and the gang of males managed to both flee and threaten at the same time, scrambling away while looking over their shoulders with bared teeth. Soon after their surprise wore off, though, the males loped back, heads bobbing nervously. Silver Stripes heaved a rock into the water, making a tremendous splash that caused Drummer to cower and drop the case. Silver Stripes and the other males started moving in on him.

*Come on, Drummer.*

Soon the males were surrounding him. Silver Stripes was on the ground a few feet away, barking while the other males took to the trees, swinging from the branches, screaming and lashing the air with their fists. The sound was fearsome and savage. Mango took her infant position on my front, shaking. I spared a moment's attention for her, stroking her little head.

A banging sound drew my attention back to the lagoon. Drummer was standing in front of Silver Stripes, the metal case in one hand. He flailed it against the side of a tree, and while the wet bark muted the noise some, the sound was still big.

Silver Stripes and his team could easily have overpowered Drummer, but for them noise must have equaled power, and they saw themselves as inferior to Drummer because they were quieter. The mothers and infants had long departed in the face of the ruckus, and Silver Stripes and most of the males now hurtled into the jungle after them, shrieking in fear.

A few young males remained. Keeping low to the ground and not daring to draw any nearer to Drummer, they made soft pleading sounds that only became audible whenever he took a break from beating the case — he was so pleased with his noise-making, though, that he wasn't about to stop anytime soon. He jangled the case in the air and then, when that sound wasn't enough, took to sitting, holding the case under the crook of his crippled leg, and beating against it with the other. That was the loudest sound yet, and he hooted proudly. Already the metal was showing dents; I hoped Drummer wouldn't destroy it before it had finished doing its work.

Finally he tired of his display and lay out in the lagoon's grassiest spot, the one that was usually Silver Stripes's. He kept the case in his lap. The remaining males timidly approached him on all fours, keeping low against the ground and making humble panting sounds. The smallest of them risked stroking Drummer's back.

When he accepted the attention, the others joined in, their faces stuck in fear-grins as they nervously groomed.

When Mango realized her brother's good fortune, she cheeped. He looked up at us, surprised; clearly he'd forgotten all about his sister and me. Typical Drummer.

He lifted the case in the air, as if to say, *Look what I found!* I waved back, and felt ridiculous as soon as I did. The other males looked in astonishment at the human at the top of the waterfall, but followed Drummer's example and stayed calm.

The metal briefcase had been more of a success than I'd expected, and (to these few males, at least) Drummer appeared to be the one in charge. I wondered if now was the best time for me to risk going down there and establishing my own presence.

Mango settled the question for me. Panting in glee, she scrambled down the tangle of liana at the side of the waterfall and circled the bank to be near her brother. I had a sudden fear that in her excitement she'd plow right into the water. So without really thinking, I crashed down from the top of the waterfall and into the lagoon.

I surfaced to shouts and cries, the loudest of which I immediately recognized as Drummer's. The chimps were running circles on the bank, hooting their heads off. All except Mango, who was clearly terrified by the noise and sought comfort by taking a flying leap from the bank to my head, nearly knocking me over. When I got my balance, I found my eyes were covered by wet whimpering chimpanzee. I pushed her hands up my forehead and waded to shore, Mango hooting in alarm.

Drummer had left the case in his prime spot, and I sat down next to it. Seeing his treasure back in my possession was enough to make Drummer overcome his fear, and he bounded back over. Teeth bared, he seized the case. I scowled at him. *I wasn't going to keep it. Calm down.*

The kingmaker back in his hands, Drummer plopped down happily. Mango hopped from my head to his, then sat on top of the case in an attempt to draw her brother's attention. When she began to play with her brother's lips I held my breath, but he seemed not at all to mind.

The three remaining males approached and sat around us, doing their best to pretend everything was normal by pulling out handfuls of vines and grass. They risked occasional curious glances at me. There was no aggression in the looks, which surprised me, since these were the same chimps who would have readily mauled me a day before. But in the face of Drummer's shocking entrance, the naked ape at the lagoon was only a minor oddity.

I knew we weren't out of danger yet — Drummer had split the troop's males, and I had no idea how the rest would react when they returned, or if the case would retain much power once the surprise wore off.

Drummer looked like he was in bliss, a chimp grooming him on either side. He wasn't going anywhere anytime soon. I decided I'd bring my belongings here, ideally transferring everything by late afternoon.

I was about to spend my first evening at the lagoon.


It took me three trips, the tent coming last. As I was packing everything up, rain began to fall, great big drops, like each one had been poured out of a cup. I looked up and caught a glob of cold water right in the eye. My face was soon drenched, and I relished the clean feeling of it.

The gulley where I'd been keeping the tent already had an inch of water in it by the time I got the canvas down and folded. I'd maneuvered Drummer into the troop not a day too soon. I threw the tent over my back and said good-bye to my second home before heading toward my third.

By the time I'd returned to the fall, the water level was noticeably higher. I'd have thought the chimps would take cover from the rain, but I found them out in the open. The weather had them entranced; they stood on two feet and swayed, barely reacting as I maneuvered down the side of the waterfall and placed my last bundle in my new home.

A kapok tree loomed over the grassy rectangle of space, keeping much of the rainwater away. Omar had found himself a particularly dry spot, hunched close over his knees and watching me with a distant, complicated expression. "I know, I know," I said. "But this is the best spot yet — you'll see. And with any luck we won't have to move ever again."

I put the tent up first so I could keep the rest of my belongings dry inside. The canvas had gotten wet through, and the air inside was intensely humid, but it would still keep everything inside from being directly hit by the rain. I shook out some fronds and tossed them on the tent floor, so I'd be sleeping on a surface that was at least partially dry. The rainy season would mean daily downpours, but also hours of daylight that would be clearer and sunnier than I'd ever had during the perpetually gray dry season; in the open lagoon space I imagined the tent might dry completely between rainstorms, which would make my sleeping much more comfortable from here on out. I kept telling myself that as I added more and more shaken-dry fronds to the floor in an attempt to spend the night without getting too wet: *Suffer this to have a better tomorrow.*

Eventually Drummer and his new allies made nests in the trees surrounding the lagoon. He must have taken Mango up with him, because I didn't hear a single cry from her all night. Omar didn't seem to want to sleep in the plastic basin in the driving rain, and instead sneaked into my tent and refused to come back out, clutching the tent floor when I tried to drag him. Once I'd zipped us in, he sprawled by my feet, hands tucked under his head like a pillow, eyes scrunched against the dampness. I stroked him until he was asleep. It took me a while to manage to relax, as I kept imagining Silver Stripes ripping the canvas and barging in, like I'd once feared a mock man would do to my mother and me in our village house. But the chimps knew better than to move about in the dark for any reason.

Come morning I was woken by their calls and hoots. I waited for the sounds to die down, figuring it was best to wait until the unfamiliar apes cleared out so I didn't surprise them. Once all was silent, Omar and I emerged, yawning, into a beautiful scene. The lagoon was sunstruck, with an oval of bright blue sky above. I enjoyed it as if from a distance, though. I'd barely slept during the night, and my nose was stuffed, my breath foul. I had trouble concentrating on even simple tasks, like finding a spot for my fire where the breezes streaming across the lagoon wouldn't put it out. I finally solved that issue by dragging a big wet log over to serve as a windbreak.

Rubbing mud off a broad flat stone, I sat on it and stoked the fire. The flames were high before I'd thought to fill the pot with water. Scolding myself for my muddy head, I left the fire and brought the pot to the water's edge. Omar toddled groggily alongside me, his hand on my leg.

I kneeled by the water. And froze.

There, reflected in the morning-still surface, were tan and black faces. I slowly turned and saw four chimps at the lagoon's edge, at the far side of my tent. First among them was Silver Stripes. They were taking great pains to make no noise.

Because they were stalking.

Me.

Despite my instinct to cringe away, I stood up to my full height. I slapped my knuckles against the pot, but the sound was muffled and did little to scare the chimps. They didn't make any further moves toward me but stood stock-still, mud-dark eyes trained in my direction.

"Drummer?!" I called. No answer. I started looking for rocks.

Two chimps began to spread out, never taking their eyes off me. The lagoon was at my back.

They were penning me in.

These chimps had a totally different attitude from when they'd threatened Drummer yesterday: They were hunting, not demonstrating. Silver Stripes's attention wasn't quite directed on me, though, but a little to one side.

On Omar. My vervet was usually so wily, but that morning he was as sluggish and foggy as I was. Even sick, though, Omar was good at escaping. Before I knew it, he'd hopped many feet into the air, seizing a branch and climbing away. There was a rush of leaves in the direction he was going, and I saw two more chimps in the trees move to cut him off.

The enemy was everywhere. There was no doubt, now, that Omar was in trouble. Brilliant devils. They'd lulled me into a weak trust; a chimp had probably killed Prof, and now they were going to get his beloved monkey, too.

I watched, helpless, as Omar fled. He disappeared into the foliage, and I could see nothing, just hear his high-pitched cries and the lower shrieks of the hunters and the branches rustling as more and more chimps took to the trees. There was a flash of fur, a hand reaching across space, silver and black emerging from green. I yelled and pounded the pot, hoping to distract the chimps, but it did nothing. *Just flee*, I begged Omar. *Forget about me. Get far away from here and never return.*

I located him on a limb directly above my tent. He might have thought he was hidden, but that lush tail of his was dangling in open air. Omar held there for a moment, swaying, then there was a black rush behind him. The vervet leaped. He was graceful and light in the air, almost flying. With an exaggerated bend of the tree, the pursuing chimp launched, catapulting after the monkey. It looked like a bird after an insect, and before Omar could escape into the tree on the other side, the chimp had him in his mouth.

In his focus on capturing Omar, though, the chimp failed his landing. He missed the tree and plummeted with his prey into the lagoon. The chimp, terrified, released Omar during the splashdown.

Within a moment, Omar had scrambled to shore and was cowering at my feet. The wet chimp struggled out of the water to face us, teeth bared. The standoff lasted only a moment before two more chimps dropped from the canopy, one of them Silver Stripes. They barked at me, virtually at once, and any thought of doing anything braver than fleeing vanished from my mind.

I backed up until my foot hit something warm and I tripped. I saw a flash of black hair as I toppled, and realized the chimps had surrounded us yet again, coming so close that I'd actually fallen over one. This was it; we were at their mercy. I might survive, but Omar was doomed.

I felt a powerful hand on my shoulder and squeezed my eyes shut, waiting for the crush to begin. The hand stayed there, and I heard sharp cries from Silver Stripes. Cracking my eyes open, I saw Drummer standing over Omar and me, shrieking at Silver Stripes. He didn't have the case with him, but the attacking chimps were backing off. All but Silver Stripes, who appeared unwilling to give up on Omar. He lunged. Omar easily dodged, and Drummer took the opportunity to bite into Silver Stripes's forearm. Drummer released quickly, but already blood was welling out of the older chimp.

Silver Stripes and the other males noisily retreated to the far side of the lagoon. Lips puffed and compressed, Drummer pivoted so he could keep his stare on the dominant chimp. I heard a rustling beside me and saw Mango crawl near, two hands around the handle of the metal case as she dragged it alongside her. *Clever girl.*

I put a hand on the case. Mango bared her little teeth, though, so I let go. "All right, all right, you and Drummer can have it."

Our attackers didn't retreat far. When barking at Drummer got them nowhere, they opted to deliberately ignore him, focusing on foraging, grooming — anything but us. It was almost as if they were trying to convince Drummer that the attack had been a prank.

Omar, however, didn't have as short a memory. He wrapped around my calf, staying there even when I returned to the tent and shakily arranged my belongings. I thought being near the fire again would make him feel safe, but he kept his head buried in my shin. I stroked him occasionally, and whenever I did, he peered up at me with worried eyes, then hid his face away again.

It took all my courage not to abandon my new home right then. The unfamiliar chimps lingered on the other side of the water, and I glanced at them frequently, alert to any sign of aggression. As if sensing the danger Omar and I were in, Drummer and Mango kept near me and the tent. Drummer seemed calm, but I soon realized it was for show: He kept peeling bark from tasty shoots and then forgetting to eat them. Mango gripped her brother so fiercely that more often than not he was walking around blind, his little sister's hands clamped over his eyes.

Throughout the afternoon, the chimps wandered in and out of the clearing. Mothers and children returned as evening neared, and their presence seemed to further defuse the males' tension. Not everyone escaped unscathed, though. I saw Silver Stripes bear down on Bad Mother, striking her quivering back with closed fists.

She cried out for a long minute, appealing to other nearby males with open hands while protecting her infant with her own body until Silver Stripes stopped. Drummer watched the incident calmly, doing nothing to intervene; apparently he didn't feel the need to go saving *everyone* who was in trouble. Soon enough Silver Stripes was calmly letting Bad Mother scratch through his belly hair. I smiled when I realized that, on my own side of the clearing, I was doing the same thing to Drummer. Attack and forgive, attack and forgive, seemed to be the way of chimpanzee life.

For the first time since I'd arrived Inside — for the first time since my mother died, really, as Monsieur Tatagani had kept his boys split up all day — I was in plenty of company. While night fell, the chimps made their cries of conflict and contentment all around me while they assembled their fresh nests and bedded down. As I lay in the tent I heard a stream of water hit the side as one of the chimps peed out of a tree and hit the (luckily water-proof) canvas directly.

Maybe it was the tension of the preceding day, or maybe I'd caught something from one of these new chimps, or maybe I was just due, but that very night I came down with my first sickness. I'd have thought I'd be immune to all illness after surviving my time in Franceville, especially after Prof's pills had cured my worms — but here I was, waking to the sharp burn of stomach fluid rising in my throat. I'd only just managed to get the tent open when I was on my knees, heaving into the grass. I only had a second to catch my breath before the next wave of nausea came. My stomach clenched, sides burning. I wanted to empty my belly more, but wasn't sure my body would be able.

Knowing how much fluid I'd lost, and remembering how quickly my mother's death-rattle breath had followed the drying out of her lips, I forced myself to take in a mouthful of lagoon water. My stomach wobbled and protested as the liquid hit. I rolled back into the tent, zipped it up, zipped it back down, and spent the rest of the night awake, hobbling over to the lagoon to take in water only to lose it in the grass minutes later. It felt like the ends of things and people came on so suddenly Inside; all I could hope was that the night I got sick wouldn't also be the night I died.

At dawn I listened deliriously to the chimps' scraping and hooting, figuring it would be safest to wait for them to clear out. But even after the lagoon had gone quiet, when I emerged I still found chimps around: Drummer and Mango were waiting patiently by the tent for me to appear. As I did a morning tour of the lagoon, chimp allies alongside me, I noticed other chimps heavy in their nests above, sleeping in. I guessed I wasn't the only one under the weather.

One of them finally descended around noon, sluggish, taking breaks on each limb of her tree before dropping to the ground. I saw the young female waver on her feet until, in a move so familiar it made me wince, she stooped and threw up. She wiped her mouth with the back of her hand and sat down heavily. "I understand," I couldn't resist saying. The young female looked at me curiously, surprised by my strange sounds. I bobbed my head and hooted softly, hoping that would sound more familiar.

I sleepily looked at the young female and she sleepily looked at me. Her hair was matted where she had gotten sick, and I was tempted to fill my pot with water and give her a rinse. But I felt so weak that I was capable only of lying flat.

An hour later, the young female did something very strange. Like a choosy browser in a spice store, she carefully selected a handful of dirt. After picking out any twigs and rocks, she ate the black soil out of her hand by darting her tongue out and slurping in a sprinkling, doing it over and over, like she was eating a handful of bread crumbs. She sprawled facedown on the grass, hands under her belly, and was soon snoring.

A second sick-looking chimp, a male who couldn't have been any older than Drummer, came lurching down from his nest. He managed to go a while before throwing up, but once he did, he did the same strange thing, taking a handful of dirt and licking it out of his palm before falling asleep.

I didn't forage anything that day, just drank water from the lagoon and played with Mango for the short spaces of time when I had the strength. That evening I still felt queasy as I got ready for bed. I knew I should eat something, but couldn't handle the idea of eating one of the sloppy black bananas in the food bag. I looked at the spot where the chimp had drawn her dirt, the surface streaked by her fingers. I looked up at her, ably constructing her nest as if she'd never been sick in her life.

I took up a handful of soil. In the semi-darkness it could be anything in my palm. Coffee. Cocoa. I reminded myself that I'd ingested plenty of dirt already, some of it stuck to nearly everything I'd ever eaten Inside. With that, I placed the handful into my mouth.

It was the taste of the jungle's smell.

Maybe the soil had some magical property only the chimps knew about. Maybe filling my stomach with something that wasn't food baffled the nausea. For whatever reason, my body accepted the dirt and I slept peacefully through the night, waking up healthy and ravenous come morning. That same mushy banana that had disgusted me the day before now sounded like a delightful breakfast.

And so I was up in the very early dawn before any of the chimps had roused themselves. It was too early for even Omar, who, outraged at being woken, burrowed under my sheet and refused to leave the tent.

I untied the food bag and lowered it, imagining the sweet soft-ness of that amazing black banana.

I peeled and ate the whole thing within seconds, licking my fingers and reveling in the oversweet rotten taste. Already I was envisioning the nearest banana tree so I could go find myself another.

Only a while after I'd swallowed the last taste of banana did I smell it.

Not a banana scent at all. More like banana beer.

I peered into the banana skin. It took me a moment to realize the odor wasn't coming from the fruit. It was like nothing I'd smelled for months. Like nothing Inside.

But it was also familiar. Something I'd once been surrounded by so much that I hadn't known until now it was its own scent.

Something Outside.

It smelled like oil and soap and the white stuff you pick out of your teeth.

From something like me. A human being.

Time slowed as I peered up at the top of the waterfall.

It was Monsieur Tatagani.

# PART FOUR:

## INSIDE

# EIGHTEEN

I got to my feet slowly, as if the Franceville moneylender were an animal I didn't want to alarm. The cooking pot tumbled, and as it clanged I heard the first calls from the chimps waking in the branches above.

The pot had fallen into the shallows, and I silently went about retrieving it before it filled with water and sank. If I kept doing this ordinary and important job, maybe Monsieur Tatagani wouldn't be there when I got the courage to look up again. But the blood throbbing through my veins told me that he was still staring down at me.

I carefully set the pot back in its drying spot, mind racing. Why hadn't he captured me right away? Had he gone blind? I could think of no reason for him to stay there watching, silent as God.

I knew I should get moving, hurl myself into the river and flee down it as fast as I could, only coming up for air once I was around the bend. But I couldn't make my body move. Even here in the Inside, I was worried about making my punishment worse. Maybe he wouldn't kill me if I didn't run. *I* hadn't been the one to give him fake money, after all. I could blame it all on Prof. Maybe then I'd survive.

Even though I decided not to flee, I couldn't wait for him to come get me, either.

Chimpanzees sometimes grunt before they start a task, as if to announce to the world, *This is me, and I will be doing this thing.* I grunted and took to the trees, like any chimp would. Within a minute I was high in the air, in one of my favorite spots at the V of an Okoumé tree. Only then, in the air with the thick trunk at my back, did I risk another look at my former master.

The Monsieur Tatagani of my nightmares would always wear that dirty shiny blazer. But the man before me was shirtless, and leaner than I'd ever seen him: a new, desperate man. Was I imagining him? I'd been sick, after all; maybe I'd fevered up a ghost to haunt myself.

All around me I heard the snores of under-the-weather chimpanzees. Soon more of them would be waking, with one of Franceville's top bushmeat traders watching from the top of the waterfall. The same man who wanted to destroy me and had sold the meat of whatever animals he could bring out of the jungle.

Monsieur Tatagani raised his arm and beckoned me to him with two sharp flicks of his wrist. I closed my eyes and shook my head, waiting for the twang of a bowstring, the pop of a rifle. I fled in my heart even as my body went still.

"Boy," Monsieur Tatagani said, voice surprisingly near, "open your eyes."

I did. He was at the base of the tree, holding his arms up to me. He'd crept up as silent as a spirit, as silent as a hunter.

"Come down," he said. "I'm not going to hurt you."

I shook my head, and Monsieur Tatagani frowned. "I have news for you. I've come all this way, and you're not even going to come down so I can tell you it, boy?"

From one of the nearby trees, I heard a hoot. We were waking more chimpanzees. "Go away," I said, for his sake and for mine.

"Your father has returned," he called. "He's paid me to bring you back to him. I don't get my money unless you come. So hurry up."

A false and queasy happiness rose in me. I didn't believe Monsieur Tatagani, but my heart wanted everything he was telling me.

I'd gone up the tree because I didn't want him anywhere near me, and also because I knew Drummer was sleeping nearby. But now I thought of all the precious things in the valise and the tent. The money. My knife. "Go away!" I yelled. Now there was shrieking from the chimps. One call, then more. The moment one of them noticed the intruder and raised the alarm, they would all be down.

"Clever rat," Monsieur Tatagani said, his eyes flicking around the canopy. "You thought you could trick your old master, didn't you? Does your new master know that? Does he know that you are a traitor, that you've destroyed every person who ever cared for you?"

I tried to stay expressionless as my mind raced. "The professor will be right back," I stammered. "Any moment."

"That is what I'm hoping for," Monsieur Tatagani said with his gray smile. "You are useful to me as bait. You are no longer useful to me as a boy."

"Prof has a weapon, like you see in the movies. The National Geographic Society gave it to him. A gun that makes a red dot and shoots a very long distance. You can't see it, but he is aiming at you right now. I can see the dot over your heart."

Monsieur Tatagani's smile broadened, though he did cast a quick glance at his chest. "Perhaps he would keep this magical weapon in a metal case? The metal case that's right by your tent? I don't see how he'd use it on me when it's sitting right there, though, do you? Where is he? Did he realize that you are an evil boy and leave you?"

"He has the rifle with him," I said. "He's putting it together right now." But I could tell Monsieur Tatagani didn't believe me. I got light-headed with panic and had to dig the edges of my feet hard into the tree to keep from tumbling out.

How had Monsieur Tatagani found me? I could only come up with two possibilities: Either Prof was alive and had returned to

Franceville — though then Monsieur Tatagani wouldn't think he was here, would he? — or after we'd chased off the forest hunter he'd gone to his markets and told about the boy and the Arab in the jungle. Once the bushmeat hunters knew, the news would soon spread to Monsieur Tatagani. I cursed Prof for tormenting that hunter.

Monsieur Tatagani's attention wasn't on me anymore. He stepped toward the silver case.

Attracted by the movement, a chimp dropped from the trees and toddled over to the case, finger in her mouth as she watched the unfamiliar person approach. Mango. Any other young chimp would have been more wary, but Mango had gotten so used to human me. She laid a hand on the handle, as if to let Monsieur Tatagani know the noisemaker belonged to her brother.

Soon I was scrambling down the tree. I lost my grip and fell the last few feet, grunting as the air pressed out of my body. I got to my feet in time to see Monsieur Tatagani reach out to Mango. She looked scared but held her ground, scanning the trees, probably for me or Drummer, her mouth opening and closing soundlessly.

I froze. I was terrified Monsieur Tatagani would seize her, but also was terrified to get near enough to be seized.

But Drummer was there before me. Hooting, he jumped between branches, and then dropped right beside Monsieur Tatagani, a tight fear-grin over his exposed teeth as he slapped the ground.

Alerted by the noise, Silver Stripes and a third male dropped from the trees. Lips bared, they joined in harassing Monsieur Tatagani, Silver Stripes nearly getting a hand around the back of Monsieur Tatagani's knee and bringing the man down. Mango was soon safely behind them. The clearing filled with chimp screams.

Monsieur Tatagani reeled toward the lagoon, retreating until he was up to his thighs in water. The chimps advanced, teeth bared. Monsieur Tatagani turned and fled, climbing the vines up the side of the waterfall until he'd disappeared over the top. The males took off after him.

Face split wide in fear, Mango reached out her arms. I took her up, and she settled tight at my back. Then I was up a tree as fast as I could, to get high enough to see what happened to Monsieur Tatagani once he and the chimps reached the top of the fall. Mango switched to my front, and together we watched.

Chimps snatching at his heels, Monsieur Tatagani hurled himself between the two boulders and into the mangroves at the river's edge. Led by Drummer, the chimps climbed to the top of the boulders and shrieked after the departing human. But they didn't pursue; their goal had been to get him out of their territory, not to kill him. Once they tired of shouting at the long-departed man, the apes returned to the hubbub of the clearing, where the females with infants were nervously milling.

The chimps were fired up, hugging one another tightly or dragging anything they could around the clearing. My tent was an early casualty, whipped around by Drummer and then stamped into the mud. Soon after, Drummer had the case in hand, banging the pot against it.

I kept watching for Monsieur Tatagani but could see no sign of him. Maybe he hadn't known what he'd be facing and was scared off for good. Until plenty of time passed without his returning, Mango and I weren't coming down from our perch.

As the tension drained, an unexpected smile spread on my face. I would have thought it impossible, but Monsieur Tatagani had been *scared*. That was why he hadn't seized me the moment he'd seen me. I'd been protected. Because of Drummer and Silver Stripes and the rest, I'd been the one terrifying *him*.

• • •

I saw no sign of him all morning. Mango eventually grew bored of the tree and climbed down to be with Good Mother and her son. Come afternoon, hunger began to nag, and since the agitated chimps had scattered and ruined my supplies, I'd have to forage if I wanted to eat. But doing so, even with fear of Monsieur Tatagani at my back, was the only way forward.

By the time I came down, the only chimp near the lagoon was Drummer. He was instantly at my side, hair raised, bristling at the memory of the intruder. I groomed him until he calmed, then I trapped and ate another small river catfish, giving half to him. Small crabs at the edge attracted my attention, and I wondered how they'd taste.

*Monsieur Tatagani is out there*, my darkest heart kept telling me, *and you're wondering how to net crabs*. But I also knew the chimps were on alert. My fear of Monsieur Tatagani was spread out among all of us, and with all our strength and attention we might keep one another safe. I didn't see how Monsieur Tatagani would steal me away, not from them.

In defiance of my fear, I traced a large rectangle in the clearing to mark where I'd someday like my hut to be. Drummer followed me, swaggering fiercely even with his lame leg curled against his hip. The first step to making my home wouldn't be building a wall; it would be planting a garden.

Feeling safe with Drummer at my side, I returned to the old campsite one last time and dug up the fragile mint I'd planted for Prof. Cradling the soft white hairs of the roots and their clumps of black soil, I walked the trembling plants back to the lagoon and planted them in a neat row. I'd have the only mint crop in this entire jungle, maybe in all of Gabon. I started imagining what else I'd plant. Banana and mango were plentiful enough nearby, so I could forage those. But I could plant the food that usually only grew in the more scraggly edges of the jungle: yams or wild celery. Maybe I'd pull up some nut tree saplings and move them here, too, so Omar would always have a supply of his favorite foods. I remembered his scarfing down bar nuts the first time I'd met him, and Prof's lenient smile. Heated by the memory, some of my fear of Monsieur Tatagani started to feel like fury.

As I finished watering the mint plants, Omar came down and joined Drummer and me. He must have just eaten a lizard or snake, as the tail was still wriggling out of his mouth. He quickly swallowed it down, then we went up in the tree, watching the top of the waterfall while I waited for the rest of the chimps to return. And return they did, noisily settling in well before sunset. With them about I felt safer. Omar and I descended.

One benefit of Monsieur Tatagani's appearance: Omar became old news. He still clutched me whenever any chimp other than Drummer or Mango appeared, but none of the apes seemed interested in him anymore. He'd gone from prey to village animal.

I managed to get the tent to stand up again, but only barely. After Drummer had dragged it through the mud, the already-bent pole nearly made a right turn. As I lined up my bedroll inside, I wondered if I'd be able to sleep that night, and was relieved to see Drummer build his nest right above me. If Monsieur Tatagani came, I'd scream, and Drummer would come protect me.

Maybe sharing my worry, Omar draped himself over my chest. Stroking the back of the sleeping monkey's head, I thought about the threats Monsieur Tatagani had made. Then I thought about the chimps all around, about the little garden I would one day have in back of my hut, the one that I'd started with Prof's mint. Those were the opposites of threats.

●   ●   ●

Monsieur Tatagani didn't come take me during the night.

Not wanting to lose the next day, too, to fear, I set to work pruning my tent site. I was worried to see a column of termites nearing the rectangle I'd made in the sand. I'd noticed they loved something about pee, so I'd started urinating in the river so as not to bring them near, but they'd come to my future doorstep nonetheless. It would have been easier simply to move the tent out of their path, but if I did that I knew I'd spend the rest of my life on the run, fleeing whenever ants or termites or wasps neared. I wanted a *home*, and I wanted it to be here. So to build my home's defense, I busied myself digging a narrow trough around the tent, using a sharpened mango stone to scratch through the soil. It seemed like it should have been easy for the insects to cross my measly moat, but they milled at the edge whenever they reached the net of shiny roots I'd exposed beneath the surface. Maybe the tree had some sort of mysterious defense in its flesh. As I kneeled, I slapped at the biting flies that took advantage of my stillness.

By dinnertime I was exhausted and sore, my fingertips punctured by termites and my backside by flies. My worry about Monsieur Tatagani, though no less present, stung a little less in comparison.

I had a half revenge by making some of the termites into my evening meal. I'd lay a stick across their path, then insert it into the fire. Most of the swarm fell away, but the fierce-jawed guards held on even in death. They were crunchy, the venom sacs as tangy as the Café de la Gare's pepper sauce.

As I ate I watched Mango lope after Good Mother, and kept imagining how easily her narrow legs would snap under an iron jaw. What if Monsieur Tatagani was waiting to catch a chimp like the hunter had, to bring it back to the market to sell to foreigners? That fear continued to seize me into the night. As I grew more tired I also grew more obsessive until, whenever fear surged, my chest got so tight, I worried I'd never sleep. And I was right.

Sometime late in the night I gave up on rest, and so did Omar. I wondered if he only closed his eyes when I did, if his life was tied that tightly to my own.

We waited by the tent exit for dawn to break. In the dark, Omar tapped his fingers against the back of my hand until I opened it, then he put his palm in mine. I closed my fingers around his hand, and he sighed. We passed a long time that way, until the sun appeared. Then, the moment it was light enough, we got out of the tent. I brewed my mint tea and ran the brush over my teeth, even though the soap was long gone. I ate a few bananas and was soon picking my way into the jungle, Omar on my shoulder.

If Monsieur Tatagani was out there, we'd locate him.

Living and eating Inside had left me light and rangy, had hardened my skin against stings and scratches; I was far more suited to this task now than when I'd first arrived. I traveled with my knife so I could cut myself free should a snare hoist me. I was careful as I went, but perfect caution would mean never moving at all.. Sometimes I'd go a full minute without imagining the twang of a bow or the click of a rifle; having been able to forget scared me all the more.

I found no sign of Monsieur Tatagani that day. The next morning Mango and Omar had a lengthy play session, then she broke off to join me as I began the day's investigating. I knew better than to try to convince her to stay behind.

We passed Bad Mother and Good Mother and their children sucking on thick green fruit along a stream, and took one each to chew as we went, sweet juice trickling into our mouths from the tough balls of fiber. I leaned over to spit out the spent fruit, then heard the sharp cry of a chimp in distress.

Mango was instantly alert, staring into the trees and making intent, almost inaudible moans. Then she went crashing into the brush.

I cursed. If Monsieur Tatagani had nabbed himself a chimp, I didn't need Mango revealing herself to him, too. I shot out after her.

As fast as I went, she was always a length ahead of me. I reached forward, grasping for the wiry hair at the back of her neck, but each time my fingers closed over empty space as Mango surged even farther ahead.

She hurtled along a game trail, so fast that she was only able to stop herself by grabbing a tree trunk and twirling around it. She plopped down in the dirt and began to moan louder. At first I thought it was from hitting the ground hard, but then I realized she was peering forward.

From her intense expression, I feared that she'd seen Drummer in trouble. Heart quaking, I risked creeping forward into the trail's open space to see.

I jumped behind a tree, heart pounding, Mango in my arms so she wouldn't cry out again. There, a ways along the trail, two men were tromping through the jungle. They looked like grown-up versions of street kids I'd known in Franceville. The same cloth pants tied with a length of scrap fabric, ragged shirts with unknowable sayings.

Monsieur Tatagani hadn't come alone.

I maneuvered around the tree so I would stay hidden, then crept along the trail to keep the men in view, Mango silent at my back. They stopped at a dark narrow clearing, where a sorry-looking donkey was tied to a tree. Food bags were lashed to its sides, and I suspected the animal wasn't long from becoming a meal itself. Behind it, rifles were propped against one another, standing up in a pyramid.

*Rifles.* These men were here to hunt. Their wandering in without permission to trap the animals who lived alongside me felt like burglary. I knew the jungle wasn't mine, but it felt like it *was* the chimpanzees', and I was furious for their sake.

Beside the supplies was a hairy black pelt that I only slowly recognized. It was Beggar's hide, which I'd pitched out on sticks in case it would be useful once it was picked clean. We were right near that spot; the hunters must have found it and decided they wanted it.

I stroked Mango as we squatted by the tree. There were biting flies in the greenery, and I couldn't risk swatting them off. One of the flies' wings opened and closed in a scissorlike motion as it bit my wrist, and I knew it was a tsetse. They hadn't gotten me sick before, so I wasn't worried, but the bite still hurt. They'd always loved me most of all, avoiding Prof's lighter skin. Mango reached out a hesitant hand and brushed the fly off my arm. She panted worriedly.

Suddenly I was in the air.

Monsieur Tatagani lifted me by the back of the neck, like a kitten. I struggled as he heaved me in the air, then there was a flurry of black as Mango bit him on the arm. He must have let go, because I fell and slid to my belly in the mud.

Something slammed me, and it took me a moment to realize it was a foot and not a log; it had the strength of something larger than a man. Blinded by the pain in my ribs and neck, I got to my feet and staggered forward. Immediately my vision went white and I was back on my knees. More hands were on me, and when I opened my eyes I was on my back, surrounded by three men: Monsieur Tatagani, a stranger, and the forest hunter Prof and I had once chased off.

Within the turmoil, I took relief that none of them had Mango. She must have escaped after biting Monsieur Tatagani.

Scowling furiously, the hunter spoke to the other men in a tribal language too distant from Fang for me to fully understand. But I could get the main point: *Is this the one? Yes. Good.*

Monsieur Tatagani placed his shoe on my throat, dirt sprinkling my neck. I gripped the sole in case he began to crush my windpipe. I noticed the hunter making silent gestures, then taking handfuls of dung to rub on his arms and clothes. The two men in T-shirts did the same. An old poaching trick, one I'd used myself back in Franceville; the dung would keep animals from scenting them.

They were here for the chimps.

I couldn't figure out what to do. I wasn't strong enough to fight them, and there was no way past that truth.

I heard the men handing out the rifles, the tip of one entering my vision as Monsieur Tatagani caught it. His boot raised from my throat and was replaced by the tip of the gun, cold against my skin. "You'll wait here for now," he said, "while they get us those chimpanzees. If the sounds of your suffering don't draw the Arab out, then the sounds of his precious monkeys screaming in pain will. I know his heart lies with them, not with you."

I turned my head away. Another fly took advantage of my stillness to bite deep into my cheek, and I wished it would go even deeper, make me more miserable, so I could accept agony as the way of the world and be done with it.

Monsieur Tatagani had found me. I'd always known he would. I was going to lose my hands. Or my head. He'd bring it back to show to his other boys. The police would applaud the message it sent to thieves and counterfeiters everywhere. *Trick us and this is what will happen to you.*

I thought about how Prof had once said our hearts were wired early, before we knew it was happening. Maybe I had the heart of an orphan. Maybe I'd always been meant to be left.

The pain from the fly became too great, so I rolled my head, the insect escaping before it got crushed. I was enlivened by the pain, by the shock of hot blood trickling down my cheek.

The men seemed unsettled by what they were about to do. They talked at length, sometimes arguing, frequently gesturing in the direction of the lagoon.

The whole time, Monsieur Tatagani kept his rifle trained on me. I couldn't even blink; tears mixed with the blood. I was furious at Monsieur Tatagani for claiming my father was alive. I was furious at Prof for doing what he'd done to the hunter, chasing him back to Franceville with a crazy tale about a boy and an Arab living in the jungle. I was furious at both of them for making my thoughts scatter. My mind no longer went in straight lines like a human being's, but instead everything I could possibly think was hitting me at the same time. These invaders with their strange language, so like Fang and yet so different, made me miss Prof. And my mom and Carine. Those were the only human family I'd ever wanted, and they were all gone. The rest of the human world could fall away, leaving only me and the chimps and this jungle, for all I cared. Because I would still have Omar and Mango and Drummer. I just needed these men gone.

They abruptly stopped talking. Overcoming my fear of the sharp metal pressed into my throat, I turned my head to see another hunter enter the clearing. In his hands was a snare with a dead furry creature. He dropped it to the ground.

It was a bushbuck. And one I'd come to know; I recognized the starburst of white spots on her forehead. The snare that would so easily have fit around a chimp's hand or foot had fit as easily around her neck, and she had suffocated and died.

Monsieur Tatagani looked at the corpse and then barked something at the man. I recognized the words *kivili-chimpenze*. The hunter shook his head. Monsieur Tatagani held out his forearm, where a neat arc of dried blood had formed from Mango's bite. The hunter pointed to me. I scrunched my eyes shut.

The discussion moved beyond me, I guessed, because their focus shifted away. I cracked my eyes open and saw the corpse of the bushbuck staring back, vacant as wood. She'd been a quiet resident of this jungle for her whole life, more fully a part of the Inside than me or the five men with their guns and snares. And now she was dead.

Something about the slow suffocation of her noose pushed my mind in new and unfamiliar directions. Not away from the current crisis, but above it. I'd spent my life struggling with questions of "today." This intensity I was feeling, this shocking newness of myself, was in trying to solve the question of "tomorrow."

Lying so still was starting to pay off. Monsieur Tatagani kept his gun trained more or less in my direction, but as he talked to the men its point would wander for long moments. If that continued, I'd be able to run. Maybe I'd snag the dead bushbuck on the way, just to keep her body out of the men's hands.

There — they moved to the edge of the trail. If I hurtled straight into the undergrowth, Monsieur Tatagani would be able to get in a shot or two, but there was a chance he'd miss. If I survived those bullets, I might make it back to the lagoon alive.

As the men got more and more distracted, I prepared to push off.

But then there was a weight on my back. Tiny rough fingers clutching at my cheek. The hooting of a scared little chimpanzee that I knew so well.

# NINETEEN

*Mango, go!* I thought. But of course she'd stayed near; she wasn't going to tramp off into the forest alone, not when I was nearby to provide comfort. She'd waited as long as she could, but the moment the men weren't looking she'd crept back.

They hadn't noticed her yet, but it would only be moments. Knowing it was hopeless to shoo her away, I wrapped my arms around the small chimp, hoping to give her comfort and enjoy her comfort during our final moments together.

I rolled over so she'd be more out of view, so they'd have to shoot through me to get to her. Maybe the noise of the first gunshot would get her to run off — maybe the bullet would end in my body and not hers. If they shot my arm, or my leg, maybe I could somehow escape and survive, too.

I looked for escape routes. And found eyes in the jungle. Silver Stripes was low to the ground, not a dozen feet off into the green. He was moving as stealthily as he could, eyes trained on the men. I had seen that look before, when he'd so quietly stalked Drummer.

I turned my head farther and saw another male, then another. I looked the other direction. Two more.

A war party.

*Mango, get ready,* I thought, hugging her tighter. And then there was a shriek from one of the hunters. Suddenly the point of Monsieur Tatagani's rifle was whisking through the air. I heard yelling, both chimp and human, and hot popping sounds.

I curled around Mango, deciding not to stand in case that would attract the hunters' fire. My vision flickered black as one of the chimpanzees leaped over me and into the fray. Their war barks were deafening. I heard another pop of the rifle, and then the shouts of combat mixed with shrieks of pain.

The chimp that had jumped over me had one of the hunters on the ground, his heavy arms clubbing the man whenever he tried to get up. While he had the hunter down, Silver Stripes was going after the man's hands, teeth gnashing. Already fingers were missing, and puncture wounds ran up and down the hunter's arms. Silver Stripes bit deeply into the man's belly, and his flailing stopped.

More rifle pops and a hot chemical smell, and then blooms of red appeared on the back of the chimp that had been holding the hunter down. He ran a few feet toward Monsieur Tatagani and his rifle and then fell, like he was drunk. Another round of gunshots. The body quivered with each one, then lay still.

Mango clung to me, shrieking, as I dragged us to one side of the game trail. The triangle of guns had fallen, and I plucked one up. I didn't know how to use it, but set myself on it anyway, pointing it at Monsieur Tatagani. When I pulled the trigger, nothing happened.

Silver Stripes and Monsieur Tatagani faced each other across open space. Fear stretched Silver Stripes's face into a grin, even as it slackened Monsieur Tatagani's. My former master pulled a piece from his gun and fiddled with an identical one at his belt, trying to insert it into the rifle. Silver Stripes clapped his hands loudly together, lips pulled back from his long canine teeth. *No, don't intimidate — attack*, I begged him.

Monsieur Tatagani finally got the piece into the gun and raised it to his shoulder.

Silver Stripes continued to demonstrate, feinting toward Monsieur Tatagani. Any second, Monsieur Tatagani would begin to fire.

But then I saw Drummer creeping along a tree branch right over him. Noticing my attention, Monsieur Tatagani looked up just in time to see Drummer drop. Shots rang out in the jungle, echoless in the dense green, as man and chimp tumbled together.

Drummer had Monsieur Tatagani's leg in his jaws. Blood spurted from the man's ankle as Drummer bit in and shook. Then Silver Stripes was on Monsieur Tatagani, too, followed by another male. Monsieur Tatagani screamed as parts of his body began to come away.

I turned to one side, pressing Mango's quivering head against my chest. I wouldn't close my eyes, though. I needed to see this finished. Once in a while the chimps would look up from the gore to assess me, their eyes hungry and demonic. But whenever one of them stepped toward me, Drummer would cuff him, and they'd return to the slaughter. Monsieur Tatagani stopped screaming long before they finished.

They didn't eat him. But the body they left behind was barely a man's.

Silver Stripes was the first to head back to the lagoon, followed closely by the other males. Drummer came to my side and sat heavily, panting in exertion. He presented his maimed leg to me, and I numbly groomed it. There was plenty of blood in his hair, but no gunshot wounds I could see. He sucked at a slash on the back of his hand, but the injury wasn't too bad. Mango transitioned from my lap to his and licked experimentally at the blood.

Cautiously, I stood and looked at the carnage.

Monsieur Tatagani was dead, as was one of the hunters. The other three must have escaped with their donkey.

Two chimps were dead. An old male, as well as the one only a little older than Drummer. Mango crawled over to him and tugged at the dead ape's lips, panting in quiet confusion.

The scattered remnants of the hunters' supplies were charcoal in the fading light. Hearing no signs of the men's return, I lashed together their small bundles of supplies and cast them over my back to haul away. I figured the bodies were far enough from the lagoon that I could leave them in the clearing without attracting predators to our camp.

I took advantage of the last light to drag a log back and forth in the soil, making a big X in case the hunters dared to return and needed a reminder of the mock men who had killed two of them. Then I stuffed Beggar's hide into one of the supply bags.

I took Mango's hand in mine. Then I took a tired Drummer's hand, too. "Come on," I said. "It's nearly dark. We have to go home."

Drummer, Mango, and I slinked up the river, our journey accompanied by the occasional distant scream of restless mock men.

# TWENTY

Because the lagoon was one of the few places in the jungle where trees didn't block the moonlight, I was able to see better once I arrived home. Drummer and Mango and I sat at the bank. Our toes dragged in the water as Mango sprawled across her brother's lap.

The other chimps were already in their nests; it would be the next day before I'd know how many of them had been injured. Gradually I skirted the edge of the lagoon, noiseless as I could be in the dim light, and unzipped the tent tooth by tooth, praying that my chimps wouldn't hear me. I didn't want them to call out in case the escaped hunters returned.

Once I'd gotten the tent open, I slumped to my belly, half in the tent and half out.

After a moment, I sat up and sifted through one bag of supplies. There was dried meat inside, a few coins, a water skin, and Beggar's hide, light and limp. When I draped it out on my knee, it no longer felt like part of the old, dead chimpanzee, but a temporary layer of the jungle, like soil or bark. I stroked the pelt and held still for a long time, thoughts circling.

I recognized Mango first by her breath, a familiar sweaty and fruity smell, a pleasant warmth not so different from the night breeze with its scents of life and rot. I opened my eyes slowly, so as not to surprise her.

She crept forward into my lap and curled tight, her long lashes tickling the exposed insides of my wrists, eyes inky in the moonlight.

It was like she'd returned to the younger Mango I'd first met, pressing into her ailing mother's embrace.

Because, unexpectedly, her mother had come back.

It seemed cruel that I'd inadvertently played with a young orphan's emotions. But Mango was so calm. She didn't have a permanent sense of Beggar's being alive or dead, I guessed; this moment in her dead mother's embrace was possible simply because it was happening. Or maybe she thought I had somehow combined with Beggar, that our two beings had tied up neatly and therefore had never been separate. I had no idea what she was feeling, and I was pretty sure Mango didn't, either.

Beggar's pelt still between us, I reached my arm around Mango to hold her tight. Sighing, she relaxed even deeper into my lap. She didn't look up at my face, just seemed to enjoy the strange familiarity of hair and skin.

So I stayed there as Beggar holding her daughter. Only when Mango was making quiet snores against my forearm did I slowly get up, sleeping chimp in my arms, and let the hide fall away. I laid Mango on the floor of the tent, pillowing her head on my only remaining shirt. In her sleep, she looped her fingers through the holes in the seams and drew it near, her nose pressed into the fabric.

Cautiously, I took Beggar's hide and crept through the night to the tumbling river. I held the skin over the water, then dropped it in and watched the black empty space it made among the moonlit waves pass around a bend and disappear.

Mango was drooling into my shirt when I returned. Drummer had made himself a nest, but Omar joined Mango and me in the tent. The bent pole made it vulnerable to the weather, and as the rain started to fall the corners grew wet. I huddled around them both. Mango sighed into my chest. It would be crowded in our little home that night, but I didn't mind. It seemed none of us did.

I spent much of the next day going through the hunters' possessions, finding among other things a knife, pills in a small oily sack, and a snare-making kit: rusty iron shears, a small tool with an eye of metal at the end, and pliers. It felt funny that these men no longer had these possessions. That I *did* have them.

I remembered the bushbuck. I'd left her body back at the hunters' camp, and didn't want to leave it there to rot. If I went back to where I'd last seen the hunters, I might also be able to see if there was any sign of their return. I could find some peace that way.

The daily storm had only begun, though; I'd have to wait until it finished. Rather than wait out the rain in the tent, I embraced it, stripping and diving into the lagoon, giving myself a surface-eye view of the drops that studded the water like hurled pebbles. The chimps stared at me while they got soaked beneath the trees, fascinated by their crazy naked ape friend. As I splashed around, unease began to spread. I kept looking into the tree line, waiting for a human face to peer back.

I knew I should have waited for morning to go back for the bushbuck, waited until the whole day was still spread ahead of me. But I was exhausted by the cringing fear that had come to stay. The moment the rain stopped, I tied my last ragged shirt around my midsection to cover my most thorn-sensitive areas, then swiftly picked my way to the hunters' camp. I went without shoes so I'd be quieter, and avoided the more exposed sections of the river.

It was even farther than I remembered, and the sun was already setting when I arrived. I cursed my foolishness, realizing that I'd be returning to the lagoon at night, this time without a rush to distract me from the snakes and meat-eating fish in the river. That, or I'd be spending the night in a strange place without a fire, with the corpse of Monsieur Tatagani for company.

When I was growing up, even the good Christian people in the village loved to tell stories of spirits that lived inside all things. It had been a while since I'd heard talk about spirits, but now, as I crept down a small path in the lost section of a lost jungle, I was sure I saw one.

Something was glowing in the middle of the woods. The small light appeared and then vanished. It came back, and then disappeared again. This time it stayed away, the ghost gone.

Was the spirit something summoned by the hunters to get revenge on me, left here to possess me if I was foolish enough to return? When the jungle stayed dark I realized it might not be a spirit at all, that maybe I was seeing some tool the hunters had left behind. Some new sort of trap. My heart tightened. Careful to make no noise, I pressed myself low to the ground. Something with many sharp legs skittered from under my chest as I lay flat, but I didn't risk moving my head to see what it was. Much as I concentrated, I could hear nothing that wasn't insect or bird. If the hunters were still nearby, they were being extraordinarily silent.

Finally I risked lifting my head. I couldn't see anyone, nor was there any glow. Edges of upturned earth were rimmed in twilight; the giant X I'd traced on the ground the night before was unmussed, with no footsteps near it but my own.

Then I saw it again — an illuminated rectangle. But no one was holding it; it was lying on the ground. A buzzing sound. Suddenly another rectangle lit up at the other side of the clearing. I started to recognize the lights and the noises, and started thinking less and less of spirits and more and more of foreigners at the hotel bar.

I crept forward and stared down at one of the rectangles. The space that had glowed was blacker than the char color of the surrounding soil. It lit up again, making a cheeping sound. I darted my hand out and grabbed it. My fingers glowed blue before the light disappeared.

I held the device high in the dusk to catch the remaining light. There was a place to speak on one end, and to hear on the other — it looked like a phone, but from what I'd picked up at the bar, I thought I was probably looking at a radio. My shoulders released. If the men hadn't come back for these precious devices, they were probably gone forever.

I left the radios and hurried about the clearing, searching the ground. Leaning against a tree, I found something far more precious than a radio: a machete!

It would be foolish to travel back to the lagoon in the darkness. I'd be vulnerable to any predator that chose to attack, or I'd step on something sharp or fall down a ravine or improvise some other way to die. So I did like a chimp. Using my prized new machete, I hacked ferns from the ground, slicing upward to make less noise. I selected a tree, kicked out the magpies that had been using it, and lay the soft ferns where two branches formed an almost-basket. I sat back. I might not manage to sleep, but I'd certainly find rest — and I'd keep out of the way of the predators that roamed the jungle floor. I smiled, pleased with myself.

Once I'd survived the evening I could rest tomorrow, sharpening my machete so I could chop down the first trees I'd use to build my hut. I'd be eating palm heart for my next meal.

As the night deepened, doves and parrots intensified their songs. Distant monkeys squealed. Even after the other animals had quieted, cicadas droned on. I lay out on my branch and watched as, in a jungle clearing many days from human civilization, little screens lit up and cheeped.

# TWENTY-ONE

The bushbuck corpse wasn't fresh, but I figured if I cut it up small and sizzled the bits until they charred, it would be safe to eat. When I got back to the lagoon I set the corpse on the drying stone, and then built the fire up as much as I could.

I'd stupidly set the meat down far enough from the fire, though, that Silver Stripes was able to reach it. He gleefully hugged the corpse to him. When I stepped near, the old chimp bared his teeth. But then Drummer came bounding over, and for a frantic few seconds the two chimps screamed at each other, tussling over the meat. Other males emerged from the tree line and pelted us with anything they could reach, making a huge racket. I watched my cooking pot fly into the jungle and made a mental note of where it landed so I could retrieve it later.

When the commotion died down, the bushbuck was in Drummer's hands. I eased over to him on all fours and reached for it. Drummer's hair raised as he turned his back to me. I crept around him so he could see me, but this time I bared my own teeth and reached my hands out. *I insist.* When he didn't give up the bushbuck, I shook my hands. Sulkily, he dropped the corpse. I picked it up, hooting softly and bowing my head. *Thank you.*

I skinned and gutted the animal, then built up the fire. When the flames were crackling and roaring, I spread the open carcass out between lagoon-soaked fronds and held it over the fire. Once the unusual smell of sizzling meat was in the air, the chimps were unable to resist approaching. Whenever a breeze batted the smoke away I could see them circled, clutching one another, many pairs of almost-human eyes staring with fear and desire. Only Omar was able to overcome his instincts, sitting beside me and leaning against my thigh, his eyes scrunching shut whenever the wind blew smoke into his face.

As I cooked, my thoughts kept returning to Monsieur Tatagani. *Dead.* For the first time in years, I wasn't living under the threat of what I owed him. I might have plenty left to fear, but not him anymore. It left me feeling pleasantly adrift.

I removed the fronds from the fire and laid them outside the tent to cool. The meat was juicy and charred, and I was tempted to pull a morsel away and place it on my tongue, even though I knew I'd wind up with blistered fingertips and a burned mouth. To busy myself as the meat cooled, I hunted the cooking pot out of the trees.

As I returned, I nearly tripped over the metal case in the twilight. Now that Drummer had less need for it, he'd frequently leave it lying around the lagoon. I lugged it back to the fireside so it wouldn't get lost — and so one of the other chimps didn't use it to take over the group.

I walked the case over to the fire and fiddled with it while the meat continued to cool. The case was looking worse for wear, massive dents along its broad surfaces and rust on its hinges. But still it was the best place to protect Prof's papers, now that the valise was falling apart. I pulled the case into my lap and input the combination. I flipped through Prof's photographs and letters twice. Then I placed them in the case and locked it, returning it to the sacred spot between the tent's fly and the interior wall, where I also kept Prof's spare galabia.

The meat was ready.

The chimps were still scared of the fire, but Omar scampered right up to the cooked meat and watched closely, hand nervously darting forward and back as I sliced it. I picked a choice morsel and gave it to him, and he gobbled it.

I knew they wouldn't understand my reasons, but I wanted to offer the chimps this meat for saving my life. I tossed a forequarter to the crowd. Instantly Drummer and Silver Stripes were quarreling over it.

While they battled, I tossed the other forequarter far away from the dominant males, landing it by Mango and Bad Mother and her daughter. They were quickly up a tree with the piece, Mango and the child snatching whatever bits dropped from Bad Mother's mouth as she ate. I continued tossing meat to chimps who hadn't yet eaten. Not everyone got some, but most did. The lagoon was full of their happy cries.

I did keep a nice hunk of meat for myself, and enjoyed my hindquarter in peace, my back against the fire so no one could beg too near me. Omar dabbed at my chin and licked the grease from his fingers.

The black coils of fat-smoke had chased off all the insects, so that night I was able to stay out after dark, blissfully unbitten.

Calmer than I'd felt in days, I lay back, Omar curled against my knees. I stared up at the stars. There seemed to be more than ever tonight, big creamy swaths. One black patch had nothing in it. It looked like a ragged mock man, all undone and open to the universe.

When I woke the next morning, Mango and Drummer were nowhere to be found. Maybe they'd taken a lengthy wander, like every chimp did from time to time. I was glad they were gone, because I could devote myself to machete-ing trees into logs without worrying about lopping off Mango's fingers. I had no idea how chimp mothers managed to get anything accomplished with their children hanging all over them.

Without Drummer and Mango to serve as a link, the other chimps were too intimidated by the fire to come very near. Now that it was he and I, Omar became more involved in my life. He kept me constant company, following behind curiously as I passed among the trees and selected my building materials. He watched me examine every detail before picking a tree, and stood back while I felled each sapling, giving me chattering monkey advice, often with his hands behind his back. Once I had enough logs to make my first wall and had stripped and cleaned enough liana vine to experiment with lashing them together, I sampled the jungle muds until I found one that held fast to the wood and dried hard in the sun. If there was anything I'd learned about the Inside's spiders, whip scorpions, and snakes, it was that cracks were their very favorite places to hide. I planned to provide them as few as possible.

My wall was a pretty good start, and the right length to stretch the distance from the lagoon's edge to my little garden. It was, I realized, about the same length as the village hut I'd once lived in with my mother.

It was time to get started on the next step. Excited, I clapped my hands. A distant chimp hooted in response.

I had to make three more walls. And a roof. As long as my blisters from the machete's rough handle formed calluses soon, I might have a home within a month! Which was good, because the tent wouldn't last much longer than that. Already the seams bowed and leaked in the afternoon rains. The moment I finished cooking lunch each day, I had to bring the pot back inside to use as a rain trap.

Once I had a second wall and had rigged a good enough corner so that the two stood upright, Omar transitioned his sleeping spot from the plastic basin to the top of the wall. I'd wake up and find him draped over the edge of the logs, his arms dangling and twitching while he dreamed away. I'd rouse him each morning by reaching up and stroking his scarred corduroy palms. As he got older he was becoming more of a homebody, I guessed, and wanted to spend his time wherever seemed most like a home. I smiled when I thought about how much he'd enjoy an actual roof. Before two more days had gone by, I'd lashed on a third wall.

By then Mango and Drummer had been on their journey for over a week, and I was lonely. I started to wander far enough away from the fire that I could be near the rest of the chimps. Good Mother and her children seemed to be thriving. Son stuck close to mom, trying to climb onto her back even though Good Mother calmly removed him each time. She had an older daughter, too, who was enjoying new attention from the males.

Bad Mother, though, wasn't doing as well. During one of the rainy season's powerful storms, the tops of the branches swayed mightily. Her daughter clung to one, crying, but Bad Mother was nowhere near. As the little chimp kept crying, I came out into the rain to see if I could coax her down. I was in time to see her lose her grip and fly through the air. She was a flat silhouette against the sky, arms out, and then she hit the ground. I knew the moment she thudded that she was dead. She cried out once and then lay still.

Bad Mother came over in the rain, shoulders hunched, and tugged on her daughter's leg. I couldn't stand to watch, so I went back into the tent and tried to fall asleep. But all I could hear were the weird whooping whiffles of a mourning chimpanzee above the drumming bass line of rain. I barely slept that night.

When I left the tent at dawn I was relieved to see that Bad Mother wasn't still out there with her daughter's body. When I didn't see her for many hours, I thought she must be off somewhere disposing of it.

I was crouched beside Good Mother, watching her crack over-ripe nuts and joining her son in trying to open a few of my own, when I saw Bad Mother descend from her nest . . . with her daughter. She cradled the corpse under her arm, like the child was younger — and more alive — than she was. She propped her dead daughter against a tree so it looked like she was sitting up.

I glanced at Good Mother to see what a normal chimp reaction was to this sort of behavior; she busily ignored the dead baby, bringing her rock down over and over against a particularly hard nut. When Good Mother's daughter came by and tugged on the body, trying to get it to play, Good Mother swatted her hard on the head. The child ran away screaming. Bad Mother propped her dead infant up again and sat across from it, staring deep into the corpse's face.

Even though she had to brush away the flies pacing the corners of her daughter's eyes, Bad Mother seemed to have hope her child would come back alive. When Good Mother left the area to forage elsewhere, and I went to work on my fourth wall, Bad Mother tucked her daughter's body under an arm and went her own way, too.

I'd gotten into the habit of talking to Omar and the chimps. Good Mother would bob her head and make pleased hooting sounds while I spoke, so she was my favorite gossip buddy. When Bad Mother was still carrying the unseeing husk of her daughter around days later, I couldn't resist leaning over to Good Mother and poking her in the ribs. "Did you *see* Bad Mother today, *mama*? I know, she's still carrying that dead baby of hers around. I know, *mama*, it's so *tacky*."

When Bad Mother looked over at us accusingly, I guiltily averted my gaze. Good Mother looked away, too, then heavily got up and went over to groom Bad Mother. As I watched Good Mother run her fingers through Bad Mother's scraggly hair while the distraught chimp hugged the dead body of her daughter, I realized how much better a person Good Mother was.

A few days later, Bad Mother came back from foraging without her daughter's body. The very next day, the males started pursuing her. On that same day of screeching and presenting and showing off by the males, Mango and Drummer returned. They seemed closer than ever; wherever Drummer went, Mango went toddling after.

When he returned to the excited males, Drummer started picking fights with anyone who got too close to Bad Mother. He displayed more than usual, running along the side of the lagoon, dragging a log I'd rejected for building. Once Bad Mother's mating signals lessened, the troop calmed. Drummer was still in charge, metal case in one hand and log in the other.

One morning, the lagoon was eerily quiet when I woke up. I thought the chimps had all left to raid a beehive or fruit grove and would soon return, but none of them came home that night. I realized they must have settled somewhere else, far enough from the lagoon that I was only just able to hear their shrieks as they bedded down.

I tried not to take it personally.

I would have been intolerably lonely if I hadn't had Omar. But within a few days of bustling about the lagoon with the vervet at my side, I was actually glad the chimps had gone away for a while, since I was now ready to put up my final wall and try the thatch. If I'd had chimps investigating the whole time, my weeks of effort would have soon wound up as a pile of splintered logs.

For a while it was only Omar and me and the *thunk* sound of my machete, the monkey's voice the only one I heard while I lay in the tent at night. Then, unexpectedly, Drummer and Mango started to visit every morning. Once we'd groomed for a while, Drummer would take to a tree and call loudly to me, as if ordering his idiot half brother to behave like the sensible chimps and follow him to the new spot. But I'd stay put, and he and Mango would finally leave to rejoin the troop.

I finished the last wall section late one afternoon, but I waited to secure it until Drummer and Mango were near. I'd rigged a door by attaching the last three logs with loose vine so I could swing them open and closed, and looked forward to opening it for them.

They weren't interested in the house, though. Drummer kept wandering in and out of the clearing, and Mango with him. I finally got his attention by picking up the metal case from its spot by the fire and strumming it. Drummer bounded over and seized the case. Mango, his little henchman, hunched down beside him and glared. I let Drummer play until he'd calmed some. Now that they were ready to watch, I lashed on the last piece of wall.

It held, and I cheered. Drummer and Mango hooted, excited by excitement. Omar made sure he was over the wall the moment I finished and was the house's first resident. I heard skittering sounds on the other side as he explored.

Drummer and Mango lost interest and were soon off to find the rest of the chimps, leaving Prof's case forgotten by the fire. I didn't have enough time left in the day to put the roof up, so as darkness fell I pitched the tent inside the walls. It felt strange, walking through the door and straight into the canvas.

I'd figure out how to rig the roof the next day. Maybe, I realized, I could pull what thread remained from the tent's ragged fabric and line the thatch with canvas to give me an extra layer against rain. For now, though, once I'd zipped the tent down, there was no sign of the walls around me. *Tomorrow I will be in a hut, a real home*, I told myself. *But tonight is a night like any other.*

If only I'd been right.

# TWENTY-TWO

The scream brought me bolt upright in the tent, gasping and groping in the dark. Then I got control and held still in the breath-close
air, trying to place the sound. There — it repeated, from somewhere up in the treetops. Omar was making a warning call. I could
tell from how constant the sound was that he wasn't fleeing, that
he was staying put a few feet away on top of the hut's wall.

Until it all cut off. Then pattering water was the only sound.

Omar made another call. This one was more familiar; it was
general distress, the same sound he'd make whenever his fur got
singed by the fire. I heard him scuttle far away, as if he was climbing
a tall tree, then return. Something scrabbled at the tent's zipper, and
I risked opening it half a foot. Omar barreled in and buried himself
against my chest. I held him while he shivered and chirped, then I
reached a hand around to slowly zip the tent back down. I examined
the skinny quivering animal as best I could in the dark, but found
no sign of injury. Once Omar had calmed, he sat quietly at the foot
of my bedroll. Eventually he fell asleep, his little hand tight in mine.
For me, though, there was only an anxious wait for dawn, when there
would be enough light for me to emerge from my new home and see
what had happened in my backyard.


The mint patch was nearly ruined. That's what I saw first.

Next I saw the animal tracks crossing and recrossing the clearing, circling the lagoon and my walls. A few of my garden plantings

had survived, but most had been smashed into the soil. I paced the lagoon as I tried to figure out what had happened. Omar followed, his hand clutching my leg. Chimps began to arrive soon after dawn and apparently decided to take the morning off; they were strewn in the clearing, dazed and lazy. What had brought them to the lagoon so early in the morning, had tempted them from the comfort of their nests to travel in the danger of the almost-dark hours? I looked for Drummer and Mango, but couldn't see them.

At the edges of the lagoon the tracks grew sparse enough that I could make out individual prints. I recognized the long-toed feet of chimps, but mixed among them were . . . paw prints. One bigger triangle, and four small pads in front of it. I'd seen prints like these before. In the clearing where Beggar had died.

They were leopard prints.

I tracked the paw marks out of the lagoon. Omar chirped in protest, but he didn't leave, instead climbing onto my shoulder and wrapping his hands around my head.

It was hard to tell at first, since the night's continual rain had ruined much of the trail, but as ridges of churned mud began to dry in the morning sun, I saw the leopard and chimp prints continued together until they emerged into a large scuffed area, and then the chimp's prints ended and only the leopard's continued. Omar and I followed on.

Part of me thought I should leave well enough alone and go back home, but Omar's odd call had opened up a puzzle that I wanted to solve. Omar and I had faced plenty of dangers together, not the least of which when the chimps had seen him as prey and tried to eat him. Even during *that*, he'd never made screams like those. He'd reserved those only for the deaths of Beggar and Prof, and now last night's attack.

With its leopard prints.

My heart skipped with unnatural speed, setting me light-headed as I tracked the paw prints. I moved on all fours to pass more easily under low-slung branches.

Then I turned a corner and found a cat on its side, with curled paws and a shattered, empty expression. The angles of its body were slightly off, like someone had drawn them from memory. There was only a little blood around its mouth, but clearly the leopard had been through something brutal. Its shoulders were impossibly hunched, its legs stretched farther than sinews and joints should have allowed. I'd seen the chimps hunt a colobus monkey, had watched them grab it by the tail and dash it to death against the ground; it had wound up with the same gaping blood-ied mouth, probably from internal wounds. I had a good hunch of precisely what kind of animal had killed the leopard.

In death, the cat had become small. Its claws had extended, and I could see black hair and red gore caked within them.

I realized with a start that Omar was no longer on my shoul-der. I yelled his name, pivoting in a circle. When he chirped back I spied him high in a tree, worrying his hands. "It's okay," I called, but he remained up there.

The leopard's front paw extended toward a hollowed tree. Figuring that might have been where the cat had been heading before it died, I investigated. The hollow smelled of urine and fur. A den. I felt a pang of sadness for the leopard, that it had died so close to home and safety.

Plugging my nose with my fingers, I crept closer. The stench was so strong that it wavered in the air. Small bones were strewn on the ground, and golden-white sheddings rimmed the hollow's edges. Using a stick to nudge aside the rotting pelt of an unfortu-nate rodent, I found two skulls in the corner. One was long and narrow, like a weasel's. Probably the same squirrel or rat that had given up its skin. I prodded it away to better see the other skull.

It was from an ape.

Maybe one of the chimps. An old one, whose canines had worn down so they looked like a human's.

I could have let myself believe that. If it weren't for the taqiyah.

Prof's taqiyah, the cap that had once been so familiar, was wadded in the back of the hollow. Even filthy as it was, it was unmistakable.

Aware of nothing more in the world than that scrap of wool, I reached a trembling hand into the hollow and ordered my numb fingers to grasp. Once I'd pulled the taqiyah out, I reached back in and tenderly placed a finger on either side of that delicate skull.

Prof's skull.

I hadn't thought of him as small — I'd only thought of him as Prof — but this skull was as light as a bird's egg. The leopard and the insects had scavenged it clean. The jaw was gone, and the teeth that remained were soft and studded with silver.

Even through tear-muddled eyes, I treasured the precious skull for its cleanness, and for the answers it gave me.

Omar's odd siren calls had been specific warnings, about a specific predator.

Drummer hadn't killed Prof. The hunter hadn't killed Prof.

This leopard had killed Prof.

Numbly, I wrapped his skull in the foul-smelling taqiyah and stumbled back to the lagoon, barely aware of Omar toddling beside me on two feet, desperate to keep up. It was only when I'd reached the hut that I realized the monkey and I had walked the whole way hand in hand.

Mango came running up, gleefully panting her greetings. I let her climb up me and clutch my back without returning the hug, barely aware of her weight as I shuffled to the waterfall. I held the skull under the water, cleaning the inside of its dome of the few caked bits of dirt and blood and cat hair. Then I rinsed out the shredded taqiyah, taking care that the threadbare fabric didn't tear under the rushing water. I carefully laid it out on a sunny rock and sat beside Prof's cap while it dried. I wanted to watch the fabric become soft and clean, and make sure that no chimp got nosy about the taqiyah and ripped it apart. Mango sniffed its edges curiously, but was more than happy to let herself be distracted by tickling.

Prof's skull in my hand, I alternated my attention between the drying taqiyah and the foraging and playing and napping chimps. The members of that family seemed both nearby and miles away. Everything about my world that wasn't Prof's taqiyah kept zooming away the moment it came into focus.

Bored by my lifelessness, Mango went off to play. Alone, I allowed my head to rest on my palms. Prof's skull was in my lap. My own head was in my hands; covered by warm blood and skin, it had a skull inside just like this one. Like my mother's and father's. Carine's. Monsieur Tatagani's.

I couldn't mope for long, though, because I recognized the pant-hoots of an approaching chimp. I watched an ape I knew well limp into the clearing, lame leg tight against his body. Drummer.

He was the last creature I wanted to see. I felt queasy and confused; I'd once been furious at him, but he hadn't done anything wrong. I'd forgiven him already, and though the forgiveness had been true, the suspicion had been wrong.

But what did it matter? What did Drummer know of my former hatred, anyway?

What did any chimp know of hatred? Nothing. The closest they knew was anger.

I pulled my attention from Drummer and returned it to the fragile skull in my lap. Prof had been torn apart by a leopard, probably while he was still alive and suffering from fever. It was no worse than being killed by a chimp — in fact, it was probably much quicker. But knowing the true killer did nothing to change the fact that he *had* died. That the person who had saved my life, who had become the purpose of it, had been taken.

He was still *gone*.

Like Carine, like my mother.

The taqiyah, so threadbare, dried quickly. I folded it on itself once and then again, holding the square of fabric against my cheek. Once I'd finished mudding my walls, I would hang it above the door. It would be the second decoration of my new home. Prof's skull might be the third. Then I'd build a mantle where I could place the hunters' radios, which had long ago stopped lighting.

I fished the machete from the valise and followed the tracks back to the hollow tree. My first decoration would be the leopard's pelt.


I examined everything I owned that afternoon, and found the taqiyah was actually among the least tattered of my possessions. In its slow but unrelenting way, the jungle was returning everything that wasn't alive to soil. The shirt I'd been wearing when I'd met Prof had lost so much thread and become so striped with mold that it looked like a decayed leaf. In a few more days, its only use would be kindling. At some point a chimp must have stolen Prof's last galabia and abandoned it somewhere; I kept looking for it but never managed to find it. The foodstuffs we'd arrived with had long ago been eaten, and the canvas bag that had contained them had turned to rot the moment the rainy season started. Even the old leather valise would have to be destroyed soon, before its lacy sides became home to mice and the snakes that hunted them.

I still had the shoes Prof had bought me, formless and yawning, but otherwise my clothing was basically gone. I was as naked as the apes — or more so, since I didn't even have their thick hair. I was the only naked ape.

Beside the machete, the only object left of any size was the metal case. Whenever another male got aggressive toward him, Drummer still braved the fire smoke to drag it away and thump the heels of his hands against it. But he only needed to do that every once in a while.

I unstaked the leaking tent and dragged it outside the hut's walls. Omar watched curiously as I laid the deflated canvas over the roof slats, then placed thatch on top and lashed it all together with liana. There were men in my old village who would have been able to weave the thatch so tight that no rain came through, but until I got more skilled I'd need a lining of tent fabric.

Once I'd finished my roof, I brought the fire-warm case inside. It made a table in the center of the floor.

I stood outside the hut. It was very small and very spare. But it was my home.

Before I knew it, Mango had wandered inside, followed by Good Mother's little son. He'd hurt his ear somehow; it was red and scabbed. But he took no notice of it as he and Mango tumbled around, gasping with pleasure as they roughhoused and rolled into the walls. I'd lashed the logs together loosely enough that they bent and held under the strain of rough play. Which was good, because soon all the chimps would be investigating, and if the adults decided to shake my home, the walls would have to be strong.

Soon Good Mother came in to fetch her child, and as she left I noticed a long red gash raking her back, three smaller gashes alongside. So she'd been the one to fight the leopard, perhaps to save her son. The wounds didn't seem very severe — maybe she'd been part of a group of attacking chimps, or she'd quickly overwhelmed the leopard with a mother's desperate strength. I'd never know.

I followed Good Mother outside, because I had work to do. Now that I had walls, it was time to expand my garden. I uprooted celery and chive plants and carried them, roots dangling, back to grow near home. I figured they had defenses that would keep them alive in my garden. And if they didn't, I would rip the corpses out and plant live ones where the dead had been.


My biggest struggle during the rainy season was to find logs dense and dry enough to smolder for days and keep Omar and me safe. I'd found that the best ones were near the river, where trees often fell over in the mud. I'd tie vines to a dead tree and cart it home like a buffalo with a plow, leaving the trunk beside the fire for days until it went from wet to damp. It would smoke dry while the inner logs burned, then I'd eventually roll the tree toward the center and keep it there until it, too, began to burn. A dense enough log under the thick leaves of the kapok tree, could stay lit through all but the worst rain showers.

One evening, though, the twilight was an eerie green, and come sundown a savage storm began. As it raged, Omar was too excited to sleep, so we stayed up, listening to the *thunk-thunk* of the pelting rain as my roof leaked into the cup and pot. The corduroy skin on Omar's hands and feet had broken out in a rash, and without a full day of dry weather anywhere on the horizon it would be a long time before it cleared up. I stroked his fur as we sat in the dark. Toward morning, I heard a loud crash and knew I'd have another fallen tree to harvest for my fire.

The dawn sky was the smooth gray-blue of a river stone. Once I'd had my tea, I went with Omar toward where we'd heard the crashing sound.

The fallen tree was massive, and I knew I'd never be able to move it, or cut off any but the smallest branches with my machete. But there was still plenty of fuel to be had; I set to work chopping off the ragged yellow pieces of wood where the tree had split and carrying those back to my fire pit. With the chimps away, the jungle was relatively quiet, and the repetitive task of going back and forth to the fallen tree put me in a trance. I got so involved in my work that I didn't notice Omar was no longer with me until I got hungry for my next meal, hours later.

"Omar?" I called. But there was no response.

Meal forgotten, I retraced my steps, calling his name. I finally heard his chirp in response, and found him in the open space along the fallen tree. He'd discovered some rotten fruit there, and was slurping down the worm-ridden globs. I dashed over and batted the mushy black goo from his hands. He looked at me in shock. I'd always counted on him to feed himself, but even the hungriest wild monkey would never eat food so clearly rotten. I headed back to camp, expecting Omar to follow. But he didn't; he sat down. So I picked him up and carried him back to the lagoon.

He was limp in my arms, like Carine had once been. As we went I examined his paws. The rash had settled into the grooves of his childhood injury and was blooming outward in bursting red tendrils. Between the red was lily-white skin, puffy with fluid. All of it was plastered together with pus. I kissed the top of Omar's head. *It's going to be okay.*

I stopped collecting wood and spent the day focused on him, massaging his tender hands as much as he would permit and holding him near the fire in an attempt to dry the rash. I chewed the leaves away from wild celery and fed the monkey the stalks, his favorite part. He held on to each piece gingerly, wincing at the pressure on his inflamed hands. Afterward I fed him from my stash of nuts, and he nibbled directly from my fingers. Before night fell, I carried him to the river and bathed his arms and legs as best I could, hoping that might help the infection. He accepted the attention, watching as I cleaned his fur and patted it dry. Then we lay out by the fire, warming our fingers and staring up into the night sky. Omar nodded to sleep in my arms, huddling near for warmth until his shivering subsided.

The next day he dozed in the house while I puttered. I tidied the site, collected more wood, filled out my garden. When he woke, Omar sat near the fire pit and its one smoldering log, his hands held out to the drying flames. The Monkey Who Loved Fire.

He sighed with pleasure when night fell and I stoked the flames higher. He edged closer and closer to the fire until I had to pull him back so he didn't singe, keeping him a safe distance only by restraining him in my lap.

The next morning Omar seemed to have more energy, sitting at the shore and enjoying the morning sunshine. I watched over him, angry with myself for not keeping better track of what he was eating. That rash had probably been limiting what he could forage for some time.

Drummer and Mango swung through for a visit that afternoon, and Omar's sluggishness finally made him the ideal plaything for Mango. When I wasn't distracting her with a tickle session, Mango was as often as not clutching the monkey to her, Omar going limp as Mango pinned him to her chest. Omar's head bobbed under her forceful petting, an unreadable expression on his face. When her affection got too violent, I'd take out a banana, and Mango would set Omar down to come get it, which would give him a chance to escape into the hut. He wouldn't hide away for too long, though — he'd come out eventually, sidle near Mango, and then complain dramatically when she picked her doll back up.

When Omar and I emerged from the hut the following dawn, the river was calm and silver. To shake up my routine, we crossed to the far side of the lagoon to fill the kettle with water to make my tea. It hadn't rained the night before, and the water was unusually still, enough to become a mirror. I was surprised to see a face reflected in the surface.

I didn't look like myself, or at least not the self I had been before meeting Prof. I had red dots studding my face, and my jaw and chin were more pronounced. Heavy lines crossed my cheeks. Muscles roped my torso.

Mango came down from her nest as soon as she spotted us and was soon force-grooming poor Omar. When Drummer came down from his nest, though, he saw me staring into the water and calmly ambled around the lagoon's edge until he was squatting beside me. He, too, stared into the river, but seeing himself clearly didn't interest him as much as it did me. He started tossing handfuls of grass into the water, ruining the reflection. I leaned into him in the glancing light. His right leg was still lame, but had healed over enough by now that I felt comfortable resting against it. His toes curled around the side of my torso, supporting my back.

I watched his open, intelligent gaze as he tracked the clouds glowing in the morning sky. I wondered what he was thinking. I wondered if he ever wondered what I was thinking.

Our dreamy state was broken by a buzzing sound. At first I figured it was a bird I hadn't met yet — the more exotic ones made truly weird noises, some of them sounding like large beasts, others like dry rasping leaves. But then I recognized the sound, and knew it wasn't a bird.

It was an outboard motor.

I thought first of my pirogue, that some animal had gotten curious about the motor and magically figured out how to start it. But I'd used up all the fuel long ago. So this couldn't be my boat.

It was someone else's.

I had a visitor.

# TWENTY-THREE

I crept into the hut and picked up the machete. Taking pains to stay low and silent, I stole along the river, heading toward the distant buzz of the motor. As I neared the sound and realized it was coming my way, I slowed down. There was no need to announce myself to an intruder. Hiding and waiting for him was smarter.

I nestled between two palms at the bank, tearing down extra fronds and jabbing them in the soil so they fanned enough to disguise me.

I jumped when there was a crash from a nearby bush. But it was just Drummer. Unfazed by my machete, he settled at my feet and started to groom. Legs trembling, I lowered myself beside him. When the termites emerged from the palms and started tangling into his hair, I plucked them off. He presented his open mouth and I placed them between his teeth. He munched them down happily.

The grooming calmed me. The chimps were rubbing off on me — no time ever seemed as important to them as *right now*. As the motor's sound intensified, birds panicked from the trees and snakes plopped into the water. It always amazed me how many animals were hidden in the jungle even when it seemed its emptiest.

Everything was fleeing this intruder. Except Drummer and me.

As the sound got louder, even Drummer grew intrigued. Alert and panting — though making no sound loud enough to give away his location — he climbed a tree. The trunk was too slick for me to follow, and I managed to grab his foot before he got out of reach. He froze and peered down at me, confused. I knew he wanted to get a better look at the intruder, but I felt safer with him nearby. He descended, apparently willing to indulge my strange needs.

We watched as a pirogue bigger and finer than mine nosed around the bend in the river. I folded down a frond and squinted, trying to glimpse any detail. Drummer was so rigid with tension that the strain set his body shaking.

Once this pirogue neared my own tethered at the bank, the rider cut out the motor. I watched as the boat coasted toward the shore. The driver was wearing bulky clothes and a mosquito net so I couldn't make out his features, much as I tried.

I kept my hand on Drummer's back, heavy between his shoulder blades. He'd lean forward and then back, teeth bared, and I knew he was torn between whether to attack or flee. If I hadn't laid a restraining hand on him, and his leg hadn't been crippled, he would probably already be charging off.

I watched the pirogue settle in next to mine, reeds sighing as they passed under the boat. Was this intruder going to steal my canoe? The only use it served right now was housing spiders, but I hated the idea of someone taking it, in case one day I had to flee back to the Outside.

But I soon saw that this person probably wasn't a thief. For one thing, it was a *she*. And white as a root!

For a mad heart-fluttering second I thought maybe it was Prof, that he had walked back to civilization and returned with a boat, and as a woman with white skin to boot. But my head told my heart it was being an idiot, that I'd held Prof's skull in my hand, and the fluttering of my heart became something I could tolerate.

The woman — narrow-bodied and rickety with age, I could now see — got out of her boat and stepped onto shore, immediately sinking up to her knees in muck. Had she never been beside a river before, that she thought she could walk there? I watched her flail, hat and mosquito net tumbling to the mud. She leaned down to pick them up, but pitched into the muck and shrieked. It had been a long time since I'd heard a person make a noise like that, and there was something quiet and vulnerable about the sound, a noise a person would make only if she thought she was alone.

Drummer sprang from under my hand. War-barking, he crashed through the brush and tore toward the woman. She fell backward into the pirogue and sat up, clutching the side and staring in horror at the beast bearing down. Drummer had his mouth wide open, teeth gleaming. The woman dropped to the floor of the boat.

If Drummer had been calmer, the woman's submissive stance might have helped her. But he was defending me and the rest of his family, and there was nothing she could do that would stop his attack.

I lunged out of hiding and staggered toward the waterline. I yelled, first in Fang and then in French once I'd gotten my wits: "Into the water! Get into the water!"

The woman rolled over, saw naked me running out of the greenery, and screamed again. But she did as I said, splashing into the river. She crashed through a raft of water lettuce, forcing a wave of murky water out to both banks.

"Farther!" I shouted, shocked by the sound of words from my mouth.

By the time Drummer reached the shore, the woman was treading water in the middle of the river, stroking against the current. Drummer paced up and down the edge, hooting and slamming his fists against the ground. His lips were peeled back so far that I could see his pink gums until they receded into black flesh far above his teeth. The white-faced woman kept her eyes locked on the hostile chimp while she swam.

I cut along the shore until I was beside Drummer. He paid no attention to me, instead focusing on throwing handfuls of soil at the woman. Sprays of gravel and debris riddled the river's surface and flecked the woman's face. "Shh, Drummer," I said, patting his back. "Shh."

"Can you swim well?" I called out to the stranger in French. But she didn't respond — either she didn't speak French or I terrified her as much as Drummer did. We would have to wait until he'd calmed down, or she'd swum to the other shore.

I took the opportunity to peek at the luggage in the woman's pirogue. The boat was full of odd, large, boxy items zipped into black cases. Once he saw me peering inside, Drummer became interested, too, seizing the largest bundle and running up and down the shore with it high over his head. The woman yelped and started swimming in.

"Come, yes, but it must be slowly, please, madame," I said, holding my hand out toward her as I crouched. Drummer was on his back, using his good foot and both hands to keep the case in the air, tossing it like he was playing with a baby chimp. Distracted as Drummer was by the new toy, most of the woman's danger had probably passed.

She stayed in the water but clutched the far end of her pirogue, peering over the top. Drummer looked up briefly from his investigation and then went back to the zipper, tugging savagely at it. I smiled at the woman. "It's okay, it's okay." What I really wanted to ask was, *What are you doing here in the jungle, crazy white woman?*

She looked like she was getting tired, legs kicking in the water as she clutched the boat. To show her I meant well, I picked the hat and mosquito net up from the mud, shook them clean as best I could, and tossed them into her pirogue. When she put the broad hat on, her head seemed to vanish and she sank farther into the water. Excited about new blood, fat bottle-green flies batted her face. She swallowed one by accident and spat it out.

"Can I come ashore?" she asked in acceptable French, sinking even more as she used one hand to swat at flies. "Is it safe for me?"

"I think you *need* to come ashore," I said. "So that is what you should do."

Drummer was still busy trying to get into the woman's zippered container. When I patted him on his head he grunted, as if to say, *Don't distract me.*

The woman was still treading water, her arms slapped over the side of the pirogue in exhaustion. Getting worried for her, I dropped my grin. "Yes, yes, of course. I'll make sure Drummer doesn't hurt you. Come in before you drown."

Keeping her gaze on Drummer, the woman made her way to shore. She stood before me, covered in dripping muck.

"Are you lost?" I asked. Now that she was near I had a sudden compulsion to cover my nakedness. I'd started plastering mud on my crotch to prevent insect bites, but that didn't mean I was wearing any clothing. I placed my hands below my waist strategically.

"The ape," she said, the words jerking as she caught her breath. "Could you get him to release my bag?"

"No," I said, looking at Drummer sadly. "I'm afraid I cannot."

The woman collapsed on the soil, breathing heavily. The noise was loud enough that Drummer again became more interested in her than the bag. He stood on two legs, panting and swaying.

"We should be quiet with each other," I said slowly, "so that he'll know that we aren't enemies. Don't move your hands suddenly, and don't touch me yet. Otherwise he will think you're attacking."

"Okay," the woman said, keeping her hands in her lap. I figured she must know chimpanzees a little; though she was talking to me, she trained her eyes on a leaf.

"You can look up sometimes. Drummer doesn't mind that."

She glanced up and gave a fearful sigh. "Like this?"

"Yes. Like that. Only less afraid." It was strange; we were speaking out loud, but I was learning so much more by looking at her stance, her rapid breathing, the expressions her mouth took on when she wasn't trying to say anything.

"You speak very good French," she said. She was staying so still that the words sounded emotionless, but I could see the tightness of her wrists, the wobble in her legs.

I nodded warily and grunted. Why should my French not be good? I was from Gabon.

"Most people who live in this region don't speak French, just their tribal language," she said.

"You're wrong. Because there aren't any people around here. There's no one for days." I wanted to add *not anymore*, but realized it might be foolish to give this woman much information.

"You mean to tell me it's just you here? All by yourself?"

I shook my head. Using words made me feel almost queasy. I didn't like them anymore; there were so many ways to be untrue. I realized that I'd let my hands fall from my crotch, and I let them stay by my sides.

"I mean, is someone else here taking care of you?"

I laughed. "No. I take care of *them*. Or we take care of one another, I guess."

"Them? Can you introduce me?"

"You've already met one."

Drummer was still crouched there, staring at us. When we simultaneously looked at him, he turned bashful. I'd never seen him with an expression like that.

The woman looked confused. "I mean human friends. Not apes."

There had been a person, of course, but I didn't want to tell this woman about Prof. I also didn't want to lie to her, so I chose my words carefully. "There are no other people here."

"I'm so impressed that you're able to survive out here all by yourself," the woman said in this warm tone that made me feel jumbled and angry.

"I told you, I'm *not* by myself," I said.

"Yes, you did tell me that," she said, suddenly cross. "And I'm telling you I'm surprised by it!"

"Are you traveling down the river?" I asked.

"Yes," she said. "I was."

"So you'll keep going." My arms crossed on their own.

Drummer came closer now. It must have been the woman's hair that he found so magical; he put his face right by her ear and lifted some of the strands — blond darkened with silver — into the sunlight and let them tumble through his fingers. The woman held perfectly still.

I knew that I'd made it sound like I wanted her to go away. I didn't, but her leaving me was inevitable; it would feel better if the idea had been mine. "You could stay here for a while," I said, voice trembling. "If you want a break from traveling." *I have a house.*

She nodded. It was almost imperceptible, but I'd noticed it, and so did Drummer. He put his face right in front of hers and delicately pursed his lips so they grazed hers. "It's okay," I said. "He's being curious."

Drummer draped a lock of the woman's hair over his own face and turned to me, his lips still pursed. I laughed. "Very pretty, Drummer. You look very beautiful."

"Drummer?" she said, staying perfectly still as the chimp tugged on her hair. "Is that his name?"

"Yes. Because he likes to drum on the kapok trees. And I think he likes you."

"I'd much rather that than he hate me," she said, looking Drummer up and down.

"Yes," I said, remembering his savage attack on Omar. "It is much better this way. The chimps are all more used to people now."

"Is your village near here?" the woman asked.

I sighed in irritation. "No. I told you there is no one else around here. I don't have a village."

She stared at me.

"But I *do* have a *house*," I said.

"Could . . ." she faltered. "Could you show it to me?"

The woman had three large bags, and as I heaved two of them across my back, my muscles seized in a way I remembered from when I'd first taken Prof's valise over my shoulder. "Are you sure that's not too much weight?" the woman asked.

I couldn't make my lungs fill enough to speak, so I grunted in response.

Drummer served as our escort. He'd bound well ahead, return to make sure we were still there, then hurtle forward again.

I stopped us before we emerged at the lagoon. "I need you to wait here for a few minutes," I told the woman. "And to keep very quiet."

She nodded, sitting against a large tree and hugging her knees to her chest.

I proceeded with Drummer and was glad to find the clearing empty. When I brought the metal case out of my hut, Drummer took my hand and dragged me toward our new companion's hiding spot. As we went, I handed over the case. Thrilled to have his tool in his possession again, Drummer bounded back and forth, banging it against anything in reach (including, painfully, my shin). Distantly, I heard other chimps call as they heard the ruckus. They'd all be here soon. We had to hurry.

Drummer tailed me when I went back to the woman, metal case dragging in the dirt. When she saw the chimp carrying a briefcase, she laughed out loud. Drummer looked at her and then at me, confused. Maybe even embarrassed.

"There will be other chimps at the lagoon soon," I said curtly; there was no need for her to make Drummer feel bad. "And that case keeps Drummer dominant. Which keeps you and me safe."

Her smile dropped. "Of course," she said.

We made our way to the lagoon. As we went, Drummer trucked the case along the ground and made terrific crashing sounds that had him hooting in pleasure. When we emerged into the clearing we found many of the chimps already assembled at the far side, agitated and making their own excited noises. Drummer did a victory lap around the lagoon, losing the case once or twice when it hit a root or rock but soon retrieving it. Silver Stripes and the other males scattered whenever the younger male neared.

The woman and I stood near the waterfall, completely overlooked. "Amazing," she breathed. "Just amazing."

I gestured proudly around the lagoon. "Yes, it's beautiful. And have you seen the house? It's around the bend!"

"No. I mean, yes, I'm sure that's impressive, too, but I mean the *chimpanzees*."

"Drummer loves that case," I said. "And you can see why."

"Is it yours?"

I didn't know. It hadn't been mine, but now I supposed it was. "Yes. It's mine."

"Amazing," the woman said. "I'd like to make a record of this."

"I've been making notes," I said. "With drawings. I can show you, if you like."

She seemed to barely hear me. "Tool use is nothing that hasn't already been observed in the wild, of course. But not in Gabon's chimp cultures. And never quite like this."

"Never with a spy case, you mean?"

She shook her head in confusion. "Was Drummer always the alpha? I'm surprised, with his leg the way it is."

"Was Drummer always in charge? No. I can tell you all about it. I can show you the *research*," I said, drawing out the word. I took the woman's wrist lightly in my hand and tugged her toward my hut, grunting despite myself. The chimps noticed us and increased their ruckus, climbing nearby trees and hooting. They were still hemmed in by Drummer, who was proudly banging the case against everything he could reach, denting trees and ripping apart bushes.

"I made this hut," I said, shouting to be heard over the noise. "From trees and vines. If you had come by a few weeks ago, it wouldn't have been finished yet. But now it is!"

But the woman wasn't looking. She was staring at the chimps, her hands on her hips. "It's amazing!"

I looked out at the apes. They were *them*. Which was amazing, I supposed.

I unhooked the door's vine handle and pried it open. Omar stepped out — I'd taken to keeping him indoors when I was away from the lagoon, in case one of the chimps got ideas and again tried to make a meal out of the aging monkey. He scampered up to my shoulder and started scolding the woman.

"This is Omar," I said.

"Hello!" she said, holding out a hand with one finger outstretched, like he was a parakeet. Omar stared at the finger, waiting for food to appear.

The woman pulled away her hand. "A vervet! He's far from his home range."

I cocked my head at the woman. "It's true. He's not from the Inside. How did you know that?"

The woman didn't answer. She was staring out the doorway, clearly overwhelmed by the sight of the chimps. The males were falling over themselves frantically, but — predictably — their displays of power were turning to play. None of them was in a position to directly challenge Drummer, which meant that after they'd finished horsing around they'd all be back to their usual grooming and friend-making.

"Do you want to come in?" I asked. "I can make you a mint tea."

"I'd rather stay out here and watch them."

I sighed and stashed the woman's bags in my hut. Shy again about my nakedness, I took my remaining scrap of shirt and tied it around my waist. We sat on the broad flat stone beside my cooking fire and watched the chimps. I made tea for her because it was what an adult did for a guest, even a guest who hurt her host's feelings by not wanting to see inside his hut.

Mango had spent the day with Good Mother and her son, and they were the last of the chimps to arrive. When she saw me she raced forward, then stopped short when she realized someone new was there. She eyed the new woman suspiciously.

"That's Mango," I said.

The woman took an orange from her bag and held it out in her open palm. "Here you go, little one," she said.

Mango looked longingly at the fruit. Oranges did not grow in our jungle, and this was a once-in-a-lifetime treasure. But when she looked at the woman, her eyes turned stormy.

"Mango . . ." I said warningly, "be nice."

Mango took the orange into one hand and sniffed it. Then she slowly and deliberately placed her teeth over the woman's wrist and bit. The woman gasped and yanked her arm away.

Mango scampered off. Then, for good measure, she kicked soil at the woman before vaulting up a tree. The dirt spray fell far short.

"Are you okay?" I asked her. "Did Mango draw blood? I'm sorry — she's never done anything like that before."

The woman examined her hand. The palm was cramped in one position, like she was trying to pick up something narrow and heavy, but I didn't see any blood. "She crunched me a little," the woman said. "But I don't think she wanted to hurt me."

Mango settled a short distance away, orange in her lap. When Drummer came near she shrieked her head off and hurled her whole body over the precious fruit. Drummer easily rolled her over and took it for himself. When she cried pitifully, he cuffed her and she fell flat. Then she turned pleading, placing her face right next to Drummer's and making cooing sounds while he bit into the fruit.

"It's amazing," the woman whispered. "Chimps clearly don't expect justice like humans do, but at the same time they show a lot more tolerance. Can you imagine any powerful human male accepting someone so close to his face while he was eating?"

"That's his sister," I explained. "He's used to having her in his face all the time."

"Even so. It's *amazing*. They'll fight and make up and be okay with having their boundaries overrun." As if to prove the woman's point, Mango pulled a slice of orange right from between Drummer's teeth. Her brother permitted it, and she turned away from him to enjoy her rescued treat, her back resting against Drummer's lame leg. The moment she'd finished that slice, she went back into his mouth and plucked away a final morsel.

"What happened to the dominant male's leg?" the woman asked.

"Drummer? He was caught in a trap. I freed him."

"You did? All by yourself? Where are your parents?"

I shook my head. The point was that I had freed Drummer from a trap. That I had made a house for myself out here in the wilderness. That I was a boy researcher.

"So . . ." she said, watching my expression. "How did you keep him alive?"

"I did what my mother once did for my father. I made a salt drip. It used up almost all of the salt I had, but Drummer lived."

"He's a very handsome chimp."

Drummer looked up, coarse black hair flopping over his forehead. "He is. You're right." We sat in silence for a while. It had been so long since I'd been around anyone who spoke a language that I had to think about how to make words work; it was like there had to be two conversations, one silent about what you were feeling and one out loud about what you were saying, and the two only rarely managed to be the same thing. It was exhausting. "It seems like you have been around chimpanzees before," I finally said.

She dragged one of her bags out of the hut. "Yes, many times. But only in sanctuaries and zoos."

"So you have come into the jungle to study them?" I asked, hoping this woman might be like Prof.

"Not exactly." She sighed, staring into my eyes. Then she clapped her hands. Mango startled and leaped in the air, then hunched down and fixed the woman with an evil eye. "Are you hungry?" the woman asked.

She unzipped the bag, and the moment I glimpsed what she had inside, I put a hand over hers to stop her. "Bring it into the hut. If the chimps see that food, it will all be gone in seconds."

I ushered her in, dragged the bag in after us, and set one of the smoldering logs on the doorstep. I did that whenever the chimps got too curious about my home. Finished with her orange slices, Mango positioned herself on the far side of the log and stared the intruder down through the rising smoke.

The woman laughed. "That little chimp is never going to come around to me, is she?"

"No," I said. "I don't think she will."

The woman lifted the bottom of her bag. Mango paced at the other side of the smoking log, trying to get a better view.

The woman dumped out the bag's contents. When I saw what tumbled out, I gasped.

A fresh bag of rice. A tin of salt (that shiny container with its sturdy lid was as exciting as what was inside). Crackers in crinkly wrappers. Strips of dried buffalo. Bandages and antibiotics. A bar of chocolate.

I was crying. The hot tears falling down my face made me feel childish, so I buried my head between my bare knees. Having that kind of food in front of me would have been overwhelming even back in Franceville, but here in the jungle the shock was even worse. "I'm sorry," I blubbered. Hearing how weak my voice sounded in front of this stranger only made me sob harder. "I'm sorry!" Then the fact that I'd apologized on top of everything else made me feel even worse.

The woman's hand was on my back. "It's okay! I shouldn't have dumped it all out at once, right here on your living room floor. That was really bad judgment. I'm sorry."

I let myself lean into the hand on my back, and it became an embrace around my shoulders. She made soft cooing sounds, completely unlike the coarse panting sympathy of chimp mothers. "Where is all that food from?" I finally managed to get out.

"The city. I flew into the capital, took the Transgabonais train across to Franceville, and came up to you by logging truck."

"That's where I'm from," I said. "Franceville. It's where I was from before I was from here."

"So you're a city boy."

I removed myself from her embrace, faced her, and sat up tall. When I stared straight ahead I couldn't see the food, and once I couldn't see the food my voice became strong again. "I grew up in a village. And then the city. And now here."

"That's a lot of traveling for someone so young." She reached down, and the chocolate came into view. She unwrapped the bar, and I tentatively accepted it. I licked an edge, and the flavor was so intense it curled my tongue. I folded the wrapper back over and put the bar to one side. "Can I save this?"

The woman nodded, her smile huge but frowning at the corners. "Of course. It's yours to do with as you like. I want you to keep all of this."

*Thank you* seemed inappropriate for something so tremendous, so I just nodded.

"I brought it for you. I bought all of this with you in mind."

I looked at her. She was a foreigner; maybe she'd messed up her French. "What do you mean, with *me* in mind?"

"I stopped here because I saw your canoe. And then I saw *you*."

"Yes . . ." I was dying to know more. But as I watched the woman choose her words, another thought struck me: I was in a room with four walls and a roof, sitting across from a person and having a conversation. *That* was a surprise and a mystery, as much as what she was saying. It made my body trill to think that a few feet away were a lagoon and lounging chimpanzees and miles of jungle with no humans in it. But here we were in a little house. This woman and I, we were people.

She smiled warmly. "I haven't even properly introduced myself. My name is Anne Osgood. I'm a photographer for the National Geographic Society."

Right as she said that, a squabble broke out among the chimps. I listened to them shriek, their calls intensifying as the whole troop became involved. Though I could see chimps running back and forth behind her, screaming their heads off, the whole time Mango sat perfectly erect at the far side of the smoldering log, concentrating on us with every jealous bone in her body. I saw her, but my thoughts were only on Prof and everything he'd meant to accomplish. I willed myself not to cry again.

"It was true," I managed to gasp. My heart was filling and bursting and filling again in a way that felt so good, it was uncomfortable. "You mean Prof didn't lie. He told the truth!"

She tilted her head. "Sorry?"

"Professor Abdul Mohammad," I said proudly. "The chimpanzee researcher! Africa's Jane Goodall! Who else could I mean?"

"I don't think I understand."

"I came here with him. I was his assistant. I'm carrying on his work."

I watched her stumble through her confusion. Finally she took my hands in hers and leaned in. Mango made defensive barks as the woman brought her head close to mine. I was worried Mango would step on the smoldering log and burn her feet, so I could barely concentrate on Madame Anne Osgood's words as she spoke: "Whoever he is, that person is not why I'm here. I'm here to photograph the boy who lives with the chimpanzees. I'm here for you."

# TWENTY-FOUR

I hadn't had the urge to cry for a long time. Not when I'd found Beggar's body, not when I'd lost Prof, not when I'd found Drummer with his leg in a trap, or Mango withering away without family, or Omar sick with his rash. But now I found myself fighting off tears for the third time in the space of an hour. "You mean . . . you're here to take pictures of *me*?"

"I gave you my name," Madame Osgood said. "Would you be willing to give me yours?"

She had a notebook out. She wanted to write down my name.

My name — it seemed such a small part of me. Prof knew it but had rarely needed to use it. Carine hadn't been old enough to even have known it. The chimps wouldn't understand what names even were. My mother was the last person who had used it often. I told it now to Madame Osgood. "Luc."

"I'm very pleased to meet you."

I mumbled "pleased to meet you" back.

"I'll tell you what brought me here," Madame Osgood said. "I'm from England originally. Do you know where England is?"

Of course I did. It was where James Bond was from.

"I've worked as a journalist in Africa, though, for many years. I've been taking photographs of logging operations, and when I was in a bar in Franceville —"

"It was probably the Café de la Gare," I supplied. "I used to work there."

"Yes! That's the one. A hunter was telling a story about something he'd been through, and it was so good that the rest of the bar crowded around to hear. Of course I listened in, too. The man told how a moneylender had hired some men to get revenge on a man and boy who had tricked him, saying that they could sell any chimpanzee infants they found. But when they'd arrived, the boy had chimpanzees on his side. He said the apes had killed the moneylender and a hunter. The man who'd survived had spent the last week drowning his sorrow at the bar.

"This all seemed very unlikely to me. So I started asking him questions, and found out more about the professor sent by the National Geographic Society to study chimpanzees."

She was getting excited, flipping through her notebooks without landing on any one page. "But here's the thing," she said. "I believed him. That man was *scared*. So when the crowd wandered off, I bought the poacher a drink, and he told me as much as he could about where to find the boy. *You*, the boy who lives with chimpanzees."

"But you also knew who Prof was," I protested weakly. "He's the real reason you're here."

She smiled softly, like she'd found something to pity. "Maybe someone at the National Geographic Society knows about him. But I don't. I came only for you."

I felt such a mix of things. The joy I'd had to know that Prof hadn't been lying was being taken away. But I also felt pride that someone had traveled such a long way to find me, and concern about what she planned to do with me and my chimps. Each feeling boiled to the top and then was pushed under by another, so the only thing constant was hot confusion.

To make the churn of feelings stop, I jumped into my story. I began not with my parents or the stolen spy case, but with Prof asking me to work for him. From there I told all the truth I could remember about Prof's and my first weeks in the jungle, about encountering Beggar and Mango and Drummer, about Prof's mysterious killing and Drummer getting trapped. I took out Prof's skull to show her, and felt awful when Madame Osgood averted her eyes. I hid the skull away in a corner.

I had to take a break, because the boil of feelings had gotten so strong that I stopped being able to form words on top of it. Madame Osgood seemed to understand, and took my hand. She and I wordlessly stepped over the smoking log and went outside to see the chimps.

Mango was upon us immediately. She gave my calf a hug, Madame Osgood's shin a good kick, and then ran away. Drummer, though, continued to adore our new friend. As soon as he saw her, he broke from a group of males at the far side of the lagoon. Hooting softly, he neared and started stroking Madame Osgood's leg. When she kneeled, he switched to grooming her scalp, examining her iron-blond hair for nits.

For most of the other chimps, Drummer's acceptance was enough to get their approval, too. First Good Mother and her son and daughter cautiously approached, heads bobbing. Then Bad Mother joined, and the other females. Finally the males joined in. They came by in small groups, curious about the new alien. Madame Osgood giggled as they ran their fingers through her hair, and was good about knowing which chimps would be fine about being groomed back and which to keep at a distance.

Good Mother seemed to take a special interest in the strange newcomer; she and her son remained beside us long after the other chimps had gotten bored and wandered away. Her constant company even convinced Silver Stripes to come over and allow his back to be scratched. As Madame Osgood ran her fingers through his gray-and-black hair, Mango sprawled defiantly in my lap, glaring at the outsider.

As the chimps began to bed down for the evening, Madame Osgood asked me to continue my story. I built up the fire, and then resumed. She listened intently, her chin resting on Good Mother's son's little head, as I told her about healing Drummer and fighting to get him and Mango accepted by the troop. Then I told her about the forest hunter, how Prof had chased him off to keep the chimps safe. I told her about the leopard and how I'd learned the real cause of Prof's death because of Omar's different alarm calls.

"That's true about vervets!" Madame Osgood said. "One call is for eagles and will send them into the bushes. The other is for leopards and will send them into the treetops."

When my only response was to stare silently into my clasped hands, Madame Osgood continued quietly. "I'm sorry about his loss," she said. "Very much."

"Thank you."

"Will you tell me your story again tomorrow, so I can take notes? And will you let me ask you more questions?"

*Tomorrow.* "You're . . . going to stay?" I asked.

"I'd like to remain here and find out more about you, if you're willing. For as long as that takes, yes."

"Of course! You can set up your bedroll in the hut, too. And I can make us mint tea in the morning. Prof used to drink it all day. And we can eat some of the chocolate and crackers you brought and some of my favorite fruits, too, and then I'll take you around. I can show you the different kinds of birds and the most beautiful trees."

"Yes, yes, we can do all that." Her smile crinkled. It was hard to tell age on someone like her, but she looked old enough that her own children were probably having children. "Will you give me permission to print your story, so other people can read it? Can I take pictures and let people know that you're here?"

"This is for other researchers?" I asked.

"Some researchers will read it, yes," she said. "And ordinary kinds of people, too. I think many, many people will be interested in what's happened to you."

"And our research, too," I said. "You could print what Prof and I did. And I can tell you all about the chimpanzees. Maybe each one could have its own story. Like how Bad Mother's daughter died. And how two of the chimps are getting cloudy eyes. Did you notice that? And I could draw you a picture of Beggar so people will remember Mango's mother, too."

"I'd love to include as much of that material as I can," Madame Osgood said. "That way everyone will know about your chimps."

This sounded wonderful. But something was worrying me, too. "Will all of this help keep them safe?" I asked.

She looked at me in surprise. "Why, yes. That's the hope. People only keep things safe if they know something about them."

"You can't write that Mango is mean," I said, stroking the chimp's head. "She's actually one of the sweetest chimps. She's being protective of me." Sensing our attention, she sulkily picked up a handful of dirt and sprayed it at Madame Osgood.

"Okay." Madame Osgood laughed. "I know she's jealous. And with good reason."

"Can I think about it? I have more questions before I decide."

"Of course. There's no rush. In the meantime, do you want to have dinner? I'll get it ready if you get the fire going a little hotter. It won't be much, but maybe some beans and a tin of salt meat?"

Now I really did cry.


Madame Osgood tacked up her mosquito net alongside mine, and for the first time the hut was truly bug free. It was bliss. Even the clever spiders found it impossible to get in — when I woke up they were stuck in the layer between nettings, coasting whenever a breeze came through. I lay there for a while in the morning light, watching with pleasure as fat flies thudded into the net. Omar was peaceful at my feet, and Madame Osgood made soft sounds of sleep beside me. Not snore sounds, but breathing. The breathing of a human.

After lying still and listening for a while, I lifted the netting and jimmied open the hut's door. I wanted to have the mint tea brewed and ready by the time my new companion got up.

The moment I was in the open I heard a creaking above, and looked up in time to see Mango bound down from her night nest. She clutched tightly to my chest while I worked, like the Mango I'd known months ago. Once I had the water heating over the flames, I took her into my lap. She was large now — still with a little tuft of hair on her rear, but I could imagine that in a year or two the tuft would be gone and the other chimps would know she was an adult. I would be proud and sad when that day came. I could someday help her keep her children safe as they, too, grew up and had children.

If I was still here.

When Madame Osgood emerged I offered her a tin cup of tea, tipping my head politely like I'd seen waiters do on the terrace of the Hôtel Léconi. She'd slept late, so the tea was no longer as hot as I'd have liked. But Madame Osgood didn't seem to mind. She clucked in delight and cradled the cup in her hands as she sat beside me and the low fire.

Now that Mango and I had passed a quiet hour together, the little chimp didn't seem as furious about Madame Osgood's presence. She lolled in my lap, peering at Madame Osgood upside down from over my knee. She ignored Madame Osgood's attempts to get her to play. But at least there wasn't any more biting or dirt-throwing.

We ate a breakfast drawn from my store of fruit, then Madame Osgood began setting up her camera equipment. I watched her, fascinated. "Tomorrow," I said while she worked, "you'll have to get up before dawn, and then you'll catch the chimps waking up. You're late. Most of them have already left for the day."

She nodded, slapping at mosquitoes. They seemed to love her, peppering her skin. Or maybe I had as many as she did, but they showed up better on white.

Once she'd gotten the camera ready, Madame Osgood started taking pictures of me. At first I stood as motionless as I could, but then she encouraged me to go about my day. Mango kept putting her hand over her face whenever Madame Osgood snapped a picture, like a famous person on the magazines in the stall outside the train station. But then she came around to the strange game, and we frolicked while the camera clicked.

Madame Osgood seemed particularly pleased with one set of photographs where I held on to Mango by one arm and one leg, whirled around and around, and finally sent her flying and shrieking across the lagoon and into the trees. Madame Osgood showed me a few on her camera's screen, and in the pictures Mango looked like a story-time creature, her outflung arms blurring into a halo as she flew. Where I stood in the background I looked like a man, wiry and weary. I gave the camera back to Madame Osgood, hoping not to have to see my image again.

After we'd broken for lunch, finishing it off with a few more licks of the chocolate bar, I brought out Prof's metal case. After the valise had fallen apart, it and the cooking tools were all that remained of the possessions we'd brought Inside.

"What is that?" Madame Osgood asked.

I input the numbers, clicked open the lid, and handed her the photographs. I decided not to give the curling letters to her; it felt like a betrayal to give Prof's private thoughts to a stranger when he hadn't even told them to me. So I left them where they were and closed the lid.

"That," I said, proudly tapping a photo of Prof beside Monsieur Baedeker, "is Professor Abdul Mohammad of the University of Leipzig."

"The man who brought you into the jungle."

"Yes."

"Can I have these photographs?"

I shook my head. "I can give you one or two, if you will print them in your magazine and tell the world about the important work the professor did."

"Thank you," she said. "I will. I'd be honored." She paused. "But I have to tell you something you might not want to hear. I've been photographing primates for a long time. I have worked with the faculty of the University of Leipzig. There is no Professor Mohammad there."

"Then maybe he wasn't officially a professor. But he did study apes, and studied them here. It was very important to him. Look, there's a picture of Prof next to a gorilla."

"The other man is Professor Rahal. I do know him."

"That's Prof's friend, in all these pictures! Ask him," I pleaded. "He knows who Prof was. I'm sure Prof told him about his mission. And ask him when he was born. Tell him Prof's combination for his case was one-nine-seven-one."

"I will do that," she said quietly, a complicated expression on her face. "I'm sure he'd like to know what Prof did for love of the chimpanzees."

Once she'd photographed the lagoon, we took a walk along the river. I showed her a nest of baby parrots, and she took many pictures of their blue feathers against the darker blue of the rainy-season sky. I'd eaten fresh eggs more times than I could count, and roasted baby parrots once or twice on hungrier days, but she seemed to adore these birds so much that I didn't tell her about that.

After I'd shown her my first campsite with Prof, Madame Osgood asked to see the spot where I'd chased away the hunters. No sign of them was left, of course. The rifles, the tents, the sad donkey, the wrecked ground, the body of Monsieur Tatagani, were all gone. But she took photographs anyway. She asked if I still had Beggar's hide, and I was glad that I could tell her it was long gone. There was no way I'd have put that dead mother's skin back on again, posed in it for photographs for readers far away.

I spent the next day showing Madame Osgood around my piece of the jungle. She claimed she was an old hand at exploring, but it definitely didn't seem that way. She fussily purified her water, refused to climb a single tree, and panicked at even tiny snakes. When I killed one, peeling it like a banana once the thrashing corpse stopped tying itself in knots, she refused the pink flesh. When she found a scorpion inside a boot, her screeches set Drummer going; he raced down from the trees and stomped on the insect so thoroughly, its corpse was pounded deep into the soil mush. He made pleased hoots at the results of his hard work and accepted a vigorous back scratching from Madame Osgood as payment.

The next morning Madame Osgood woke up with a rash all over her feet. Prof had gotten the same rash once or twice, and while it went away soon, it made it painful to walk. So we stayed around the lagoon that day. I told her more of my story and learned about some of the many places she had been.

For a while we sat quietly, watching the chimps. Whenever one or two would wander by as they foraged, I'd tell her what I knew about their histories and personalities. I told her how I'd noticed their wrists didn't bend back like ours, so they could hit a branch at high speed and hold on. I told her how I'd noticed their jaws went farther up and down than ours, which made them so good at stripping bark. She asked to see the records I'd kept. I shyly brought the observation notebook out of the metal case.

She read it silently. Intent, I watched her face as the moisture-soft pages turned. I could barely stand the wait to hear her thoughts. Then she finally looked up. "This is terrific. Surprisingly rigorous work."

"Thank you," I said, deciding *rigorous* was something good.

"I noticed it's all pictures and marks. Have you considered writing down each chimp's name instead of using pictures? It might save you some time."

I shook my head.

She paused, her bottom lip disappearing behind her teeth. "Do you know how to read?"

"Yes. I went to school. I got a twelve mark on my primary exams," I said proudly. "But I haven't read for a long time."

"Would you like if . . . Could I help you remember how to read and write?"

I had said no when Prof had offered the same thing. Reading had seemed like part of my life with my mother, impossible now. But I could imagine this nice woman helping me. And once I was reading again, I'd be able to understand some of Prof's letters. "Yes," I said. "Yes, please."

One by one she created words, and we practiced how to say them. She showed me how to make *Drummer* and *Mango* and *Anne*. And my name. She suggested I write our names over and over in the notebook, but I didn't want to waste those pages. So I wrote those names in the dirt until I'd scratched away all the soil in a large area. Omar took advantage of my reading practice to eat any earthworms I turned up.

"It's coming back fast," she said. "I think you were always able to read, and were just afraid you'd forgotten. You read very well."

"Thank you," I said.

She wrote some sentences in her notebook, keeping her writing small, using a pencil that made clicking noises and looked like a pen. I practiced saying the words.

*Luc.*

*Luc is not lonely in the jungle.*

*Luc is not lonely in the jungle because he has so many chimpanzees.*

*Luc is not lonely in the jungle because he has so many chimpanzees and also because he is a special boy.*

It was hard not to roll my eyes. She was trying to send me a message, but she was telling me something I already knew. Of course I knew that a boy who had made his family out of chimpanzees was someone special.


Come evening we sat around the smoldering fire for a long time. It was a lovely quiet, the kind that felt permanent.

"I have to tell you," Madame Osgood said, finally breaking the silence, "that I can't stay here forever. I'm going to have to leave at some point."

There were no clouds in the sky, so the sun didn't change color as it hit the horizon. There was only its yellow sliver, surrounded by ash, then coal, then black.

"Will it be hard for you to leave with me?" she asked.

To say yes or to say no — both were lies. How did people say anything in words without missing the truth? "I'll never leave," I said. I hadn't really known that until I said it.

"What do you mean?" she asked. "You don't really mean that you'd stay here, that you'd be okay going forever without seeing another person again. What about everyone who misses you?"

I shook my head. What I was really feeling — that the nearest I had to family was all around me and nowhere else — was too hard to explain. Or it was easy to explain, but hard to risk the feelings that would follow. I worried she'd laugh me off, that she could take my decision away from me and make me feel like an idiot.

"You're very lucky to have survived this long in the jungle without getting into serious trouble," she said. "There are many diseases here and many dangerous animals."

"I know that," I said hotly. I knew that far better than she did! And *I* didn't shriek at scorpions in my boots. Though somewhere my heart screamed about how nice it would be to be somewhere where everything wasn't wet all the time. To sit with people and talk about weather and radio programs.

"If you stay here, then you won't live as long as you would if you returned to the real world. People are not meant to be alone like this."

"This *is* the real world. And I'm not alone."

"You know what I mean."

"I know what you mean, and you know what I mean!"

She sighed. "You fought off grown men who were threatening chimpanzees you'd grown to love. That's a very special thing. People want to hear about brave orphan boys doing things like that."

I nodded, even though something about what she was saying didn't make me feel good.

"I can understand that staying here might seem like the best idea to you right now. But. My editors are going to love this story. Our readers are going to love this story. You could leave Africa. You could go somewhere with a lot more opportunities. You could be interviewed by famous people. Please listen to me when I promise you that."

"Gabon," I said.

"I'm sorry?"

"I'm from Gabon."

She sighed in frustration. "Yes, and also Africa."

I knew what she said was true, that I was from Africa as well as Gabon — but it didn't feel that way. Africa was a big thing that meant nothing to me. It scared me to continue arguing about this, because with all her education she probably knew something to say that would make it very clear that I should leave with her. But I had to tell her why I was staying.

"This was Prof's mission," I said. "I'm finishing it for him."

"Okay," she said. "But you see, I can't in good conscience leave you out here. And you could do even *more* good for your chimpanzees by leaving them. You could make the world listen to their story and their plight. Wouldn't that make Prof happy, too?"

I considered what she said. "Africa needs its own Jane Goodall," I said grudgingly, repeating what Prof had once said to me. "But if these chimpanzees became famous, wouldn't people want to come here?" I asked. "I wouldn't want that. It wouldn't be good for them."

"We don't have to tell anyone exactly where this place is. Only you and I would know."

"But I would want to come back to see Mango and Drummer, and other people could follow me in secret. Then more and more people would come here, and men would set more traps for the chimpanzees."

She poked at the fire, turning over a charred piece of wood so it glowed red in the night air. We stared as the ember grew hems of white, then gray, then black. "You truly don't want to leave, do you?" Madame Osgood asked.

"No, I don't."

"I wish I could do something for you."

"You've done a lot for me," I said. It was true, but what I really wanted to say — *The best thing you could do for me is to decide not to leave* —

261

was too hard to say. I knew she would answer *no*, and hearing that would be too big a grief.

Madame Osgood rummaged through a bag. "I'm going to leave you everything I can, everything I don't absolutely need."

Piles of belongings began to accumulate between us. A spare mosquito net. Women's T-shirts and underpants. Pill bottles. Sleeves of cookies. A flashlight with a strange panel that let the sun charge it. Novels in French and English. And, most precious: two fresh notebooks. I would make them last years each. I hungered for them.

I closed my eyes so I wouldn't have to see the pile. There was no chance I was going to refuse Madame Osgood's gifts, but I was embarrassed by how many there were and by how much I wanted them after I'd come to believe want was no longer part of me.

I was wearing the shoes Prof had bought, and used the sole to nudge the blackening ember closer to the fire so it would glow again. "The man in those photographs, who was so often with Prof. It's because of him that Prof learned about chimpanzees. I imagine that man is scared about his friend. Will you promise to tell him what happened? I will give you a photo of them together to bring to him."

It had become so smoky and dark that I couldn't see Madame Osgood's face. Firelight glinted in her eyes. Far above, a chimp made a call as she settled in her nest, and I recognized Bad Mother's whining voice.

"Okay," Madame Osgood said. "I'll make that happen."

"Also," I continued, "you could tell him that Prof's life was a success. You should tell him our story as best you can, so he will know that Prof did the job he came to do."

"I will," Madame Osgood promised. We listened to the logs crackling in the night. Great moths flew into the whirl of smoke rising from the fire, circled and dived and caught the orange light on their broad white wings, some finding too much heat and falling, sizzling, to the ground.

"I will miss it here," she said with a sigh. "I do understand why you'd want to stay."

I didn't say anything. I was staying because the life I'd been handed had never left me any options. I was finally making a choice of my own, and it made me feel a contentment that lived right next to terror.

"It might take a long time," she said, "but once I've gone back to England and submitted my pictures, would you mind if I returned and tried to find you? Even if it's a year from now by the time I make it?"

Tears stood in my eyes. From now on there would always be a person out there who might be thinking of me when I was thinking of her. When life Inside got hard, I could hold on to the thought that a visitor would return during the next rainy season. "Yes," I said. "I would like that."

The next morning, Madame Osgood took some final photographs and then showed me what the camera had seen. I was holding Mango close to my chest, Omar perched on my shoulder and silhouetted in the dawn light. I asked Madame Osgood to wait to leave, so I could sketch a copy into my notebook first. I drew a picture of her, too, to put up on the wall of my hut. Once I was finished, she packed up her belongings and left.

Moments after Madame Osgood motored away, the chimps started acting up. One chimp followed her along the bank and came home with a new orange-brown rock, and the excitement of it got Silver Stripes and his closest allies more aggressive than usual, bullying the females and showing off all day. When Drummer took the rock for himself, he almost lost a finger in Silver Stripes's jaws when the older male and a partner pinned him down. Drummer's allies rescued him, but I realized Drummer's dominance might not last forever. Especially given his lame leg, which he still held tight against his body. If any ambitious male got over his fear of the metal case, Drummer might lose his position.

Maybe I was a fool to have stayed.

I'd been lucky until then, with the rainy-season storms starting only late in the afternoon, but at midday the sky grew dark as evening and began dropping a rain that felt thick and heavy and endless. The chimps must have sensed this, too, because they stopped their eating and socializing and built day nests, something I'd never seen them do. As Omar and I retreated into the hut I motioned for Mango to join us, but she ignored me and built a nest near her brother.

I worried about Madame Osgood, but figured she'd be fine journeying the river in the storm as long as she remembered her route well enough to follow it when the rain limited her view. As for me and Omar, if we snacked sparingly on the provisions she'd left, we'd be able to survive for weeks in the hut — a good thing, too, as I didn't relish the idea of going out into the driving rain, what with the risks of getting lost or slipping into a ravine or being crushed by a falling tree.

As he hobbled around the humid hut, Omar had the stiff movements of an old man, and I knew his monkey life might not have more than a few years left. I wanted him to enjoy the gifts we'd been given before any of the chimps took them away, so I decided to open a can of anchovies, slicing along the edge with my bright new camp knife. Every hour or so I pulled out a new dripping strand of fish, ate the glistening body, and offered the head to Omar. He'd eat it eagerly, lick my palm clean, and then recline in my lap, giving fishy burps.

We could be days inside this hut before the storm let up. I

wondered how the chimps were faring, but they had been making it through rainy seasons for years and decades and centuries and longer. I had little doubt that the whole group would be waiting for me when I emerged — a little wet, maybe, but ready for life to resume.

But for now, it was me and Prof's monkey and four walls.

And books.

They were mine, and no one could take them from me. I'd never possessed this much luxury, even in Franceville.

I stood the metal case up lengthwise, so it rose as tall as possible over the mudding ground. Delicately, I opened the notebook, flipping past the drawings I'd made of Drummer and Mango and the rest. I opened it to the page where Madame Osgood had written down all the letters of French, and remembered her descriptions of how they sounded when they went with other letters. I *did* remember how to read. I would just have to go very slowly.

The novels she had left me were on top of the pile. Books that took many, many pages to tell one story. I decided that before any of those, though, I would read Prof's Baedeker. Then I would start the French novels, going however slowly I needed to get every ounce of story from them.

Only then, once I'd sucked all the sweet company I could from those books, would I read whichever of Prof's letters were in French. As slowly as the whole process would go, as many words as I wouldn't know until I'd seen them many times over and puzzled through their combinations, it would be a long time from now before I got to Prof's letters. I might be as old as Prof had been in those happy pictures, when he'd traveled far from Egypt and sat beside a new friend in front of a building made of brick.

I liked the idea of it, that a long time from now I would sit down one morning, make a mint tea from the patch behind the hut, and spend time with Prof.

But first the Baedeker. I picked up the guidebook Prof had always kept close, lifting its spine up into the scant rain-dappled light that leaked through the walls of the hut.

"Behdek . . ." Finally I was able to read the whole title aloud. *"Baedeker's Guide to Civilized Life in the Jungle."*

I had my thumb at the cover's edge and was about to lift it when I heard a crashing sound. Scared for my chimps, I stood by the door and listened for any screams. But there was nothing.

My curiosity overcame me. I tugged open the door and looked out into the rain-dark clearing, water streaming down my limbs. Lightning flashed across the sky, and in the quick white I saw two black shapes skirt the lagoon. Blinded, I wiped the rain from my face and tried to blink the purple fuzz from my vision.

I felt a hand on my leg and instantly knew it was Mango. I leaned to pick her up, but she dodged my grasp and skipped into the hut instead. I turned to follow her but was startled by another hand working its way into mine. Looking down, I saw a full-size chimp struggling to keep his balance, hopping with one leg on the muddy ground. I smiled.

"You too, Drummer?"

His hand still in mine, we went inside and closed the door.

The rain picked up harder, and even though it was mid-afternoon, the light grew stark and sparse. I clicked on the sun-charged flashlight, and Drummer and Mango were instantly fascinated by the ruddy glow behind the plastic. Drummer sat right beside me and placed his hands over mine so we were holding it together. He stared into the light, panting in confusion and blinking rapidly as it blinded him.

Soon Drummer was leaning against me, waiting to be groomed. As I picked through his hair, Mango huddled in alongside us, and Drummer started running his fingers through her hair, too. Omar sat on the case, but with one leg outstretched so it rested on my knee. Though the day was wet and dark, it wasn't too chilly with so many warm bodies around.

I risked taking the Baedeker back into my lap. Right away I had to start batting away Mango's fingers as she tugged on the pages. Drummer, though, seemed happy just to look at the strange lines on paper and feel the vibrations of my voice while I read aloud.

All around me was the fertile smell of mud, the scent of decay drummed into the air by the heavy rain. There was a whiff of smoke from the extinguished fire, an almost chemical tang from the chocolate bar, and above it all the smell of wet chimp.

I showed Mango, Drummer, and Omar the cover and repeated the title aloud: *"Baedeker's Guide to Civilized Life in the Jungle."*

Then my family watched as I opened the book.

# AUTHOR'S NOTE

The chimpanzees got a bad rap in my previous novel, *Endangered*. I couldn't help it — compared to the peaceful, matriarchal bonobos, they seemed like abusive villains. But that was before I read the gorgeous memoirs of Jane Goodall. Vivid and specific and lovely, Goodall's nuanced accounts turned chimps in my mind from brutes to delicate, poignant creatures full of wants and needs, who live in a more hardscrabble social world than the comparatively bourgeois bonobos. Our two closest relatives serve as a terrific double lens through which to examine our own human natures. Chimps, like bonobos, share 98.7 percent of our DNA — making them closer to us than they are to gorillas. Our kinship is about a lot more than numbers, though. In their book *Demonic Males*, Richard Wrangham and Dale Peterson point out another startling similarity between our two cultures:

> Very few animals live in patrilineal, male-bonded communities wherein females routinely reduce the risks of inbreeding by moving to neighboring groups to mate. And only two animal species are known to do so with a system of intense, male-initiated territorial aggression, including lethal raiding into neighboring communities in search of vulnerable enemies to attack and kill. Out of four thousand mammals and ten million or more other animal species, this suite of behaviors is known only among chimpanzees and humans (24).

Like science fiction can provide a way to isolate and examine the realities of our everyday world, Goodall's accounts of chimp behavior provide a new way to examine our own tendencies to destroy, and the benefits and costs of in-group, out-group aggression. Chimps would recognize the pattern, so common to human cultures, of a young wife joining her husband's village. They'd recognize the male-generated violence of humans who fixate on vengeance and go to long lengths to hunt down their betrayers. Chimps would understand, too, the caring side of human nature: In them we find deep compassion and intimacy and a selfless devotion that looks a lot like love.

There is no actual *Baedeker's Guide to Civilized Life in the Jungle*. The Baedeker guides existed, and led many a turn-of-the-twentieth-century tourist on cautious travels around the globe. But those tourists never had a guide to Gabon, and even today those who visit Gabon from abroad generally do so because of logging or oil, not sightseeing.

I titled this book *Threatened* in order to distinguish it from *Endangered*, but make no mistake about it: Chimps, too, are endangered animals. They're doing marginally better in Gabon, however, than elsewhere. Gabon's deepest jungles are home to roughly sixty thousand of the world's chimpanzees, thought to be the largest concentration of the imperiled species.[1] Gabon is also one of the least populated countries on Earth. With only 1.6 million residents in a country the size of Colorado, it averages only two people per square mile outside of its urban centers.[2] There are areas of the country, it's said, where no human has set foot. Because of the revenue coming into Gabon from oil and logging, the president in 2002 was able to afford to set aside an unprecedented amount of

[1]Dale Peterson, *Chimpanzee Travels: On and Off the Road in Africa* (Page 210)
[2]CIA fact file (www.cia.gov/library/publications/the-world-factbook/geos /gb.html)

the land for national parks — 10 percent.[3] Gabon is a reservoir of endangered species and forms a positive note in ape conservation and a caution to those who too readily lump all the varied stories of Africa into the single tale of a doomed continent. In Gabon you can find gorillas, hippos, and forest elephants on the same beach. What better place for an animal story?

One unattractive trait Gabon does share with the United States, though: Of all the countries of the world, ours are the only two that still sanction medical testing of chimpanzees. One of Gabon's major primate testing centers, the Centre International de Recherches Médicales, is actually in Franceville. No great medical advances have ever come from the testing of chimpanzees, and yet research chimps are isolated in tiny chambers with barely enough room to stand or turn around, spending decades without sunlight or trees or even solid ground under their feet as they undergo hundreds of painful medical procedures.[4] If we choose chimps to test because they're so similar to humans, it follows that their very person-ness also means that we should make every attempt to eliminate their torture and distress. At the very least, mustn't we provide these highly social creatures with the comfort of fellow chimps? Strides have recently been made toward ending medical testing of chimps in the United States, but we're not out of the woods yet.

Of course, one reason some scientists support the idea of medical testing of chimps is that we can use them to find a solution to some of our most dangerous viruses: hepatitis and HIV. It's an irony that chimpanzees hold out (unrealized) hope for breakthroughs in diseases — particularly HIV — that have ravaged the very human populations pushing chimps to the edge of extinction.

[3]*National Geographic Explorer,* "Gabon"
[4]Roger Fouts and Stephen Tukel Mills, *Next of Kin*

There are over fifty million AIDS orphans in sub-Saharan Africa: over three hundred for each of the estimated 150,000 remaining wild chimpanzees.[5] Outlooks for both of those populations are grim. Forty percent of Gabon's people are under fifteen, in large part because AIDS decimated a generation of adults.[6]

In 2001 Klaus Toepfer, executive director of the United Nations Environment Programme, articulated the magnitude of the crisis facing the great apes: "The clock is standing at one minute to midnight." At the rate their habitat loss is going, creatures that have been on Earth for millions of years are heading into their final decades. To Luc, chimpanzees were humans caught out after midnight. But what will happen at midnight to the chimpanzees?

[5] Jane Goodall Institute
[6] *Africa's Orphaned and Vulnerable Generations: Children Affected by AIDS* (UNICEF)

# FURTHER READING

When I was writing *Endangered*, I found a wealth of literature about Congo and relatively little about bonobos; this time, almost the opposite was true. I benefitted from a preponderance of terrific books about chimpanzees; Gabon was a different story.

## Chimps

I started with Jane Goodall's work, spending particularly large amounts of time with *Through a Window: My Thirty Years with the Chimpanzees of Gombe, Jane Goodall: 50 Years at Gombe, Africa in My Blood,* and *In the Shadow of Man*. Though no chimp in *Threatened* is directly based on any of Goodall's chimps, I took frequent inspiration from her accounts of the fortunes and misfortunes of the Gombe apes. Similarly, Dale Peterson's *Jane Goodall* was a great introduction to Goodall's life.

The non-Goodall book I turned to most was Roger Fouts and Stephen Tukel Mills's *Next of Kin*. It's both a fascinating account of the United States' challenged history with chimpanzees and an exploration of the startling links between our two species. It's hard to finish that book and not start to think of chimps as having personhood. Striking a similar note was Dale Peterson and Jane Goodall's *Visions of Caliban: On Chimpanzees and People*.

*Demonic Males: Apes and the Origins of Human Violence*, by Richard Wrangham and Dale Peterson, is similarly important reading. It provides a gripping way of examining chimp and human cultures as similar histories of in-group, out-group conflict dominated by bonded males. That's a metaphor that couldn't be more widespread or more telling.

More technical, but still very useful, was *Chimpanzee Cultures*, by Richard W. Wrangham, W. C. McGrew, Frans B. M. de Waal, and Paul G. Heltne.

More generalized accounts, but helpful nonetheless, were *Among the Great Apes: Adventures on the Trail of Our Closest Relatives*, by Paul Raffaele; Desmond Morris and Steve Parker's *Planet Ape* (textbook style, with lovely photos); and *Walking with the Great Apes*, by Sy Montgomery.

My primary source on the behavior of vervets was the charmingly titled *How Monkeys See the World*, by Dorothy L. Cheney and Robert M. Seyfarth. I love those crazy monkeys. I should point out, though, that their leopard alarm calls aren't quite as dramatic-sounding as I've made them in this book.

We benefit, too, from a wealth of filmed chimp behavior. I recommend *Chimpanzee* (dir. Alastair Fothergill, Mark Linfield), James Marsh's *Project Nim* (based on Elizabeth Hess's *Nim Chimpsky: The Chimp Who Would Be Human*), and the "Social Climbers" episode of David Attenborough's BBC series *The Life of Mammals*. The Animal Planet reality show *Escape to Chimp Eden* was useful for its wealth of filmed human-chimp interaction.

## Gabon and Its Natural Environment

My first exposure to Gabon was Jan Brokken's *The Rainbird*, a book of anecdotal accounts of his experiences in the country. My reading about nearby Congo (listed in *Endangered*) proved useful, as did other books about Africa more generally, such as Paul Theroux's *Dark Star Safari* and Colin M. Turnbull's *The Forest People*. *National Geographic Explorer's* episodes titled "Gorilla Murders" and "Gabon" were particularly useful. For more general reading about surviving in a jungle environment, I turned to Yossi Ghinsberg's *Jungle* and David Grann's *The Lost City of Z*.

*Gabon, Sao Tome of Principe: The Bradt Travel Guide* (2003) is out of print, but provides a dose of information about one of tourism's most far-flung frontiers. There is no Baedeker guide to anywhere in sub-Saharan Africa, but I took much of my inspiration for the fictional *Baedeker's Guide to Civilized Life in the Jungle* from *Baedeker's Upper Egypt*, first published in 1892.

## AIDS and Its Impact

*Children of AIDS: Africa's Orphan Crisis*, by Emma Guest, is a terrific, balanced, and harrowing account of the many facets of the AIDS orphan crisis.

Of the plentiful articles about AIDS orphans in Africa, I found particularly useful "Streetchildren and Gangs in African Cities: Guidelines for Local Authorities" (published by United Nations Human Settlements Programme) and "Africa's Orphaned and Vulnerable Generations: Children Affected by AIDS" (published by UNICEF).

The South African film *Yesterday*, a 2004 Academy Award Best Foreign Language Film nominee, is about a South African woman whose husband brings AIDS into her life and then disappears. It's beautifully written and directed by Darrell Roodt.

# HOW TO HELP

During school visits I'm often asked what the average person can do to help the great apes. If the answer is hard, it's only because the possibilities are so plentiful.

What chimps need most are impassioned people willing to devote their time to their care. That means many different types: field biologists, nongovernmental organization managers, and veterinarians, but also lawyers, lobbyists, and lawmakers. Some of the young people who care so much about apes now will one day come to fill these roles.

Most of us, though, won't devote our lives to conservation. There are many ways to help, even so. Conservation is expensive, so one way to contribute is to pitch in to adopt a chimp at an African sanctuary. Through the Jane Goodall Institute (www.janegoodall .org), you and a group of friends can support a chimp and keep her supplied with care and bananas and everything else she needs to survive, while simultaneously contributing to the local economy. Also through the institute you will find resources on forming a Roots & Shoots society, clubs focused on identifying conservation issues of domestic concern and taking action to help them.

Another charity I've come to greatly respect is the Animal Legal Defense Fund (www.aldf.org), which undertakes the representation of animals in court. Its goals are varied: securing the release of chimps from medical testing facilities, ceasing cruel maternal deprivation studies in research centers, ensuring animal abusers are prosecuted, and making sure livestock is treated as humanely as possible. Within a highly ordered society like ours, legal action is often the most effective way to protect vulnerable and mistreated animals. Pursuing justice isn't as romantic as bottle-feeding baby chimps, but it's even more vital. ALDF also maintains a great list of ways you can help animals in your own community under the "Resources" heading of their web page.

Every once in a while (like at the time of this writing, February 2013), the National Institutes of Health puts out Requests for Information (RFIs) about guidelines for the use of animals in medical testing or research. These are solicitations for opinions from experts and the general public alike. If you have something to say about how we treat animals, keep a lookout for these RFIs on their website (www.nih.gov) and write a letter. Have your friends sign it with you, and copy your congressional representative. If you need extra ammunition on the cruelty of such research, or its far-reaching impact on the wild chimp populations of Africa — whose infants are hunted to become test subjects — I suggest turning to Peterson and Goodall's *Visions of Caliban: On Chimpanzees and People*.

The cure for cruelty is expanding the moral imagination. The great civil rights struggles have always been about taking a group that has historically been seen as "other" and learning to see it as "self." Whether it's about stopping cruelty to animals or helping AIDS orphans a continent away, the best side of humanity lies in expanding our empathies as much as we can. Helping the chimpanzees is but one of those paths.

# ACKNOWLEDGMENTS

My biggest thanks are due to someone I haven't met. For years I had only a vague sense of Jane Goodall's awesomeness. I knew she'd been somewhere in Africa working with the chimpanzees, and that she'd helped a bunch of them. But then I read her memoirs, and her world swallowed me up.

Goodall's writing is as observant and nuanced and elegant as the best fiction. What was most striking, though, was its breadth. She followed chimp families for decades. Kings and queens rose and fell at the hands of heroes and villains. Promising infants found greatness or died early, whether at the whims of nature or the schemes of conniving aunts. Her characters lived lives worthy of Shakespeare; only they were real, and they were apes.

I still owe immense gratitude to Claudine André and the staff of Lola Ya Bonobo in the Democratic Republic of Congo for hosting my visit to the "pygmy" chimpanzees, the bonobos. The chimps may have won me over far more than I expected, but bonobos will remain my first love.

I typically spend a quarter of my writing time drafting and three-quarters revising. I'd be blind to *Threatened*'s early rough patches without my contingent of savvy readers. Maggie Stiefvater: I may have played it cool, but I teared up when I realized you were really going to spend some of your talent on me. Justin Deabler, you've got one of the sharpest minds I've known. Marie Rutkoski, I was jealous of your Skyped-in brioche but grateful for your insights. Donna Freitas, same goes for you and your Manchego. My writer's group, Jill Santopolo, Betsy Bird, and Marianna Baer: You da best.

Eric Zahler, my partner: My first gauge of a book is how late you keep the bedside light on. Thank you for helping me see that animals don't need to talk or sing or wear hats or secretly be people inside to be worthy of our compassion. Thank you for helping me find my heart and cut through my excess. Thanks, too, for Chester, Ludovic, Little Bonobo, and Little Pook.

David Levithan, my editor: You may claim you're not an animal person, but no one could tell it by the amount of attention and empathy you've given the chimpanzees of this book. I consider myself so lucky to have you in my corner, and I know I'm not alone: You might be the most thanked person in young adult literature. If this genre is experiencing a golden age, you're its emperor. (The benevolent Augustus kind, not the icky Caligula kind.)

Scholastic Press is more of a bonobo culture than a chimpanzee one, I have to say; that is one strong alliance of powerful females! Lizette Serrano, Ellie Berger, Lori Benton, Stacy Lellos, Tracy van Straaten, Candace Greene, Emily Heddleson, Erin Black, Rachel Coun, Bess Braswell, Emily Morrow, Rachael Hicks, Jazan Higgins, Sue Flynn, Nikki Mutch, Chris Satterlund, Barbara Holloway, Terribeth Smith, and many more: Thank you. (John Mason, Alan Smagler, Charlie Young, and Antonio Gonzalez — being favored males among powerful females isn't so bad, is it?) Kate Hurley, you are a champ. Whitney Lyle, your designs are museum-worthy. Becky Amsel, you are a miracle of a publicist, and with rocking glasses to boot.

Richard Pine, my agent: You are one stand-up guy, and way more bonobo than chimp. Thanks.

Thank you also to my mom, my first editor and a great writer, who tirelessly explains the difference between a monkey and an ape to the various residents of Clearwater, Florida.

And to the librarians and booksellers who have worked so hard to get good stories into the hands of young readers, thank you. We are the blacksmiths and you are the knights.